DATE DUE APR 0 6

6-12-06			
AUG 10 06			
2-27-07			

GAYLORD   PRINTED IN U.S.A.

RANDOM HOUSE

LARGE
PRINT

AN UNFINISHED LIFE

AN UNFINISHED LIFE

A NOVEL

———◆———

MARK SPRAGG

R A N D O M   H O U S E
LARGE PRINT

A portion of this work previously appeared in
Colorado Review.

Grateful acknowledgment is made to Alfred A. Knopf
for permission to reprint an excerpt from the poem
"Not Dying," from Selected Poems by Mark Strand.
Copyright © 1970, 1990 by Mark Strand. Reprinted
by permission of Alfred A. Knopf, a division of
Random House, Inc.

*The Library of Congress has established a Cataloging-in-
Publication record for this title.*

0-375-43433-X

www.randomlargeprint.com

FIRST LARGE PRINT EDITION

10 9 8 7 6 5 4 3 2 1

This Large Print edition published in accord with the
standards of the N.A.V.H.

For Virginia,
because of Virginia,
always,
and
for Kent and Cathy Haruf,
and
Nancy Stauffer,
with my love

These wrinkles are nothing.
These gray hairs are nothing.
This stomach which sags
with old food, these bruised
and swollen ankles,
my darkening brain,
they are nothing.
I am the same boy
my mother used to kiss.

—Mark Strand, "Not Dying"

AN UNFINISHED LIFE

ONE

———

THE SAPWOOD SNAPS and shifts in the low-
bellied stove, and the heat swells up against
the roofboards and weathered fir planking, and
the whole small building seems to groan.

It's the first cool night of the fall—a good
night for a sweat—and Einar adjusts his wet
back and ass in the webbing of the lawn chair.
He feels the full weight of his seventy years and
wishes he'd thought to bring a towel to drape
over the webbing, but he was in here just this
spring and hadn't remembered one then either.
He scoops a dipper of water from the pail beside
the chair and casts it across the stovetop where it
sizzles and steams.

He wishes he'd have known this was the way
it was going to be.

"Some old son of a bitch should've explained
getting old to me," he says aloud and then
bows his head against the wet pulse of heat.

"Some old son of a bitch probably did and I wasn't listening."

The sweat drips from his nose and chin.

He reaches his denim shirt from where he hung it on a nail, soaks it in the bucket and then stands to wring it and mop his face and chest.

He spreads the shirt over the chair and sits back down, staring at the chair that stands empty before him, both chairs raised up on this platform into the heat.

Through the west window he watches the amber moonlight on the pasture and remembers the fall they skidded in the fieldstones and mortared them into the foundation under this board floor. The building was Griffin's idea. He'd said: "Dad, I need it. I really do."

"You need a sauna?" Einar had asked.

"I'm a Viking," the boy said. "It's what the Vikings did."

All of this twenty years ago, Mitch helping them frame the walls and the headers for the door and windows, and Griffin just a boy, but already used to working with the diligence of a man. And not a boy who'd ever asked for much.

They put in a south-facing window, this one to the west, and a square of double-pane glass in the slanting roof so they could see the stars. And a smaller pane low in the east wall for the benefit of the boy's dog, so Karl could lie on the porch and stare in at them.

When they were finished, Griffin took each man by a hand, standing between them, and bowed his head. "God bless this place," he said. He was serious, original, not just repeating something he'd heard.

"Is there anything else you need?" Mitch had asked.

The boy shaded his eyes, looking up at the man. "You could sit in here with us."

Mitch's face shone even blacker in the sun, like wet obsidian. "Even though I'm no Viking?" He bent down over the boy. "Even though my great-granddad was an African man?"

"Does that mean no?" Griffin asked.

Mitch shoved him away playfully, the way men roughhouse with boys. "I guess I won't," he said. "I believe I've sweated enough in this life already."

Einar smiles at the clarity of the memory. He works his jaw, and his ears pop as if he were descending from a great height. The old dog fidgets on the porch, then settles its grayed jowls on its crossed forepaws and stares in through the little window. His name's Karl, but it's not the original Karl, just another dog taken from the town shelter, worked and fed and given a place to rest and grow lame. The first Karl lies buried behind the barn. Dead and buried like his son, Griffin, and his wife, Ella.

He straightens in the chair and wonders if the dog wishes it had a boy for company. Not his boy, just some other kid. He wonders what it is that dogs long for, or if they long. Maybe they just wait patiently for some improvement in their lives. He thinks he's a man who knows something of waiting, but the heat's gotten to him and he feels his stomach come up and shorten his breath. He cracks a window and sucks at the draft of night air. He drops his head back and stares through the window in the roof.

Pegasus has risen in the dark sky, poised as if for a run of magic, or that's what he used to think. Now he looks at the stars and sees only a silent, uncaring witness, and tonight feels this press of steam-thick heat, smells the odor of living wood reduced to ash. No magic.

He pops a wooden match with his thumbnail and lights a candle on the shelf by his elbow. He shakes the match out and looks down at his shriveled thighs and worn knees. His legs are white as summer cloud, blue-veined. At least his arms and shoulders are still strong, and he tightens his chest, the muscles in his neck. To the empty chair he says, "I've always been puny through the hindquarters, from the get-go. That's not news."

He scoots forward on the chair and takes the quart Mason jar from the shelf, holds it below him and pisses it half full before setting it down by the water bucket. He thumbs the sweat from his eyebrows and blinks at the walls and shelves, at the fist-size chunks of agate and quartz, the petrified wood and half a dozen of the boy's favorite books. There're the hawk feathers he'd hung on the walls. The skull of a black baldy bull. A map of Norway cut out of a **National Geographic,** carefully, with a razor blade. One of Iceland. The picture of a bearded man in a horned helmet, and another of a tall black man with a spear, balanced on a single leg. Both from **National Geographic,** the Norseman and the Senegalese hunter. The boy saw himself as dangerous, raised as he was by the descendants of warriors.

Einar stares down at the dog again and thinks it would be a fine thing to have that kind of focus. To have a small window, with something to stare at on the other side. He wishes for his own window and wonders what he might see. He wonders if Mitch has gone to sleep for the night.

He pushes out of his chair and opens the

door. He carries the jar at his side and steps to the edge of the porchboards and sloshes the piss out into the darkness. He stands steaming in the cool air. The dog shifts but doesn't rise, its hips so brittle with arthritis that it moves only when it must. Einar turns back to the doorway and says, "Just like old times."

The dog blinks its clouded eyes and yawns, and Einar thinks this is an animal that should be called out into the tall weeds and shot in the head and buried next to its namesake. But he knows Mitch would never stand for it. Mitch believes in suffering as a right, a burden, even sacred, for both man and beast.

TWO

———

S HE SITS ON THE SIDE of her bed and
reaches back to run the flat of her hand over
the sheet. She'd slept on her back, legs straight,
arms at her sides. She can feel where the fabric's
cool and where it's warm, just there, where her
fingertips edge into the outline her sleeping
body has made. She imagines the warmth whispering softly that she was here, but in a minute
or two there'll be no proof she was ever in this
bed, or even this trailer house, like she's invisi-
ble. She likes thinking that she can't be seen. It
makes her smile.

She listens. There's the noise of her mother in
the kitchen, the gurgle of the coffeemaker, water
running at the sink. She stands and smooths the
wrinkles on the bottom sheet, pulls up the top
sheet and cotton blanket and tucks them tight,
then fluffs the pillow at the head of the bed, her
small hands working in the dim light.

She climbs onto the bed and edges a fingernail under the heads of the thumbtacks pressed into the wallboard above the window. The tacks hold the brown bath towel she puts up every evening for a curtain, and they've worn divots in the wallboard, and little particles always fall out when she removes them, like sawdust, but she doesn't think the wallboards are made of wood. She doesn't fool herself about much. She knows everything in this trailer's fake, that it just tricks you into thinking it's real.

The window faces west, and she started putting the towel up in the summer so the setting sun wouldn't overheat her bed. But now it's the end of September, and she's grown used to sleeping in the darkened room. She folds the towel and places it on her pillow. Outside, a tractor is pulling a machine along the edge of a field, the cornstalks falling as it passes. She thinks she might ask Roy what this machine is called, not today, but sometime later. Roy puts guardrails up along the county roads, and since he needs machines to do that she thinks he might know what this one is called.

On the north side of the cornfield there's the interstate, with the cars and big trucks heading east and west filled with people who know nothing about her. She wonders if anyone ever looks her way, or imagines what it's like to live here. If they even notice the three crooked rows of old trailer houses, whose trees aren't big enough yet to climb or to shade the flat metal roofs. The dog next door barks, and she remembers it's Thursday and the garbage truck has turned in off the lane. She's never heard the neighbor dog's name.

She kneels by the bed and pulls out her suitcase and lifts it up on the blanket. Its clasp is rusted, its corners scuffed and peeling.

The first Thursday morning she saw the garbage truck she thought it looked a lot safer than the trailer houses, and all summer she prayed that if a tornado came it would be on a Thursday morning when she could hide in the garbage truck. Then the tornado could crumple this fakey trailer and suck Roy right up from the broken trailer parts and put him down somewhere else. She knows there's no use in killing the man who lives in the trailer. Dead or alive, her mother would just replace him. Before Roy in this trailer in Iowa there was Hank in the trailer in Florida, and before Hank there was Johnny in the little house that smelled like cat pee, and before Johnny there was Bobby. She can't remember Bobby very well, but there've been four. Everybody's mother is good at something. Her mother's good at finding the same man, no matter where she lives.

Her mother tells her that children are a calendar. She says it at least once a month, like it's some new idea she thought up all by herself. Her mother says that if she, Griff Evans Gilkyson, had never been born, never learned to walk, dress herself and speak, then she herself could still think she was a young woman. Griff thinks her very own calendar is her mother's men. Four men. About a year and a half for each one, and before that she was too little to keep track. She shrugs and whispers, "So, I'm nine and a half."

She strips off the T-shirt she slept in and folds it and lays it in the bottom of the suitcase. The suitcase smelled of mothballs and mildew when her mother bought it at the John 3:16 thrift shop, and it still does. She opens her hands flat and presses down against her chest. No titties, she thinks. She's still safe. She thinks that one morning she'll wake up with breasts, maybe the start of hair between her legs, and everything will begin to go wrong. Just like things have gone wrong for her mother. Breasts attract trailer houses and pickup trucks and lots and lots of tears. She wishes her father were still alive. If he weren't dead it would be safe to let her titties grow.

She puts on a pair of tan corduroy pants, a ribbed cotton chemise and a striped polo shirt. She laces her tennis shoes and opens the bottom drawer of her dresser. The dresser and the desk are made of the same pressed particleboard, and she likes them because they don't even try to look like wood. The drawers stick, so she has to be careful to keep them quiet.

She empties all the dresser drawers into the suitcase, every piece of clothing she owns. When she gets a bigger suitcase she'll get more clothes. No sense in owning something she'd need to leave behind. That wouldn't make any sense at all.

She slips her schoolbooks and notebooks into a small backpack. The backpack is orange, with zippered pockets on its sides for her pencils, pens and Magic Markers. Roy bought it for her. He told her orange was a good color for Iowa. "You'll be easy to spot whether there's snow or not," he'd said. "Some hunter won't think you're just a little brown rabbit and shoot you for dinner." She hates the backpack. She prays the tornado will get that too.

She kneels beside her bed and slips her hand between the mattress and box spring. When she feels the coolness of her diary she stops and listens. There's still just the sounds her mother's making in the kitchen, so she slides it out. The cover is lavender patent leather, so shiny she can see her reflection in it. She sits at her desk and opens the diary to its last page: THINGS I HATE ABOUT MY MOTHER.

1. I hate that she's pretty.
2. I hate that she thinks she's not pretty.
3. I hate that she works at the dry cleaners. (But I like Kitty, her boss.)
4. I hate that she doesn't know karate.
5. I hate that she likes the same music Roy likes.
6. I hate that she doesn't believe in God or angels.
7. I HATE that she makes us live in Iowa.

And this morning she adds:

8. I hate it that she's not really, really hairy. So hairy that only kangaroos would fall in love with her.

She's always especially liked that kangaroos travel with their own little pouches, like luggage. She closes the diary and puts it in her suitcase and cracks her door open, then steps into the hallway and holds her breath. She listens. Her mother shuts off the water in the kitchen. Her mother and Roy's bedroom is at the end of the hallway and the door's closed. The bathroom is the next room toward the kitchen.

In the bathroom she washes her face, brushes her hair and teeth. She puts the washcloth and her toothbrush and toothpaste in a Ziploc bag she hides every night under the clean towels, then returns to her room and eases the door shut behind her. She packs her hairbrush and the plastic bag and puts the pillow and the brown towel on top of everything else.

"Griff," her mother calls from the kitchen.

She has to sit on the suitcase to get it closed and clasped. She thinks she might have to leave behind a sweater. Sweaters take up a lot of room. She looks around the room, turning. That's everything. The dresser and desk are empty. The fake-wood walls are bare. She saw a poster she liked of a white baby seal at the mall in town, but there's no way to pack a poster.

"Come out here and have breakfast with me."

She steps into the hallway, holding the orange backpack by one of its shoulder straps.

In the kitchen her mother sits sideways on her

chair at the kitchen table sipping a cup of coffee and smoking a cigarette. "Good morning," she says, and blows the smoke toward the sink.

"You promised," Griff reminds her. Her mother always promises and never remembers. She thinks when she writes in her diary again she'll say she hates it that her mother doesn't remember her promises.

What her mother does instead is brush cigarette ash from the front of her white polyester dress. Her name is embroidered above her left breast and it's not a dress, not really. It's a uniform that looks exactly like the ones all the women wear at the dry-cleaning shop.

On the table there's cereal and a carton of milk, a white insulated pitcher of coffee and a plate of toast. Griff sits down across from her mother and fills her bowl, pouring in enough milk to float the cereal up near the rim. This is the breakfast her mother makes every time after it happens, like she has to prove to Roy that he was wrong about her.

The door opens at the end of the hallway and then she hears Roy in the bathroom peeing.

"You promised," she whispers. She wants to help her mother remember.

Her mother nods.

"How're my girls this morning?" Roy asks.

She doesn't have to turn to know he's standing at the end of the hallway adjusting his belt. It's where Roy stands and what he says after his morning pee.

Clear across the table she feels her mother stiffen, and watches her stub out her Old Gold cigarette.

Roy puts his hands on the back of her chair, leans over and reaches around and takes the spoon from her hand. He ladles up a spoonful of cereal. She can hear his mouth crunching just above her head, and she can smell him. Roy smells like he puts up guardrails in Iowa. "Everybody sleep okay?" he asks. When he drops the spoon back in her cereal, she pushes the bowl away and laces her fingers together with her hands in her lap. She thinks she'd rather eat the neighbor dog's poop than use a spoon with Roy-spit on it. She wasn't really hungry anyway.

Her mother turns in her chair. "Everybody slept just fine, Roy." She looks at her daughter with her good eye and the blackened one. Under the blackened eye her jaw's swollen and dark, and at the edge of the dark part it's colored a pukey yellow. Both of her mother's eyes ask her to say she slept all right.

"I slept fine," she says. She thinks this is how her own personal calendar is broken down into parts. This is how the last year and a half is reduced to once a week, or once every two weeks, or once a month. The marks on her mother's face are how she knows exactly how old she is.

Roy sits between them, and she asks, "Can I be excused?" It's safe for her to leave, because Roy's making nice.

He pours a cup of coffee from the white pitcher. He says, "What'd you do, little girl, fart?" He's smiling like it's not the dumbest thing she's ever heard, but he's still using his make-nice voice.

"I just want to leave the table, please."

"Sure you can," her mother says.

She takes her backpack from the back of the chair and walks into the hallway and stands holding it at her side.

She hears Roy ask, "You hate me, don't you?"

Her mother says no, she doesn't hate him, and Roy says he hates himself.

"You know that's the truth, baby," he says. He stirs a spoonful of sugar in his coffee. "I hate when you back me into a corner." He sips his coffee. "I don't know why I come out swinging like I do. I wish I didn't. Tell me we're still in love."

She thinks her mother must have nodded

yes because Roy says, "That's what I can't live without."

She hears Roy get up from the table. She hears him pick up his lunchbox where her mother leaves it packed by the door next to his hard hat. She doesn't know why Roy needs to wear a hard hat working on guardrails. She's never seen a guardrail that was tall enough to fall on somebody's head.

Roy says, "Baby, I love you more'n my own life. If I thought you hated me I don't know what I'd do."

She hears Roy open his lunchbox like he does every morning. He always checks to make sure there's something inside.

"I packed you a Snickers bar with the sandwiches," her mother says.

Roy snaps the lunchbox shut. "What do you say I pick up a pizza after work? Hell," he says, "I could rent us a video."

"That'd be real nice," her mother says.

Roy opens the door. "That's my girl." He makes it sound like he means it. "That's my baby." She hears the door shut, and the side of the trailer shudders. She hears Roy start up his shiny red pickup.

She walks back into the kitchen. Her mother's

still sitting at the table in her polyester uniform with her name embroidered above her left breast.

"I wish you were a lesbian," Griff says.

Her mother lights another cigarette. They both listen as Roy backs the pickup out of the carport. Her mother exhales as the truck idles away from the trailer.

"What do you know about lesbians?"

"Miss Crowder's one."

"Your teacher Miss Crowder, or some other Miss Crowder?"

"My teacher. I saw her kissing Miss Zimkowsky."

"Who's Miss Zimkowsky?" Her mother stubs out the cigarette even though she just lit it.

"The girls' PE teacher. For the junior high. They don't even work in the same building. When I see them together they look happy."

Her mother gets up and walks to the sink, leaning over it to watch Roy turn his truck into the lane at the entrance of the trailer park. "I'll drop you off at school," she says. She's still looking out the window like she thinks Roy might turn around and drive back.

"You promised," she says. Her mother turns around. She doesn't just look bruised and swollen, she looks tired too. "You promised after the next time it happened we'd go. That's what you said."

Her mother stares down at her shoes. The shoes are white, and they've got thick white soles. "How long will it take you to pack?"

She says, "Not very long." She's careful with her face. She doesn't want her mother to know she packs every morning.

THREE

—————

EINAR SLEEPS IN LONG UNDERWEAR, tops and bottoms both. They're off-white, a wool-and-cotton blend he orders by the dozen from the L.L. Bean catalog. And a pair of thermal socks. From first frost to last.

He knows how he looks—like some nosepick old rube—but he's past caring about appearance. He'd rather be warm. One of the few gifts of age, he thinks, is that the essentials rise to the top, and sleeping warm's essential. Anyway, it's not like he lives in town. If he lived in Ishawooa he'd buy a robe. A man couldn't do his morning chores in a bathrobe, but if he lived in town the only thing he'd be required to do before noon is read the newspaper.

He checks the thermometer outside the kitchen window. This morning it's thirty-eight. If the temperature is above thirty and there's no wind, he can get right out to the barn without the bother of a jacket or jeans.

He starts a pot of coffee and loops a kerchief around his neck and seats his hat. He's dialed his hot water heater to high, and in the evenings he scalds out the stainless steel pail and a few jars and turns them up to drain. He takes the pail from the dishrack, then sits in the straight-backed chair by the front door and pulls on his boots and steps out onto the porch. There's a light dew, and the silvered grass damps his boots on the way to the barn.

In the barn he breaks a leaf of hay into a manger, and the milkcow lumbers to the hay and stands eating. He hangs his hat on a nail and pulls the milkstool to her side. He enjoys milking the cow. Besides the old dog, an older horse named Jimmy and the mob of cats he's never stopped to count or name, she's the only stock left on the place that would miss him. She needs him alive. She needs to be fed and watered, and twice a day her udder strains low with milk.

She lashes her tail and it catches him on the back of his neck, and he hunches forward against her warm flank. He considers himself fortunate the tail isn't wet with fresh shit and snorts a laugh, that this is what his life has come to. An old man who's happy not to have cowshit on his neck. The cats roil against his legs, mewing, wriggling on their backs in anticipation. He guesses there're about three dozen of them. They keep the place mostly free of mice and voles and packrats, and the coyotes and owls keep the cat population pruned down to just this core of smarter, luckier animals.

He pulls harder on the milkcow's teats and says, "Stand now," and the cow turns her head from the manger to stare at him, shifting her stance, her mouth full of hay.

When he's done he stands the three-legged stool in a corner of the stall and puts his hat back on. He takes the pail up by its bail and carries it to a row of saucers lined against the wall opposite the stalls. There's always a catfight, sometimes two or three. The older, more experienced cats simply stretch up against his legs, purring. The cats love his habits and don't care how he's dressed.

He spills the saucers full of milk, pours a heap of dry Cat Chow from a forty-pound sack onto a rusted cookie sheet and starts for the granary, then stops and looks back at the humped bodies of the cats. They're inbred and ragged and battle-torn and lined out at the saucers, lapping milk. The loft stands open and shadowed above them.

It's warmer in the granary. Its east-facing window catches the morning sun, and the room smells sweet with oats.

He lifts a tin bowl down from a shelf and fills it with milk and steps away from it. He stands next to the oak rocking chair by the window to watch the pair of raccoons shoulder out of the hole in the granary's floor. They grouse, chatter and move cautiously around the bowl, their backs arched. They're shier than the cats, and Einar doesn't count them in as livestock.

He sets the pail on top of a grain bin and takes down a thick white crockery mug, dips it full of milk and sits in the rocker. "I heard you little bastards snuffling around in the yard last night," he says. The raccoons look at him, their noses white with milk. The larger of the two wipes its muzzle with a forepaw and licks the milk from the pads of the paw.

"Thanks for keeping the owls off my cats." He sips from the mug, sucks at his milk-slick tongue and rocks back slowly in the chair.

Even when it's well below freezing and the radio weatherman has warned of windchill, this is where he sits in the early mornings.

Last January he fell asleep in this chair. It was

ten below zero, and he wore insulated overalls pulled over his long underwear, a woolen cap and felt-lined boots. When he woke and looked down at his gloved hands, the mug of milk was frozen solid. He wove a netted sock from baling twine and hung the mug from the granary ceiling, and it didn't start to drip until the third of March. It had been a hard winter, and he'd sat through part of every morning of it watching the sun strike his pastures, sipping milk from a second mug he carried down from the house. He was careful not to doze again.

This morning he sees Curtis Hanson skirt the timber at the far end of the east pasture mounted on a young, edgy bay colt. Curtis works hard and he works his horses hard. He's out checking the Hereford cows for signs of illness or accident. The cows fan away from Curtis and the colt, quick in the morning chill, puffing funnels of breath and bawling at the inconvenience.

The Hansons' ranch, the Triple C, is the next place north along the front range. Curtis's two older brothers have moved away, one to Billings, the other to Denver, but Curtis can't think of anywhere he'd like to go.

Old Dan Hanson turned sixty this spring, ten years younger than Einar, but he hasn't been worth a shit since he fell off his tractor and let it run over him and snap his back. That was twenty years ago and the back healed crooked, but the truth is he's never been worth a shit. Einar's known Dan his whole life, known him to be stove-up inside and out. The tractor wreck's just his excuse to cripple around like the cranky asshole he was born to be.

He won't deed the Triple C over to this son who's stayed, who can tolerate him enough not to leave, and instead said he might will the whole place to the Hutterites if God tells him to. Einar leases Curtis his hay meadows to irrigate and bale, and his pastureland to run Hereford cows on when the farming's done. The lease allows Einar an income and Curtis a living while he waits for his dad to die. Everybody knows the only thing Dan Hanson's ever had to do with the Hutterites is to buy their butchered chickens.

Every evening Curtis rides back to the Triple C, where he's made to feel like a guest. He's told Einar he has to knock at the door of his own house. If the old man's on the john he has to stand on the porch until Dan gimps to the door and lets him in.

Einar doesn't feel sorry for Curtis, or like him any better than his dad, but the man's never been late on a lease payment. He's polite, doesn't bitch about the weather and gets a good spread on the irrigation water.

The Hansons have been good neighbors, even Dan with all his broken-backed whining. They're stout and plain men, all of them dull and honest. Einar thinks if the whole clan were the size of barncats they'd have been killed and eaten by predators years ago. Dan would've got dragged down first, and Curtis could've had a good year or two on the family place before the coyotes got him too.

Einar finishes his milk. He pulls a sleeve of his long underwear over a hand and wipes the mug clean with the webbed cuff, then starts back through the barn with the half-filled pail. The cats have cleaned their saucers and the cookie sheet and moved out to find spots against the barn where the sun's warmed the dew off the grass.

In the house he takes two scalded jars from the dishrack and fills them with the last of the milk. He screws the lids tight and sets them in the refrigerator. Every second day, if there's any milk that he and Mitch haven't drunk, he sells it in Ishawooa to a co-op of young married couples who've moved to Wyoming for a more natural life. Their big houses dot the foothills, their twenty-acre ranchettes fenced with buck and rail. They drive brand-new SUVs they don't put in four-wheel-drive more than half a dozen times a year, and Einar rightly blames them for the spike in real estate prices and property taxes. But there's also a big-deal veterinarian in Ishawooa now, and both cafés in town serve better coffee than they used to. It's fine by Einar if rich dudes want to drink his milk. He's not about to pour it on the ground.

He fills two insulated mugs with coffee and seats their lids and takes a vial of morphine from the compartment on the refrigerator's door where it says he should store butter. He holds the vial up to the window to check its level and opens the cabinet above the sink and takes one of the plastic-wrapped syringes from the box.

He walks out through the mudroom and exactly thirty-seven steps down the path he's worn to the bunkhouse. Karl watches him come. The old dog's gotten too crippled to want to use himself up doing chores. He sleeps on the bunkhouse porch, and in the winter Mitch moves him inside day and night.

Einar steps onto the porch and pulls the latchstring and eases the door open, then sidesteps the floorboard that creaks and stands and listens.

"I'm awake," Mitch says.

"You hear me coming back from the barn?"

"Of course I did. I'm not deaf. Karl out there?"

"Yes, he is."

"Tell him I'll feed him in a little bit."

"He knows you will." Einar sets the coffee on the workbench and sits on the edge of the bed. "How was your night?"

"As long as I'm asleep I like it fine."

Einar snaps the nightstand lamp on and tears the plastic away from the syringe.

"Don't just leave that lying around," Mitch says. He's turned away from Einar, on his side. "I found the one from yesterday where you let it fall."

"I'll put it in my pocket."

"It isn't cold enough for you to have a pocket. What you're doing is sitting there in your long underwear, and long underwear doesn't have pockets."

Einar holds the vial of morphine up under the lampshade with the needle stuck in through the rubber stopper. "I'll put all this in your trash can." He thumbs the plunger back to the right dose.

"Put it in your boot and walk it out of here

when the rest of you leaves. Litter your own goddamn place up. I like mine the way it is."

Einar opens the drawer in the nightstand where he keeps the cotton balls and a razor. Underneath the drawer there's an open shelf with shaving cream, a bottle of rubbing alcohol and one of horse liniment. He plucks out a cotton ball and turns the rubbing alcohol up against it and tucks the blanket back. "Left or right?" he asks.

"My left needs a rest. Let's work on the right awhile."

Einar scoots Mitch's shorts down and sticks the needle in with just a flick of his wrist, like he was in the Spur Bar in town throwing a dart at a board, and Mitch exhales all at once, just like he does every morning. Einar presses the cotton ball against the puncture and caps the syringe with his other hand. "How was that?" he asks.

"Smooth," says Mitch. "So smooth I thought my mama'd done it."

Einar drops the capped syringe, its plastic wrap and the cotton ball in his left boot top. He shakes some horse liniment into a cupped palm and rubs his hands together and works the greenish liquid into Mitch's lower back. The smell of it makes his eyes water and his nose run.

"They've got morphine in drops now," he says. "I could get you a bottle, and you could keep it out here with you. It's got a little squeeze dropper, and you could drip some under your tongue anytime you liked. If you had a bad night it might help."

"I don't need to be an addict," Mitch says. "I don't want to get like you were with booze."

"You never have been like me."

"I never said I was. I'm just saying I probably like morphine better'n you ever liked the bottle."

Einar works his thumbs deeply into the slick, wide ribbons of scar tissue that puzzle Mitch's back, healed purple-black, and then gentler into his sunken side where his right kidney used to be. Mitch groans. Just like he does every morning. He groans as he breathes in and out, and the sound gets into Einar right below his sternum and catches there. Not like a fist, but like the empty place inside a fist.

He spills more liniment into his hand and works the undamaged flesh of Mitch's shoulders. The man still groans. The skin's smooth, hairless, a deep, rich amber. The empty place in Einar starts to spread, and he breathes in deeply and holds his breath and tries to push it lower, toward his gut, away from his heart.

Every morning it shocks him. He watches his white hands massaging Mitch's black skin and can't seem to look at anything else, the difference in the colors fixing his attention, and he knows if he shuts his eyes he'd forget they weren't the same man, that he wasn't working the liniment into some scarred part of himself.

"The pain bad all the time now?" he asks.

"It gets my full attention." Mitch rotates his shoulder so Einar can work deeper along the bone.

"How's that morphine doing?"

"It must be getting a grip." Mitch turns further away so Einar can get at both shoulders, then shifts his head a little to look back. "I'm not so worried now about where you keep the trash."

Einar stands and wipes his hands on his thighs and arranges both pillows up against the bed's headboard. Mitch rolls onto his back, and Einar hooks him under the arms and muscles him upright against the pillows, then pulls the bedcovers to Mitch's waist. The right side of his chest is pocked with puncture wounds.

"I dreamed about the sea last night."

Einar walks into the bathroom. His father had built just one large room with a crew of Finns down from Red Lodge, Montana—the same gang who'd skidded in the lodgepole pine and put up the main house and barn. And now there's this bathroom they added on when they plumbed the whole place in the late forties, a small room made of milled lumber and fir paneling.

"What was it like?" he calls. He's set an enameled basin in the sink, filling it with hot water, and steps back into the doorway to hear Mitch's answer.

"Just a regular sea. Blue and green. Whipped up here and there."

Einar shuts off the water and carries the basin out and levels it on the side of the bed. He drapes a towel across Mitch's chest and dampens another towel in the basin. He presses the damp towel against Mitch's face with both hands, over his cheeks and mouth and chin, to soften the whiskers.

He feels Mitch smile beneath the towel and thinks what he's often thought when looking at the man: that Mitch's eyes appear exactly like those of a deer, with the same kind of innocence. He thought it the first time he met Mitch in Korea, and fifty-one years later, he's still thinking it.

But now the eyes sit slanted in his friend's

face. When the shattered cheek and jaw and skull healed together, the left eye settled lower. Still the same innocent eye, just an eighth of an inch lower than the right. Einar can feel the ridges and grooves in the bone under his right hand. With the tips of his fingers he can feel the hole where Mitch's left ear used to be, and above it the jagged furrows ripped back through the nappy white hair.

Einar takes the towel away and fills his left palm with shaving cream and dabs it over where the whiskers grow, then wipes his hands on the damp towel.

"You get wet? In the sea you dreamed about?" He draws the razor down Mitch's cheek and rinses it in the basin.

"Walked right in. Easy as falling in love." Mitch purses his lips to stretch out his upper lip, and Einar scrapes it clean. "Smelled like a woman. Tasted like one."

"I don't believe your memory's that good." Einar swishes the razor in the basin again.

Mitch tilts his head back so Einar can get at his throat. "I don't mean it like some lame kid-joke." His Adam's apple bobs. "I mean it smelled fine. Like the way a woman's skin does when she's been working outside in the sun. Maybe working in her garden. The way Ella's skin smelled." He drops his head, and Einar hands him the towel to wipe his face.

"I was the one married to Ella." Einar stands with the basin and carries it to the bathroom.

"Just because you marry someone doesn't mean everybody else in the world has to hold their noses when they're around them."

"You hungry yet?" Einar calls.

"I guess I'm not. Just that coffee'll do."

Mitch pushes himself to the edge of the bed and drops his legs over its side, then takes up the canes that lean against the nightstand and gets to his feet. He uses the canes to shuffle to the chair at the workbench, and when he switches on the shaded light above the bench, it illuminates an elk antler clamped in a vise. Mounted on the wall and swung over the vise are a foot-wide magnifying glass and the arm of a dental drill. He adjusts the magnifying glass over the antler and squints through it and sips his coffee from the mug.

The main body of the antler's carved into a stream of running horses, shoulders flowing into flanks, their heads and tails up, their manes flecked like sea foam. The herd separates, still running, into the larger tines. Mitch eases the pad of a thumb against the place where yesterday's work stopped.

Einar pries off the top of his mug and stands beside him. "You warm enough?"

"I'm fine." Mitch still stares down through the glass. "That morphine's got fire in it."

"Then you'll get dressed when you want?"

Mitch looks up him. "You got someplace to go?"

"I thought I might run into town for breakfast. I've got to go anyway. Jimmy's licked his mineral block down to nothing. I need to go to the feed store and get him another."

Mitch turns the light off and the room falls back into shadow and slants of morning sunlight. "It's the getting-up part that's hard," he says, running his hands over his undamaged thighs. "Hell of a deal, isn't it?"

Einar nods. "You've got those horses just right."

Mitch looks up. "By God, I do, don't I?"

"You want Karl let in?" Einar looks up at the carved antlers displayed across the log walls. More horses, geese, coyotes, wolves, deer, elk.

"He'll come in in a minute. You think you might eat at Nina's?"

"That's what I was thinking."

"I like her pancakes. If you remember you could bring me back a stack."

"I thought you might want seafood." Einar smiles.

Mitch turns the light back on over the bench. "That was just a dream." He peers down through the glass.

They hear Karl get up on the porch, whining.

"Well, I guess he'll come in now," Mitch says, and Einar opens the door, and the old dog pads inside and lies down on the carpet scrap Mitch keeps for him by the workbench, looking up at him. He knows Mitch will feed him once Einar's gone and they're alone. Karl won't eat unless no one's watching.

FOUR

———

GRIFF CARRIES her suitcase and backpack to the car and then helps her mother fold all of her clothes into two black plastic garbage bags. They drag the garbage bags to the car and stack everything in the backseat. They don't pack any cookware or knickknacks or appliances. They leave with only their clothes, which is what they came with. All of it together doesn't rise past the seatback.

The car's a 1984 Chevy Impala with exactly one hundred and forty-seven thousand and one miles on the odometer. Griff checks. It still has Florida license plates and her mother still has a Florida driver's license in her purse. The car was paid off before they left Florida. And Jean's always chipped in half the rent, from the very first month with Roy. Griff watched her write the checks.

When she stands with her mother next to the

packed car she thinks it's like they've never even lived in this trailer house in Iowa. They owe Roy squat.

She looks up through the carport's roof. It's made out of wavy blue-green plastic, slanted so the rain runs off. This morning it's beaded with water from the drizzly little storm that sputtered through before dawn. She holds her hands out under the aquamarine light. "Look at this," she says, turning both hands slowly in the strange light cast by the wavy roof.

Then she faces the trailer and points her index fingers, cocks her thumbs and shoots from the hip, boom, boom, boom. She empties both hands and blows the smoke from the tips of her index fingers and reholsters. This old trailer was already dying, she thinks. A faded brick-colored red and rusty. Two panels of skirting around the base of the wooden stoop are missing and the paint's peeled up at the edges of the decking. She smiles at her mother, ready to tell her that she just put this butt-ugly trailer house out of its misery, but Jean's eyes are filled with tears, even the blackened one.

Griff thinks when she unpacks her diary she'll write that she hates it when her mother cries. "We should leave right now," she says. "Before we change our minds."

"You aren't worried a bit about changing your mind." Jean wipes her cheeks with the back of a hand. "It's me you're worried about."

"If we leave right now, what's the worst thing that could happen?"

Her mother takes a tissue from her uniform's pocket and blows her nose and puts the tissue back in the pocket. "The worst thing is"—she waves her arm toward the trailer—"this is apparently the best I can do."

THEY DRIVE to the dry cleaners first, and Jean walks right in and says this morning is the last time they'll see her sorry butt.

Kitty just laughs, then asks her if she wants her back wages in cash instead of a check. "So you won't have to stop at the bank," Kitty adds. "If you're really leaving that Mickey Mouse son of a bitch, the less stops the better."

Jean starts to cry again, and Kitty hugs her, and Griff watches carefully as her mother tries to smile. "He might not even miss me," her mother says.

"That's just bullshit," Kitty tells her. "You're not that lucky. Roy'll miss whatever he can't eat, beat, or screw."

They drive to the women's shelter next. It's

just an old house, but it's on a street of old houses that have all been fixed up and it's made of real wood, with a fresh coat of yellow paint, and it has a yard.

They sit on a couch in the front room. Griff thinks it was probably a living room when a real family lived here. She can see three women in the kitchen. When Jean knocked and a fat lady named Janet opened the front door, all three of them in the kitchen looked out like they expected to see Freddy, the cut-you-up guy in the horror films.

Janet sits on the edge of an easy chair across a coffee table from them. Griff thinks she just sits on the edge of the chair to look like she's really listening, that if she sat back in the seat she'd probably get stuck.

On the wall behind Janet there's a poster of an x-rayed skull that's cracked open at the top. On the bottom of the poster it says: **Some men break more than hearts.**

Janet says, "I'm sorry, Ms. Gilkyson." She pulls her dress away from her breasts like it's a real hot day, but it's not. "If you'd come in a week ago we could've had a relocation set up for you. You could've called ahead, even."

Her mother says, "It was a snap decision." She touches her swollen jaw, not to make Janet feel sorry for her, just remembering. "We sort of snapped."

A woman comes out of the kitchen with a plate of cookies and puts the plate on the coffee table. Janet says, "Thank you, Cynthia," and the woman smiles at Jean and Griff like they're starved dogs out looking for a turned-over garbage can.

"I can find work," Jean says. "All we need is a place to go."

Griff picks up a cookie from the plate and puts it back. With three women in the kitchen she expected something freshly baked, but these are just like the cookies Roy bought.

"We have a reciprocity agreement with Kansas," Janet says. She calls into the kitchen to make sure they do, and leans over and plucks up three cookies.

Cynthia comes into the doorway and says they have agreements with Kansas and New Mexico both.

Janet's chewing, and brushing cookie crumbs off her big saggy breasts and looking down to see where they went, when she says, "If you stay here in the shelter for a week, I'm sure we can find you a place in Wichita."

Her mother snorts and stands up and glances at Cynthia, who's still propped in the kitchen doorway. Her mother doesn't look like any lost dog. She looks like the kind who might bite. "Every goddamn man in this town who beats a woman knows where this shelter is," she says.

"Is there anyone you could stay with?" Janet leans forward and takes another cookie from the plate.

"We could stay with you." Griff can't help herself. She widens her eyes and makes her face go blank in innocence. Janet looks like she's got a cookie caught in her throat.

Griff says, "We wouldn't bother anyone." She looks up at her mother, proud of her. She wants her to know that she's not a lost dog either.

Janet sits all the way back in the chair.

THEY GAS UP the car and have the attendant check the oil. Jean buys a road atlas, a big one with a different state on every page.

At the edge of town they stop at the Mc-Donald's and get Egg McMuffins and chocolate shakes, then find the ramp onto Interstate 80 heading west. Every time they pass a stretch of guardrail Griff feels a little better. She gets up on her knees on the seat and sips her shake through the straw. She looks at the people in the cars that pass, and if there's a kid in the car she waves.

Jean asks, "What are you doing?"

"I'm just being friendly."

When they pass a farmhouse along the interstate Griff closes her eyes and tries to picture the family who lives inside. She sees them all at the kitchen table, the platters of hot food, the mother with an apron on, the father cracking jokes.

Jean's got her dress hiked up and her chocolate shake stuck between her legs. The back windows are down, and the warm morning air swirls in the car and lifts their hair. Jean brings the shake up and sucks at the straw and drives with one hand.

"We should've done this a long time ago," she says, and when Griff doesn't say anything like "I've told you that a hundred times," Jean asks, "Where to, madam?"

Griff settles on the seat and opens the atlas on her lap. She flips through the pages, looking for towns to live in. "What about Carefree, Arizona?"

Jean doesn't miss a beat. "How about Bountiful, Utah?"

Griff turns to another state. Every one seems

filled with good places where kids don't have to live in trailer houses and pray for tornadoes. "Loving, New Mexico."

"Keep going, girl."

She's never seen her mother this happy before. Not even when they left Florida.

Griff puckers her lips, her eyes forced squinty. "Who'd want to live in Butt, Montana?" she asks.

Her mother pulls into the faster lane to pass a corn truck.

"It's pronounced 'Beaut,' not 'Butt,'" Jean says. She laughs and says, "Maybe there is a Butt, Montana. Hell, for all I know, maybe there's an Asshole, North Dakota." Griff laughs too. She's never heard her mother cuss when she wasn't crying or nervous or sad. She thinks she might start a new list in her diary. Things she likes about her mother. She likes it that her mother can cuss and laugh at the same time.

They still aren't all the way around the corn truck when they hear the honking start behind them. Her mother has just finished her shake and is lifting the empty cup to drop it over the back of the seat. She looks in the rearview mirror. "Shit," she says, and she's not laughing anymore.

Griff turns in the seat. The grille of a red

pickup's right on their bumper, but she can't tell for sure if it's Roy's. Her mother speeds up and pulls in front of the corn truck, and they don't breathe until the red pickup goes by, fast, and the man driving shoots his arm out the window, his hand above the truck's cab, and gives them the finger. It's not Roy, Griff thinks, but probably someone just like him.

A sign says it's thirty miles before they get to Des Moines. Griff opens the atlas to Iowa and bends over the map. "There's lots of littler roads," she says.

Jean checks the rearview mirror again. She puffs her cheeks and blows. "You mean roads Roy might not think we're on?"

"Yeah." Griff doesn't look up from the atlas. "We could take a right when there's an exit for one. And then, when we find a road going west, just take a left."

Jean reaches in her purse and pulls out her cigarettes and lights one. She cranks her window down an inch and holds the cigarette up by the crack. "You're damn right we could."

She clenches the cigarette in her teeth and tilts her head back from the smoke. She's smiling again, around the cigarette, as she flips on the turn signal and pulls off the interstate onto Highway 65 North.

She flicks her ash through the crack in her window and drives slower, like they're on their way home. For miles the fields spread away from both sides of the road. They're striped green and tan, and real dark where they've been plowed.

"This is a lot better," Griff says.

"Why don't you decide when we should take a left."

"Any road I pick?"

"Just say when."

Griff looks back down at the atlas. "I can feel a good road coming up."

Jean holds the steering wheel in both hands and pushes back against the seat, wriggling back and forth like she's got an itch. "I guess about any road heading west will get us to the Pacific."

Griff closes the atlas. "Is that where we're going?" She never thought they were going that far. "We're going to the Pacific Ocean?"

"Why not? We're wild things, aren't we?"

Griff can't think of a single reason why they shouldn't live by the ocean. She cups her hands over her ears to hear the waves, but can't remember who taught her to do that. "Is it warm there?"

"It is as long as we don't get too high up on the coast."

Griff points at a highway sign that says 20 West. "There."

"Are you sure?"

"I'm positive." She smiles as if she were already standing on a beach.

Jean turns west. She's smiling too. To the north there're whole pastures filled with pigs, dotted with little plywood A-frames so the pigs can stay warm in the winter.

"Do we have enough money to get to the ocean?"

Jean snaps her purse open and takes out her wallet and hands it to her. "I can't count and drive."

Griff counts out the bills, twice. "Eighty-two dollars," she says, opening the atlas to California. She evens the stack of bills across the state, like x marks the spot.

Jean pulls a folded white envelope out of her dress pocket. It's the envelope Kitty gave her. "How much in there?"

Griff counts. "Two hundred and twenty."

"Are you sure?"

Griff counts the bills again, out loud this time.

"That's about sixty dollars more than she owed me in wages."

"Maybe Kitty lived with Roy before us."

Jean pushes her hair back from her face. "Maybe she did."

"Is three hundred and two dollars enough?"

"Sure it is."

Jean lights another cigarette.

"You sure?"

"It'll be tight, maybe. We might have to sleep in the car."

"I can do that."

Her mother turns to study Griff's face, then reaches across the seat and holds her hand against her daughter's smooth cheek. "So can I," she says.

FIVE

―――――――――

EINAR'S NOT SURE it's a good idea anymore, but Curtis has already seen him and he doesn't feel like turning around and pedaling back to the barn. The bay colt's trying to get out from underneath Curtis, to get away altogether, snorting and rearing and skittering sideways into the brace at the fence corner. Finally Curtis steps down, and the colt stands quivering, pulling back against the bridle reins.

Einar coasts to a stop. He thinks of the half-dozen favorite horses he's ridden in his life and remembers every one of them as well mannered. He knows Curtis as the type of man to imagine a horse only as transportation, that he'd never put in the effort to turn this colt into a gentle-man. "It's a tricycle," he says, louder than he has to.

Curtis looks at the bright-red pennant on top of the fiberglass pole mounted against the basket between the tricycle's back tires. "Kind of like a kid would have?"

"Yeah, like that," Einar says. "Only bigger." He turns on the seat and sets the jar of milk upright in the basket. "I never had one when I was a kid, but it's that kind of outfit."

"I never had one either."

Einar takes off his jacket and stuffs it in the basket around the jar so it won't fall over again. He's overheated and wishes he'd taken off his long underwear before he got dressed to go to town.

"Where would a man find a trike like that?" Curtis isn't trying very hard to hide his smile. The colt's stepped forward, his ears pricked, and there's some slack in the reins.

"I bought this one from Nancy Sidwell." Einar squeezes the blue bulb on the handlebars, and the horn toots.

The colt pulls back again at the sound and Curtis steps to his head. "That's enough now, goddamnit." He grips the bridle's cheekpiece. He's not smiling anymore.

"Nancy had it shipped up from that retirement village in Arizona where Ernie died."

Curtis loops the reins at the fence brace and squats on his heels to have a ground-level look.

"I always liked Ernie Sidwell," he says. "You think that tricycle's what killed him?"

"He probably died of criticism, if you're any example."

"Hell, Einar, give me a minute. I've never seen a grown man on a trike before. Did Jimmy die?"

"He's thrown a front shoe."

"What about your truck?"

"My truck's fine." Einar lifts his hat and drags a forearm across his forehead. "I guess you've never heard of exercise either." He seats the hat and spits over his shoulder and stands up on the pedals to get himself going. "You're a dull man, Curtis. You know that?" The tires bite into the skim of gravel on the dirt road.

Curtis stands, smiling again. "I like your flag," he calls. "Without that red flag you might look ridiculous."

Einar toots the horn and doesn't turn to see what the bay colt thinks of it.

When he gets to the blacktop the pedaling improves. He stays on the highway's shoulder, and his neighbors slow and turn on their truck-seats when they pass. They wave and he waves back. It's only half a mile into Ishawooa, but he thinks he's seen damn near everyone he knows by the time he coasts to a stop at the Conoco station at the west edge of town.

He carries the milk in, and Jimmy J. gives him three dollars for it and sets the jar in the cooler with the Cokes and Dr Peppers. The food co-op's in the failed diner next door, open only on Tuesdays and Thursdays, and Einar likes to bring in his milk when it's closed. Jimmy J. pays him and gets his money back from Joyce Thompson, who runs the co-op. The other three workdays every week, Joyce sits at home with her laptop and trades stock. Einar imagines she must be good at it, since she drives a canary-yellow Hummer and each January goes to some island in the Caribbean to scuba dive for a month. Einar doesn't think you should call yourself a resident if you don't spend Januarys here. Joyce came from Maine, and he thinks there ought to be some mention of that too.

Last winter Jimmy J. said, "I'll bet down there in the Caribbean she's thought of as a real good floater." That's his way of saying Joyce has about forty pounds she could lose.

She wears sleeveless blouses and flower-print skirts year round and doesn't shave under her arms. Or her legs, either. It makes Einar less sure about the benefits of natural food, and once when he delivered the milk Joyce said, "Here we are in the wild, wild West, old-timer. Where the men are men and the women smell like 'em."

That's not something he ever wants to hear again, which is why he never delivers his milk on a Tuesday or Thursday.

He pedals down Bridger Street and stops at Ishawooa's single traffic light and waits for the light to turn. Front Street runs north-south, and what businesses are left line one of these two streets. The First Wyoming Bank building is diagonally across from him, and on the corner straight ahead there's Ishawooa Drug. The residential streets, most of them unpaved, clot around this intersection. The grade school and junior high and high school are in a new brick complex south of town in a pasture Ed Hasslebeck farmed his whole life. The town council didn't know they needed a new school until Ed got elected mayor. The new football field's there too, the bleachers painted blue and gold.

There're two attorneys in town, a Republican named Brown and a Democrat named Hooten. John Hooten, one of only a dozen local Democrats, was a Republican for most of his life, but when his mother retired at sixty-five from the brick factory and started waiting tables to keep herself busy, the government told her she was making too much money to collect Social Security, and that's when John switched.

Ishawooa's got its own undertaker, but up until 1989 when they built the little ten-bed hospital there never was a full-time doctor. Before then, if you got hurt, someone drove you the twenty-two miles southeast to Sheridan. If you were sick and expected to die there was the hundred-and-twenty-mile trip north to Billings, Montana. There always was a dentist, but Ray Dawson's wife made him quit drilling teeth when he couldn't remember the names of their three kids anymore, even when they were lined up for holiday photographs. For thirty-five years Ray mixed his patients' fillings right in the palm of his hand, the silver and mercury both. The doctors found out even before Ray's family became strangers to him that the mercury had leached right in through his skin and never come out again. Jimmy J. claims Ray weighed eight pounds more than he should've when they buried him, but Einar always liked Ray, light or heavy.

There're only two churches, a Missouri Synod Lutheran and St. Anne's for the Catholics, and four bars that everyone can use.

Einar raises his arm to signal and turns right

and parks against the curb in front of Nina's Café. He stretches his legs before he steps off the trike. The tops of his thighs burn, and he wants to make sure he can walk before he tries.

He crosses the street to get his mail from his post-office box and crosses back to Nina's.

Only one table's occupied. There's a blond man sitting there tucked up close to his plate, his shoulders nearly as wide as his side of the table. His sleeves are rolled and his forearms are roped with muscle. Ten years ago Einar saw this man squat and hug a fifty-five-gallon drum filled with grain up against his chest and walk away with it. He did it because the drum needed to be moved, and he looks like he still could do it. An Indian woman sits to his left, and across from her a boy's pinching up French fries one at a time from a red plastic basket. His hair's so black and clean that when he turns to look at Einar it catches the light and reflects in a flash of sapphire, like a raven's wing would.

Einar nods at the man. "Morning, McEban."

McEban wipes his mouth on a paper napkin. "Good morning, Einar."

The woman sits back in her chair because she holds a child balanced on her lap, asleep, turned in against her belly, the fingers of its right hand clenched into a fist, sucking its thumb.

"You get married while I wasn't looking?"

"These are friends of mine." McEban glances at the woman like he hopes she might correct him. Like she really is his wife and he'd somehow missed the ceremony and reception. "This is Rita." He motions toward the boy. "And there's her brother, Paul."

Rita looks down at the child's sleeping face. "I named him Kenneth."

Einar tucks the mail under his arm and takes his hat off and holds it at his side. "He looks just right," he says. The child doesn't look a year old yet.

"Thank you." Rita smiles with pride.

Einar asks Paul, "McEban working you hard?"

"I like it," the boy says. "I even have my own saddle."

"You still have an old man out there at the Rocking M?"

"Mr. Ansel Magnuson." Paul says the name slowly, reverently, like he's announcing their resident movie star. "He lets me crawl under the baler if the twine gets tangled in the gears and stops it. That happened this summer. He says I'm better at it than anybody, but he doesn't let me do it if the baler's still running."

"You can't beat that," Einar says. "You tell

Mr. Ansel Magnuson that Einar Gilkyson says hi."

"Yes, sir, I will."

Einar nods his good-byes and takes a seat at the next table over. He lays his mail on the place mat and starts through it, and Nina approaches with a small metal trash can and a glass coffeepot.

She sets the trash can on the floor beside him and fills his cup. "Good morning," she says. She's more than six feet tall, as tall and lean as Einar. Her face is tanned, and she's drawn her light brown hair into a ponytail. She wears a chambray shirt and jeans, and an apron imprinted with cattle brands. The brand pattern was her idea, as were the rodeo posters, spurs, lariats and saddle blankets that decorate the café's walls.

"Morning yourself, Nina." Einar tosses an advertising flyer in the trash can and holds up an envelope. "You believe they're still sending junk mail to my boy?"

"Maybe the dead like getting mail."

"I'm the one who needs mail." He slips the envelope in his shirt pocket and sips his coffee. "Am I in here too late for breakfast?"

"Just tell Charlie what you want."

She motions toward an open rectangle cut into the kitchen wall behind the cash register. Charlie leans on the countertop in the opening, a rounded, mostly hairless little man with a white bandana tied over his head.

"A couple of eggs sunnyside," Einar tells him. "Buttered toast and some fried potatoes if they're handy."

"It's all handy," says Charlie. "You want meat?"

"I'm fine without it this morning. But I need a stack of pancakes boxed up for Mitch."

"Coming your way in a jiff." Charlie pushes back into the kitchen, and they can hear the grill sizzle. He whistles while he cooks. Not tunes exactly, just whistling.

"How's Mitch doing?" Nina asks.

"He had a dream about the sea last night."

"No shit? I lived right on the beach in Oregon for a year before I moved home. Did I ever tell you about living in Oregon?"

Before Einar can say he can't even remember that she was ever gone, McEban gets up and walks past them toward the restroom, and Nina steps aside to give him room. Then the bell over the front door jingles, and two boys in their early twenties come inside. One of them stumbles into the table by the door and knocks the salt and pepper shakers over. He and his friend laugh, and then slide into the far booth against the wall. Their clothes and caps and hands and faces are stained with drilling mud, and Einar guesses they've driven in from the oilpatch east of Gillette.

Nina looks at them, then at Einar. "What do you think? Do you think those assholes drove over here just to give me a big tip?" She doesn't wait for an answer. She pulls a pencil from behind her ear and a pad out of her apron pocket and walks to the booth, standing there with her hip cocked. "So tell me, boys," she asks, "how hard is it to get this drunk before noon?" Mostly she just sounds impatient.

The stouter one laughs hard and pounds his fist on the table, and the child in Rita's lap begins to cry. She unbuttons the front of her blouse and settles the child on a breast, rocking in her chair while he nurses.

The thinner boy widens his eyes, looking up at Nina. "Hell, it's easy. But you've got to keep at it all night."

"And you can't pussy out just because the sun comes up," the bigger boy adds.

Charlie sets Einar's breakfast and the boxed

pancakes on the countertop in the window and slaps his palm down on a little domed bell.

Paul's quit eating his French fries. He sits very straight in his chair, staring at the drunk boys.

The stout boy pulls his belt away from his belly and looks down in his lap, then up at Nina with his mouth hanging open in amazement. "I've got something else here that's come up just for you, darling."

Einar watches Rita nurse the baby. He looks at Paul, and then at the empty place where McEban was sitting. He remembers what it was like to be drunk in the morning.

He takes his breakfast plate and the box of pancakes from the countertop and walks to the boys' booth, sliding in next to the big one. "You fellas take catsup on your eggs?"

The boy next to him snorts a laugh. "Why don't you just blow me, you old fuck."

Einar smiles and takes a piece of toast from the plate. "I think if we had some catsup here everything'd be just fine." He turns his head to Nina and she nods and steps away from the booth, but not very far. "I used to drink some," he says as if he'd just remembered. He knows everything is not just fine. He can feel the violence in these two, and how desperate they are to break the routine of their lives, like lightning splits a tree all at once. He's felt the same himself.

He breaks an egg with the tines of his fork and watches the yellow yolk spread and remembers waking drunk in his truck, or where he'd fallen in the house, and not knowing where he was, who he was or what he could expect from himself. Not knowing what pain he'd caused. "Wasn't anything for me to be drunk this time of day."

The thinner boy rolls his eyes.

Einar points the fork at the boy's chest. "Aren't you Jess Shepard's son?"

The boy holds his eyes steady and sits back in the booth, trying to recognize him.

"Ricky, or Dickie, or . . ." Einar wags the fork at the boy.

"Richard," the boy says. "I don't know you."

"Sure you do. You've just forgot." Nina sets the catsup bottle on the table, and Einar picks it up and smacks the bottom of the bottle with the heel of his hand. "Liquor hits everybody different." He pours the catsup over his eggs and potatoes. "When I was drinking I just got quiet. And then I mostly got quieter." He looks up from his breakfast. "Sometimes I didn't."

The big boy next to him says, "You ought to save your sermon for someone who gives a shit."

Einar turns to the boy. "I don't believe I know you." He's got a mouthful of potatoes and catsup.

He's watched the boy's movements and gestures, and thinks if he's lucky he might just handle this one, with his slow arms and wit, but he knows he can't take them both.

"Fuck you, Granddad."

Einar nods, wondering if these boys'll hurt him badly enough to put him in the hospital. He still stares at him, chewing his potatoes and hoping the boy can't read that thought in his eyes. "What you forget when you're drinking is how fast your life can change." He swallows and tries to think of someone who'd take care of Mitch. He can't think of anyone. "You believe me?"

The boy spits against Einar's chest. "What I believe is that I'm going to kick your shriveled old ass."

Einar lays what's left of the toast on his plate, staring at the boy next to him but watching the other one too, mostly waiting for what he knows is going to happen next.

"No you're not," McEban says.

Einar turns, as do both boys, to look up at where McEban stands at the end of the booth. He's bent forward slightly at the waist, and Einar and the big kid together aren't wide enough to fall out of either side of McEban's shadow. The thinner boy stares straight down at the table, and the other slumps all the way back into the corner.

Einar stands out of the booth. He pulls a bandana from his back pocket and wipes the spit from his shirt, then lays a five-dollar bill on the table. He takes the box of pancakes and holds it against his side.

McEban picks the bill up, still leaning over the table, and extends his arm behind him to Einar. "I think this fella here wants to buy your breakfast. Don't you, son?"

The big boy says "Sure" and shifts enough in the booth to get his wallet out, looking like he might cry.

McEban hasn't once looked away from him. He says to Einar, "I never did thank you for helping Ansel bring our cows down off the mountain last fall."

"It just took a day," Einar says. "They practically came down all by themselves."

"Nothing happens all by itself."

Einar tips his hat to Rita. "Nice to meet you."

"You too," she says. She's still nursing her child, rocking in her chair.

Paul's gotten up. He's not much taller than the back of the chair, but he looks ready to help.

Einar opens the café door and the bell jingles. "That's a good boy you've got with you."

McEban swivels his head just a little and looks at Paul. "Yes, he is. He's first-rate."

Outside, Einar sets the pancakes in the trike's basket and backs it away from the curb. When the light at the corner turns green he pedals east at the intersection and back out on the two-lane. He leaves the tricycle in the barrow pit by the turnoff to the ranch and walks up a path worn through the sage to the top of a rise. There's a single cottonwood and beside its trunk a wicker chair, the cane weave weathered bone-white. Below the rise are his pastures and house and barn and the sweep of prairie beyond.

He sits in the chair and leans back into the shade. His legs feel used up. He tastes his breakfast in the back of his throat and swallows and pulls the bandana from his pocket again. He lifts his hat and wipes his forehead and puts the bandana back in his pocket. "Well, here I still am," he says, and looks around as if someone were there to hear him.

Two grave markers stand just before him, side by side. His wife and son.

He takes the envelope from his shirt pocket and slits it open with his pocketknife and shakes out the contest entry form. He squints at the grave marker on his right. "Says here you might've already won fifteen million dollars." He holds the contest announcement out toward the stone, then folds it back into the envelope and returns it to his shirt pocket. "I probably ought to send it in for us." He looks to the west. The Bighorns rise up into the blue sky, dusted white with an early snowfall. "The odds can't be any worse than losing a kid early, and we got that done." He looks back down.

GRIFFIN GILKYSON
BORN 1972 DIED 1993
AN UNFINISHED LIFE

He slips forward in the chair and rubs the burn out of the tops of his thighs. "I almost got my tail whipped a little while ago," he says and stands up out of the chair as though waiting for some kind of response. There's just the chatter of the wind in the papery cottonwood leaves. He takes his hat off and holds it against his belly, staring down at the polished marble of Ella's marker and the dark lettering. Dead at forty-one. That's nothing, he thinks. That's just getting started.

"What were you thinking?" he asks. "I mean goddamnit, did you think I couldn't use you around here? Do either one of you think this is easy?"

Dead isn't the same as if they'd said they'd had all of Wyoming they could stand and moved to Tucson, but that's how it feels. Like they're just out of reach, and won't call or write, and he's the one that's left behind.

He reseats the hat and turns away and starts back down the trail slowly, on the heels of his boots. His legs are tired enough to quiver as he comes down the slope.

SIX

———

ROY DOESN'T HAVE TO get out of his truck to know they're gone. He knows what alone feels like, and this is it. It doesn't mean a thing that Jean's car isn't there.

She finds any excuse she can to work late at that piece-of-shit job at the dry cleaners, and then she's got the balls to act surprised he's got half a load on when she drags her ass home. You might as well stick in an IV of pure sour mash as drink on an empty stomach. She knows that as well as he does, and she still can't get home on time to fix dinner. She knows he works out under the hot sun all day. He's said out loud how hot it gets, and it's not news either that one of the few fucking pleasures he has in life is a cold beer when the work's done. What did she say? She said it ain't exactly frigid in the back room at the dry cleaners. Great, so have a beer right along with me, is what he said. He could see she wanted one, but that would fuck up her master plan. What she said was she thought she wouldn't have a beer. Thought she wouldn't? What she really thought was she couldn't rag his ass if she was drinking too. There's the master plan.

Just last Thursday she tells him the high-school band leader came in to the dry cleaners with his car trunk loaded with black and red uniforms and said he needed the whole batch right away. Turns out he had to haul his little flute-playing cocksuckers on some road trip first thing Friday morning for a football game in Ottumwa. But it also turns out a freshly laundered brass band don't mean shit. The Trojans lost thirty-five to seven.

And what did she break her back to fix old Roy for dinner when she got home at eight o'clock at night? A goddamn can of Campbell's Hearty Vegetable, that's what. Hearty-Goddamn-Vegetable, even though she looked right at the coffee table and could count the five empties. But did he make a fist when she said he could've fixed the soup himself? No, he did not. Only a lame out-of-love motherfucker would pull a stunt like that. This is the woman he loves. He just let her stand there and feel superior, which is what she wanted anyway. It'd take a hell of a lot more than telling him to make his own soup to get him backed into a corner. What does get him there is her yapping mouth, when she's got to point out every little fuck-up that ever happened and drop it all in his lap. Where the hell does that leave him?

What he did that night was watch **Close Encounters of the Third Kind** on TNT. And he did it just for the benefit of that weird-ass kid of hers, so she could watch it with him, even though she's just a miniature version of her mother and he wanted to watch **The Godfather.** He'd been looking forward to seeing Marlon Brando and Al Pacino take care of business.

Didn't he ask the kid to sit on the couch with him? Of course he did, but she says no. Didn't he tell her she could put her legs up on the coffee table if she wanted and she still wouldn't say shit? The truth is she wouldn't say shit to him even if she had a mouthful of it. She knows how to get in her digs. Anyway, she was leaning against the wall in the hallway when the final credits started, and he wasn't even pissed anymore. In fact, he looked back to tell her it was just a movie and not to be scared, but she's already in bed, thank you very fucking much. He hoped she lay awake all night waiting for the mother ship to come get her. He'd thought about driving his truck around to the outside of her room and shining the high beams through her window and pounding on the side of the trailer, but she's so much like her old lady that she'd have just rolled over and pretended to sleep.

He finds his money right on the dresser where he left it. That doesn't surprise him either. Jean left it there so even gone she could stick her nose in the air and let him know she didn't need anything he had to give her. His dad's watch is still there sitting in his little change dish and he picks it up and sits on the edge of the bed, dangling the watch and watching it spin at the end of its chain. He's checked everywhere else. No note. No hi, bye or kiss my ass, Roy.

He didn't have to bring her in his own home—and not just her, but her kid too. He didn't have to provide a home. She would've done fine in some little hole-in-the-wall apartment, and he could've gone over and fucked her anytime he wanted. But he wanted more for her. He wanted to give her kid a chance at a family. And this is the thanks he gets.

He stands up fast and throws the watch as hard as he can against the bedroom wall, watching the watch-parts spring back across the carpet. Right there's one more thing she can add to the goddamn list of things she's made him do that he didn't want to.

He doesn't bother to close the door when he leaves. He sits in his truck and swivels his head all around to ease the tension out of his neck, then walks back into the trailer and hooks a finger in the plastic webbing of a six-pack of Milwaukee's Best and walks right back out through the open door. He leaves the fridge door open too.

Backing out from the carport he thinks that leaving the door open might just air the place out. Jean and that kid can take their stink with them.

He parks across from the dry-cleaning shop and drinks two beers, one right after the other, until he starts feeling a little better and his neck limbers up. He opens a third beer and says, squinting at the parking meter at the curb, "There were good times, plenty of them." He sucks the foam from the top of the can.

Hell, he thinks, when she first moved in didn't he pull his drawings out from under the bed? Didn't they sit together on that bed until he'd let her look at each drawing he'd made over the years? He remembers how she held each one on her lap. Didn't she say she thought he ought to go to school, maybe learn to paint too? That maybe he could paint pictures full-time for his living? Didn't they make love like mink that night, right on top of the drawings? Didn't he make her come? Goddamn right he did. Good goddamn times.

He bows his head and thinks of the pleasure of drawing, about what painting might be like. Okay. Fine. He makes a good living just as it is. Right now he needs to find out where Jean's gone. Get her back and show her they're a family, even if she does pull a stunt like this. What the hell's he so upset about, anyway? This right here is part of a man's job. It's how things work. It's the woman who gets her nightie in a knot, and the man who gets it untangled. There're lots of situations worse than this. It's what relationships are all about. It's give a little and take a little. He may not like it, but life's no fucking rose garden.

He sets the beer can on the dash and starts across the street to the dry cleaners, taking deep breaths in and out. It settles him, helps him remember that he's part of a family. The head of a family. And now is just one of those times to take command and set things right. The plain truth is, and Jean knows it too, she'll never find another man who loves her like he does.

When he walks into the shop and smiles at Kitty he knows that he's a man filled up with love. "Is Jean still around?" he asks.

Kitty stands sweating behind the counter. Like she's been working hard. She says, "Jean never came in today, Roy."

He can tell the old bitch is lying, but she doesn't get to hear everything he knows. "You're kidding me," he says. "Jesus." He leans into the counter to show how worried he is. "I was just at the school, and they said Griff never showed up either. Not for a single class all day."

Kitty stands behind the counter ringing out the till, keeping her eyes on the cash drawer because she doesn't have the guts to look him in the face. She says, "I don't know anything about Griff either."

"Jesus, Kitty," he says, "this isn't like Jean. I'm worried something bad's happened to her." He catches her eye, to let her know he's not just killing time. "I'm not sure you really understand how worried I am."

Kitty looks right at him. He'll have to give her that. And then she points across the street with her chin—the lazy bitch won't even lift a hand—and he sees the cop car pull in behind his truck. He won't look back at her right away. He'll give her enough time to figure out that cops don't mean shit to him. He asks, "You call those boys?"

He hears her say that she called the cops just as soon as he stepped out of his truck. He smiles and waits another minute until he turns. He wants her to know she doesn't mean shit to him either.

"You know, Kitty." He plucks up a pencil and taps at the counter with the eraser. "You and me could probably find Jean all by ourselves." He looks up at her and smiles right in her face. "If you weren't a two-bit lying cunt we could probably drive right to her."

He sees her eyes flicker, and it's only the two fat cops walking across the street that keeps her from crying and slobbering Please-don't-hurt-me-Roy-please. The cops make her brave. "I'm like you, Roy," she says. "I got worried."

He pushes away from the counter and hitches up his jeans. "Well, I guess I better go tell those boys that my true love and me had us a little argument." He turns back to her and makes a sucking sound with his cheek like he's just had a good meal and there's something tasty stuck between his teeth. "They can follow me on over to the house, and I'll show 'em where she got so mad she threw my dad's good pocket watch against the wall." He smiles his best smile through the window at the cops. "These here po-lice and me can probably sit right down at the kitchen table and fill out the missing-persons report. Then you know what I'm going to do, Kitty? I'm going to find my sweet Jean. Just as sure as God made little green apples. Don't you think I won't."

SEVEN

———   ·   ———

THERE'S A SERIES of grinding smacks followed by three high-pitched shrieks, like
R2-D2 might be giving that annoying C-3PO
the good whacking he deserves—Griff's always thought C-3PO way annoying—and her
mother coasts to the side of the highway. The
smoke doesn't start coming out from under the
hood until they finally stop, and then they both
get out quick and run up to the grille, just looking at the smoke for about two seconds, and
then Jean uses the hem of her dress to protect
her hands and unlatches the hood. When she
leans forward to push the hood open the flames
singe her bangs, and she slaps her forehead and
screams, "Holy fucking shit," and then, "Am I
on fire?"

She's not, but Griff runs to get the water bottle on the floor of the front seat anyway, because

the car definitely is, and Jean pours the whole bottle over the flames but it doesn't help much. Then she throws the bottle down and strips out of her uniform, right there on the side of Highway 9, and spreads it over the flames like a tablecloth, like company's just rung the doorbell and she's running late. And then she closes the hood and stands back in her bra and panties and clunky white shoes, the sun setting at her back.

They listen to the flames crackle for a minute, then it stops and there's a hissing sound instead. When Jean opens the hood again, the uniform's burned a little but mostly just melted, and the fire's out.

Everything suddenly feels funny to Griff, and she says, "At least we weren't in an airplane."

Her mother looks at her with real astonishment, and then the look changes to something like appreciation. She's still mostly pumped up and jumpy from being scared and almost set on fire. "You've never been on an airplane," she says.

"I know I haven't. But if we were on one, this would've been really bad."

That's when Jean starts to laugh, hard enough to get Griff laughing too. Griff watches her mother's little pooched belly jiggling, and her titties, and for a minute she even wishes for titties of her own.

Jean pulls a black garbage bag from the backseat and finds a pair of jeans. She takes her shoes off and she's stepping into the jeans as Griff slides in behind the steering wheel to look at the odometer. "One hundred and forty-seven thousand and three hundred and thirty-four," she says. "We've gone three hundred and thirty-three miles."

"Since where?" Jean's buttoning her shirt.

"Since the trailer house. I wanted to know how far away we got."

Jean sits in the backseat with the door open, tying her shoes. "We aren't done yet," she says. "The next time you look at your atlas, see if you can find Better Luck, Nevada."

Griff looks at her mother in the rearview mirror. "There's no ocean in Nevada," she says, and when her mother just shrugs and says that at least they'd be closer than they are now, Griff goes around the car and drags the rest of their belongings off the backseat and piles them next to the plastic bag already sitting by the edge of the highway. "Now there's room for a picnic," she says. She knows she didn't have to tell her mother where the ocean is, and where it isn't.

They sit together in the backseat and make

sandwiches out of the bread and lunchmeat they bought in Fort Dodge and pass the milk carton back and forth. They watch the farmland get all hazy as the sun sets, and when the crickets start to chirp her mother asks, "Did you pack a flashlight?"

Griff shakes her head.

"Well, me neither. So, if there's anything you need to do, you'd better do it before it gets dark." Jean sniffs at the last bite of her sandwich like all of a sudden the meat's not very good. "I'm not even sure we had a flashlight to pack."

Griff wades into the tall weeds at the bottom of the barrow ditch and stomps down a little circle, looks up and down the highway, then squats to pee. The broken weeds smell musty, like wet leaves. When she gets back in the car she says, "I didn't have anything to wipe with."

Jean stares out at the cornfields. "I won't tell if you don't."

Rows of corn stretch in every direction, as far as they can see. On the hills it doesn't look like corn at all, there's just lines of yellow shadow, and in between the hills, the lines turn a browner yellow. When a breeze rattles the dried husks, stalks and leaves, the sound makes Griff shiver.

"I guess they harvest a week or two later up

here," her mother says. "Maybe we should've stayed farther south, down on Highway 20."

Griff wishes there were men out now, up in their yellow-and-green machines with the headlights on, mowing down the corn. Farm lights come on in a small cluster of buildings to the north. "Do you think we'll have to walk up there?" she asks.

"Not tonight." Her mother sounds more tired than she was before the sun went down. "If nobody comes by and gives us a ride tonight, we'll go in the morning."

Griff can see the outline of her mother's body and face, but it's too dark to see the singed hair or the bruises.

"Do you think anybody will come?"

"It's not like we got here in a covered wagon," Jean says.

Griff nods and lies down on the seat with her head in her mother's lap.

"This is the best day I've had in a long time," Jean says.

Griff smiles but doesn't raise her head. "It's not your fault the car broke," she says.

Her mother combs her fingers through Griff's hair, hooking the hair behind her ear. "Hell's bells, baby, this old car didn't just break. It up and died."

"That wasn't your fault either." Griff tries to remember if she's ever heard her mother say "hell's bells" before.

"Well, it sure wasn't the car's fault," Jean says. "I probably forgot to have something checked, or add something."

Griff turns on her back, her head still on her mother's leg. "If anybody asks," she says, "I'll say that it spontaneously combusted."

Jean rests her hand against her daughter's cheek. "That's what I'll tell them too," she says.

IT'S STILL DARK when Griff wakes. Her mother isn't there, and for a minute she thinks it's time to get up and take the towel down from her window. Then she hears an engine and sits up in the seat.

"I'm right here," Jean says.

Griff can see the approaching light flicker against her mother where she stands beside the car.

"What time is it?"

"It's not morning yet."

Griff gets out and stands beside her, and they watch a single headlight bobbing toward them from the east, and finally have to bow their heads against the glare, and then the driver stops and cuts the engine and puts the kickstand down. He eases the big bike over at an angle, but keeps his headlight pointed at the raised hood. He sniffs loudly. "Smells like you had some car trouble."

Jean nods. "I think what we have is a dead car."

"Spontaneous combustion," Griff says.

"That's what it was." Her mother smiles. "Death by combustion."

The man lifts his helmet off and sets it on the gas tank right in front of him. "How long have you been stuck out here?"

"Just three hours so far," Jean says.

"This road doesn't get a lot of traffic." The man turns on the seat and looks up the empty highway as if to prove his point. "It doesn't get much traffic even in the daytime."

"I believe you," Jean says.

The man nods. He's got a full beard and hair as dark as his leather jacket, clear to his shoulders. When he nods his beard looks like it's bouncing against his chest.

"Are you a Hells Angel?" Griff asks.

The man smiles, and even in the reflected light she thinks he's got the whitest teeth she's ever seen.

"I'm from outside of Estherville."

Griff points at the lettering on the gas tank. "It says Harley-Davidson."

"They don't sell these just to Hells Angels," the man says, rapping the tank with his knuckles. "My name's Marvin. Even if I wanted to be a Hells Angel my mom wouldn't stand for it." He grips a fistful of beard and tugs it. "She isn't real sure she likes this or my long hair either."

"I'm Griff."

Marvin flashes his white teeth again. He pulls off a glove and reaches toward her, and Griff shakes his hand. She really just shakes the first two fingers because his whole hand's too big to shake.

"Griff's a nice name," he says. "I wish I was Griff instead of Marvin."

Her mother steps around in front of her. "What are you doing out here after midnight, Marvin?"

He puts his glove back on real slow, taking his time. "I'm riding up to Sioux Falls." Then he rests both hands on top of his helmet. "I've got a girlfriend there. I got a late start."

They listen to the crickets for just a minute before Jean asks, "Is there a bus station in Sioux Falls?" She's looking at the car's raised hood.

"Yes, ma'am, there's a good one."

Marvin reaches back and takes a flashlight out of the saddlebag mounted just behind him and shines the beam over the black garbage bags, the suitcase and the backpack, then raises the light toward Jean. "I really wasn't planning on making more than one trip."

She holds up a hand to shield her eyes, and Marvin shuts the flashlight off and puts it back in the saddlebag. He sits bent over staring down at his side and when he looks up, says, "I wouldn't do nothing but give you a ride, ma'am. And your daughter."

Her mother holds a hand over the hurt side of her face in case he gets the light out again. "This was an accident," she says.

Marvin strokes his beard, then tilts his head back and looks up at the stars. "Well, I hope there's some son of a bitch out there having an accident of his own." He looks down at Griff and smiles. "Like an accidental spontaneous combustion."

Griff smiles because she likes this idea even better than the tornado getting Roy.

The wind rattles through the corn again, and Jean shivers and says, "What the hell." She turns and shakes her clothes out of the garbage bags and snaps the suitcase open, then calls over her shoulder. "Shine your light over here again, Marvin." To Griff she says, "Just take something clean for tomorrow. We can get new stuff in Sioux Falls."

Griff dumps her books out, and together they stuff the backpack with clothes and toiletries and all the underwear that'll fit.

Marvin plays his flashlight over the heap of clothes that's left. "You better put on jackets," he says. "When I get us up to speed it'll be chilly."

Jean and Griff find their jackets, and as Jean shoulders into the backpack and climbs onto the Harley behind Marvin, Griff turns away and slips her diary under the waistband of her pants. She holds her pillow against her chest and squeezes her jacket over it and can barely get it zipped up. Then she turns around.

"You look like my uncle Tommy," Marvin says, righting the bike and snapping the kickstand back.

Griff pats the pillow like it's a big friendly belly. "I don't want to get cold."

It's hard to bend over, but she sets her suitcase on the backseat and starts picking up the clothes they can't take and even the empty garbage bags.

Her mother asks, "Why don't you just leave all that stuff?"

Griff looks at her sitting there behind Marvin. "I don't want to leave a mess." She steps to the front of the car and extends her arms, "I can't reach the hood."

"Are you coming or not?" her mother asks.

Griff drops her arms. She thinks her mother looks good on a motorcycle, but there's no place left to sit. "Where do I go?"

Marvin pushes his helmet down on his head and thumps the gas tank with a knuckle. "Right up front."

She looks at her mother again and Jean nods, so she steps forward and lets Marvin lift her up. When he starts the engine she leans back against him. She likes the view over the handlebars.

He asks her if she's ready, and she turns. "Do you live in a trailer house?"

"Do I live where?"

His beard brushes against her cheek, and she pushes it aside. "I want to know if you live in a trailer house."

"No, I live with my mom."

Griff holds his beard away, and it's softer than she thought it would be. "Does she live in a trailer?"

Marvin's smile looks good even with the helmet on. "Nope, in a farmhouse. I help out at the farm since my dad died."

Griff drops the handful of beard. "I'm ready now." She turns forward, and Marvin eases them out on the straight stretch of pale-gray highway.

WHEN THEY GET to Sioux Falls it's like they're the only ones awake. Marvin drives the motorcycle real slow through town, and there's no traffic. He puts his feet down when he stops at a light, to hold them all upright, and keeps his hands on the handlebars, and Griff stays leaned back against his chest. She can just see over the big arms on either side of her head, and she feels like there's nothing in Sioux Falls, South Dakota, that can touch her. She feels like she's just passing through, with Marvin all around her and her mother right there behind him.

Some of the streetlights are bright white and others are tinted yellow, and the blue and gold and red neon signs are reflected in the dark shopwindows. Her eyes water in the cool night air, and if she squints and lets the motorcycle jiggle her, all the colors blur and jump around, and it's not like really even being in any town at all.

It's like being locked up safe in a big glass box, she thinks, just looking out at a world of colored lights.

She sits up straight and clenches her teeth so the motorcycle doesn't make them chatter. Their reflection passes across the tall clean windows of a bank, and she raises an arm and watches herself wave. She wishes Marvin didn't have a girlfriend or a mother, because then the three of them could sleep hidden in cornfields during the day and ride the motorcycle at night, the big boom, boom, boom of the engine blocking out the whole world, with everybody asleep in their beds as she watches herself passing through in the dark store windows, all the way to the ocean.

She turns to Marvin and says, "It's like being a ghost," and he nods like he knows exactly what she means.

She feels her life belongs just to her. She doesn't have to smile or be polite, have the right answer or even think of the perfect thing to say, so nobody gets mad and yells and sends her to her room. She doesn't have to worry about how men look at her mother, or wait around all tense for the next bad thing to happen. She hugs her arms tighter across the pillow under her jacket and promises to remember this night, so when she's a woman this will be her example. All she'll have to do is remember this one night and she'll know how to make herself happy. She shuts her eyes and whispers a little prayer that she won't have to actually be a ghost to belong just to herself. Now she knows she wants to feel like this in the daytime, when everybody's awake.

MARVIN'S GIRLFRIEND'S name is Mary, and she doesn't look like she's ever been on a motorcycle in her life. When she sees Marvin she squeals like he's Santa Claus and she's been waiting for him all year. She's short and white as cookie dough, and pudgy but not fat. She smells so sugary Griff presses her tongue against the roof of her mouth and swallows.

Mary's wearing a pink robe tied loose at her waist, with lacy red underwear on underneath that Griff thinks she probably bought just for Marvin. Her lipstick is the same red as her panties, and her pretty blond hair's piled up on top of her head.

She runs down the hallway and jumps up into Marvin's arms like a little girl would, and he holds her like that, even though she's not a kid. He doesn't try to put her down, just holds her up against his chest with one arm behind her knees and the other around her back. She kisses him all over his face and doesn't care that the back of her robe falls open with her red-pantied butt sticking right out.

When Marvin introduces Griff and her mother, she doesn't ask where they came from or where they're going. She just says, "If the heat's on too high for you, the thermostat's over there."

She points at the little box, then Marvin carries her down the hallway and back, and she's got folded sheets stacked on her belly. She hands the sheets to Jean and says, "Isn't Marvin the best thing in the world?"

Jean says he sure saved them from a bad night, and Mary giggles and starts kissing him all over again.

When she's done, Mary points at the couch in the living room. "That foldout's real comfortable," she says. "Lots of them aren't. Help yourself to the bathroom and the kitchen, and don't worry about sleeping late because I took tomorrow off work."

She loops her arms around Marvin's neck and he carries her back down the hallway, Mary switching off the lights as they go.

Griff helps her mother make up the couch and goes to the bathroom to brush her teeth.

The toilet seat has a fuzzy red cover, and so does the top of the tank. Pictures of kittens are hanging on the pink walls, and the plastic shower curtain shows kittens playing with balls of yarn. Behind the curtain Griff finds bowls of bath-oil balls and about twenty bottles of shampoo and conditioner. She picks up a bath ball that's the same color as her diary, and it smells as sweet as Mary.

She sits down on the padded toilet seat and digs her toes into the little red carpet in front of her. She thinks Mary would be a good friend, and that when they get to the ocean she'll have time to find a good friend, and she'll look for someone like Mary, only her own age. She flushes the toilet and keeps the door shut until the tank fills up. She can hear Mary giggling with Marvin in her bedroom.

When she gets back into the living room her mother's already under the covers, so she kicks off her shoes and folds her clothes on the arm of the couch, then turns off the lamp and lies down. At Roy's the light from the streetlamp felt like hard liquid metal, but in Mary's house it's soft as firelight, and she gazes around at the pictures and shelves on the walls. On all the shelves, and on the tables too, there're dozens of ceramic figures: sheep and shepherdesses, kittens and puppies, and four pink pigs on top of the clock radio. They're all painted bright and cast little shadows, and the film of dust on every one of them proves they're here for good. Mary doesn't pack her things in the mornings. If she did, Griff thinks, she'd need a whole truck.

She turns on her side, and her mother snuggles against her back with her knees drawn up against the backs of Griff's legs and an arm around her, holding her tight. Her mother feels warm, even hot.

"Are you hungry?" she whispers.

Griff shakes her head. "No, I'm just excited."

She thinks this is how it should be. Not as good as if her father was alive, but the next best thing. She's here with her mother, and if Marvin wanted to get mad he's had plenty of time to and still hasn't. She thinks Marvin's big enough to keep them safe, and Marvin already has Mary and his own mother.

"We can't stay here forever. You know that, don't you?"

"Sure." Griff twists around, and her mother's face looks dark and smooth and relaxed in the light from the street. "But I can like it while we're here, can't I?"

"I just don't want you to be disappointed."

"Are you disappointed?"

Her mother kisses her on the forehead. "I'm never disappointed," she whispers. "I've got you."

After awhile Griff feels her mother's lips part against her forehead, her breaths deepening into sleep, and she kisses her back.

MARY'S BOSS CALLS before anybody's up and asks her to come in for just a little bit. Marvin tells her to go ahead, that he'll get everything squared away here.

He puts on a pot of coffee, and Griff goes to take a bath. When the water's real hot she drops in the lavender ball of bath oil and watches it dissolve, hoping Mary won't mind. And when her mother's done with her coffee she says she might not get another chance for awhile so she takes a bath too. After they pack, Marvin takes them on his motorcycle to a Perkins' Restaurant for lunch. They all have the special, which is a cheese sandwich with ham in it, and Marvin orders pie for everybody even though Griff told him she's full.

And then he takes them to the Wal-Mart so

her mother can buy them each some clothes. While she's shopping Griff and Marvin take turns in the blood-pressure chair at the pharmacy, and her mother finds them there, sitting together comparing readouts. She has a blue plastic bag full of outfits, and Marvin carries it to the parking lot for her.

When Marvin drops them at the bus station he asks Jean if she wants him to come in and wait with them, and she says no and gives him a kiss, but not the bad kind. And then Marvin kneels down and hugs Griff real tight. He calls her Little Sister and tells her to take good care, then waits by his motorcycle as they go inside. She stands at the window and waves, but he's already pulling away. She thinks she probably won't ever see Marvin again, but there're lots of people she'll never see again, and riding through the night on his motorcycle, then sleeping at Mary's, will be a good time to remember. She squeezes her eyes shut tight, to fix the picture of Marvin in her brain. He's proof that not every man's like Roy.

They sit on a bench that looks and feels like a church pew. Griff keeps the shopping bag from Wal-Mart on the floor between her feet. They sit watching the people because her mother says that's the best thing about bus stations. There're a lot of kids and young mothers. Most of the kids are crying, or just sitting dazed and waiting for something to cry about. The single guys all sit or stand by themselves. But mostly there are old men, none of them dressed very well. A cop wakes one of them up and makes him stand against the wall, then walk with his arms held out to his sides, and when he does the cop leaves him alone.

Over all the noise of people talking there's a man's voice on the loudspeaker saying when buses are coming or leaving, where they're from or where they're going.

Her mother slides the orange backpack against her leg and says, "I'll be right back."

Griff watches her walk to a phone booth and close the hinged door behind her. She doesn't make a call, just sits hunched over the purse in her lap with her back to the door. When she comes back, she sits with her arms folded across her chest.

"Do you know where we're going yet?" Griff asks.

"I'm still thinking about it."

A man and a woman are leaning against the wall in front of them, standing face-to-face, and the woman waves both arms in the air and talks right into the man's face. She scoops her hair away from her eyes so she can see him up close, then stomps her foot.

"We don't have a whole lot of money," Jean says.

"Is that what you did in the phone booth?" Griff thinks about the gas and food and clothes they bought since she counted the money in her mother's purse back on Highway 20, before they went north and west again and rode on Marvin's motorcycle to Sioux Falls. "Count how much we have left?"

Her mother nods, still watching the couple across from them. When the woman turns to walk away, the man catches her by her arm and pins her up against the wall. Griff can feel her mother wince. The man holds the woman by her arm. He won't let her go.

"Just watch our things," she says, then walks to the counter and comes back with two tickets pinched between the thumb and forefinger of her right hand. She glances at the couple and says, "We're going to Wyoming."

"Wyoming?"

"That's what we can afford." Her mother looks at her and grins. "Unless you've been holding out on me."

"That's just one state over from here."

"It's like two states," her mother says. "We're on the eastern edge of South Dakota."

Across from them, the woman slumps down against the wall and just sits there on the floor. The man stands over her, looking embarrassed, glancing around to see who was watching.

"Where in Wyoming?"

"Your grandfather's."

Griff waits for her mother to smile and say "Gotcha," but now she's staring down at the bus tickets in her lap.

"I have an alive grandfather?"

"Not much of one."

Griff feels panicked, like she does when Roy's done yelling and ready to start hitting. She looks at the old men slumped in their seats and then back at her mother but she's still staring at the tickets. A long time ago, Griff knows, her mother's dad died of something called an aneurysm. Her mother told her about it. And she knows her mom's mom died because she didn't want to live without her husband. Her mother told her that too.

She stands up and moves right in front of her mother, but she still won't look at her. "You mean my dad's dad?"

Her mother nods.

"When were you going to tell me?" Her whole arms, from her shoulders down, are pressed hard against her sides.

When her mother lifts her face, she looks old and ugly. "I never was."

Now her mother's curled asleep on the bus seat, and Griff wishes her face looked this relaxed and unworried when she was awake.

She turns to the bus window. The driver told them on the loudspeaker that they're in Wyoming now, but the moon's already gone down and she can't make out the landscape. She cups her hands around her eyes and presses her face against the glass, but all she can see is dark, flat land, with gullies and little hills. She'd like to see Devils Tower. They showed it in the **Close Encounters** movie, but she bets it's better in real life.

She drops her hands and stares at her reflection, just inches from her face. She huffs and the window fogs, and she watches as the reflection clears. It stays right there in front of her, like a sister, she thinks, just at the tip of her nose, the world outside moving past. She hears the people around her, the muttered conversations, the people turning in their sleep. A man coughs.

She whispers aloud, "Grandfather." Then, "My grandfather." Her reflection smiles. She closes her eyes and tries to imagine the image of the man who raised her father. What he looks like. If he'll be able to tell right away that she belongs to him.

EIGHT

———◆———

THE LAST HALF of the night Jean stands in the aisle, holding on to the rails that front the luggage racks above her head. When her arms get tired she braces herself against the seatbacks. Griff sleeps across their seats, her knees pulled toward her chest.

They stop every fifty miles or so in some Podunk town to take on a passenger or let someone off. Between stops, on the straight stretches, she does squats or bends forward and touches her fingertips to her toes for a count of twenty. She knows she's got an ass men like. When she looks between her knees she sees a man shifting in his seat, as though shifting in his sleep, but watching. Have a good look, she thinks. She doesn't want him to notice anything else, like the bruises on her face.

She doesn't even try to sleep. Her eyes burn and water and her mouth tastes dry, and she wants a cigarette. She doesn't know why she decided she could quit on this bus trip. What did she think—that this was going to be some new beginning?

Just before dawn they pass by Sheridan and head northwest off the interstate, then west, and Griff wakes up. Jean sits down beside her, and laces her fingers and stretches her arms out until her knuckles crack. She asks, "Are you still mad at me?"

Griff sits blinking. Her cheek is creased with the diamond-shaped pattern of the seat cushion and the hair on that side of her head is curved up.

"I'm not awake yet." Griff yawns. "I don't know how I feel."

The sage flats out the windows appear gray and mildly aqua, the rocks gunmetal and greenish. The trunks and branches of the cottonwoods and brush willows, as severe black lines against the landscape, as if something large, something with claws, has tried to scratch its way out. That's how Jean feels inside, and it's not just that she wants a cigarette. What do the dry drunks say in their meetings? This may not be what she wants, but it's what she needs? What she needs is a car she didn't have to leave on the side of a highway. That's what she needs. And she could really fucking use a cigarette.

She leans into the aisle and through the windshield can see the dawn sun lighting the tops of the Bighorn Mountains. White snow, green meadows, green fir and pine, yellow scoops of turning aspen. All that and the smell of diesel and the sour odor of strangers. Welcome home, dumbass. She should've found the money somewhere to take them over these mountains, to cross the Continental Divide and just keep going. Stolen the money, if she had to. What did her dad say? He said shit in one hand and wish in the other and see which one fills up quicker.

The driver downshifts, and then again, and they coast through town and stop at the Conoco station. The driver turns on his seat and says, "Ishawooa." He doesn't use his microphone when there are passengers still asleep. She stands and waves her hand to let him know this is where they get off.

No one's waiting to board, and she and Griff stand by the gas pumps in the gray light and watch the bus turn and head back through town, then hear it gear up on the two-lane that leads toward the interstate and on to Billings, Montana.

Griff walks to the curb and looks up the

main drag. She kneels on her left knee and knots a shoelace. Across the road a sign reads ISHA-WOOA, elevation 5,313, population 1,783.

"Is this it?" she asks.

"This is it."

They watch a man unlock the glass door in the front of the gas station and prop it open with a metal Pennzoil sign.

"Just stay here," Jean says. "I'll be back in a minute."

When she enters the station the man has the radio on and he's pulling cash out of a stained blue velvet Crown Royal sack and slotting the bills into the open cash register. Jean stares at the money, can feel the freedom in it.

"What can I do you for?" he asks. He's skinny as a girl, and his dark hair's lank and greasy.

"A package of Old Golds," Jean tells him.

"The hard pack okay?"

"Whatever. And one of those rolls of white-powdered donuts."

He sets the cigarettes and donuts on the countertop, and Jean takes her wallet out of her purse and counts out four ones. She's got her last two twenties folded and stuck behind her driver's license.

"That's all I've got." She looks out the front windows at Griff standing at the curb.

The man takes the bills from her and wets a thumb to straighten a wrinkled corner. He hasn't said anything about her face, but she probably isn't the first beat-up woman he's ever seen.

"Hell, you're close enough," he says. "I mark up everything in this place. This won't hurt me."

"I'll just take the cigarettes."

"You take these donuts too." He waves toward Griff with the bills in his hand. "For your girl. I'm not shitting you, there isn't anything in here that's not priced double what it's worth."

He moves to the end of the counter, and Jean picks up the pack of cigarettes and opens it.

"I'll have some coffee made in a minute. I don't charge nothing for the coffee."

She watches him measure out scoops from a Folgers can into the basket of a drip coffeemaker that sits on a little stand by the door to the garage bays, with Styrofoam cups and packets of creamer and sugar.

"I'll pay you back," she says.

"Well, you can or you can't. It's up to you." He doesn't stop counting out the scoops. "Go on and light up if you want—there's a good breeze through here this morning."

He steps into the bathroom behind the counter to fill the glass carafe, and Jean lights a cigarette, her hands shaking as she cups the match. When she looks at the cash register, the drawer's closed.

"You're that Evans girl, aren't you?"

He's standing outside the bathroom, smiling at her.

"I don't remember you," she says.

He hooks a thumb under the pocket flap of his shirt, where his name's sewn on. "I'm Jimmy J.," he says. He walks over to the coffeemaker and pours the water in. "I'm an easy one to forget. I've got a good memory myself, but I don't make much of an impression." He looks back over his shoulder. "Anyway, welcome home."

Jean can feel her heart race and her arms tingle. She thinks she'll never go this long without a cigarette again. Not ever. She takes another drag.

"I'm just visiting," she says, stepping toward the door.

"Don't forget those donuts," he says.

THEY WALK in the apron of road cinders along the highway. Griff follows with their shopping bag. Jean can hear the plastic swishing against her corduroy pantleg.

They cross a slough that drains through a culvert under the road, and the warm water steams in the chill air. Cattails crowd the berm, already gone to seed, swollen and pale in the mist. The sun still hasn't reached them, and the air smells of pine, sage, live water and earth. She hears the three ascending notes of mead-owlark song, the descending trill, and closes her eyes and breathes deeply. The morning smells and tastes and sounds like home, but she wishes it didn't.

She tears the package of donuts open and pops a whole one in her mouth. She presses it against the roof of her mouth and feels it soften and dissolve, sweet and gummy, and she swal-lows. Griff stops beside her.

"It's not far," Jean tells her. She coughs and powdered sugar puffs from her lips, and she holds out the roll of donuts. "You want one of these?"

They sit together on the roadside and eat the donuts in silence, one after the other.

"They're really good," Griff says.

Jean lights another cigarette. This time her hands don't shake. "I'm glad you like them," she says. "I'm afraid the rest of today's going to be downhill."

They watch the sun gain the rim of the hori-zon, and squint against the glare.

Griff says, "You can see a long way here."

Jean flicks her ash between her feet.

"Can you always?"

She looks at her daughter, glowing suddenly in the low light. "It's clear here," she says. "I read somewhere that if you're in Yellowstone Park you can see for a hundred and two miles. That's the good part of being here."

For a single instant Griff appears lit from within, struck by this sun angled just a degree above the two hundred miles of prairie to the east.

"This isn't Yellowstone, though, is it?"

"Not quite." Jean points toward the Bighorns. "It's over there, but this is nearly as clear."

Griff looks back at the mountains, a little sandy-haired, brown-eyed girl sitting in the morning light in clothes that are too big with powdered sugar on her chin.

"I wish we had a bottle of water," she says.

Jean stands and extends her hand and pulls her daughter to her feet. "Well, what you do," she says, "is wish in one hand and poop in the other and see which one fills up first." She's smiling.

"I don't get it," Griff says.

They continue along the highway and then turn onto a dirt lane. It's rutted, the center grown up in weeds trimmed evenly by the undercarriages of trucks. To the northwest a man is riding a horse, and Jean shades her eyes with a hand. It's one of the Hansons, she thinks, one of the brothers. She's surprised she can still identify a man by how he sits a horse. She waves, but he doesn't wave back. She's probably wrong. It could be anybody.

Griff points to a sign bolted to the corner brace of the fenceline. The board is weathered gray, the top edge scalloped white with dried birdshit, but the routed name is plain: GILKYSON.

"Is my grandfather as big as Marvin?"

"No," Jean says. "He's smaller."

She walks in a single rut down the lane, Griff following close behind, and soon a dog starts barking from the buildings below them. She can't see the dog, but it sounds old, capable only of short, strained woofs without strength or threat. She guesses he can't even see them and just knows something's wrong.

They stop at the edge of the lawn. Overgrown in end-of-season dandelion and yarrow and crabgrass, it looks like it hasn't been mowed all summer. She sees Einar before he notices them, coming back from the barn with a pail in his left hand.

"Is that him?" Griff whispers. Jean can feel her daughter's excitement, and she nods.

She's surprised he still walks with such ease,

an old man's ease, but purposeful. He's kept his shoulders, his gait. Then he stops and thumbs his hat back from his face.

She takes her daughter's hand and they walk toward him. She feels light-headed and stops ten feet away, and pulls Griff to a stop. Sweat runs down her sides, and she presses her arms against her ribs.

She says, "Was that Curtis Hanson on that horse?"

Einar tilts his head, staring at them, and she wonders if he needs glasses. She also wonders how long it's been since he's seen someone he hadn't expected. She can hear herself breathing, and Griff too. The dog barks again, out on the porch of Mitch's little cabin, and Einar turns and shouts, "Shut up, Karl." And now Jean wonders why it wasn't Mitch out in the pasture instead of one of the Hanson boys.

"Is that the Karl I know?" she asks.

Einar says nothing.

"I see you still keep a milkcow," she says. She's trying, isn't she? Still, what in the world was she thinking when she told her daughter about this man?

Except to yell at the dog he hasn't looked away from her. "That's what I'm down to," he says. "One old cow. An older horse."

"Those aren't your cows in the pasture?"

"Just leasing to Curtis," he says. He comes half the distance toward them and stops, then steps forward and grips her chin with his free hand, and his touch sends a shock down through her chest. He turns her face up in the light, to the side, then back again so he can look right at her. "I don't want you here."

She steps back, and his hand falls away. "It's good to know we agree on something, Einar." She rubs her chin. It feels like it's burning where his thumb pressed into the cleft. "I wasn't sure we would."

He sloshes the milk pail toward Griff. "That yours?"

"She's yours, too." Screw this, she thinks. She can feel her face flush.

Karl barks again, and Einar doesn't shout for him to shut up.

"You're here first thing in the morning to tell me I have a grandchild I don't know about? That about it?"

"I was pregnant at Griffin's funeral." She watches him closely for any changes in his expression. She's been saving this. She wants it to cut. "It didn't seem like something you wanted to hear at the time."

He brings a hand up to clear the corners of

his mouth as though he's tried to spit and made a mess of it, but that's all he does. He doesn't look at Griff. "What's her name?"

Griff drops her mother's hand. "My name's Griff Gilkyson."

Einar sets the pail to his side and squats down in front of her. He pushes his hat back further on his head, and his forehead's white as the milk in the pail.

Griff asks, "Do you wear your underwear all day long?"

Jean wants to laugh out loud. That's my girl, she thinks. Einar just cocks his head. He seems truly surprised she can speak, staring at her like she's some blemish he's just noticed in the bathroom mirror.

"I wasn't expecting company," he says. And then, "Griff's not a usual name for a girl."

Jean wants to tell him that Griff's not a usual girl, either, but instead says, "I need to lie down, Einar. We've been on a bus for sixteen hours."

"So lie down."

He presses on his knees with his hands to get his back straight and then stands up. It's the only thing she's seen him do so far that would remind her that he's aged ten years since she was last here.

"Can we go in the house?" she asks.

Karl's come off the porch, but only far enough to stand where the sun's warmed the workyard.

Einar takes up the pail again. "How'd you get here?"

Griff says, "We walked."

"I can see that you have. Where'd you walk from?"

"From the gas station where the bus dropped us off," Griff says, looking down at his boots. "We started the day before yesterday in Iowa."

Einar scuffs a boot at the shopping bag, and Griff looks up at him. "You must've come from the trendy part of Iowa," he says.

Jean hears her daughter tell him that their car caught on fire, spontaneous combustion, and then they got a ride on a motorcycle and that's why she couldn't bring her suitcase. She hears her tell him about Marvin and Mary and the shower curtain with cats and balls of yarn on it, even about taking her blood pressure in the Wal-Mart in Sioux Falls. Griff doesn't say anything about Roy.

Jean takes a step toward him, wanting to draw his attention away from her daughter. She's the one who deserves his hate.

"I never thought I'd see you again," he says.

"I'm asking for a month, Einar. Just until I can earn enough to get us out of here." She clears her throat. She turns completely away from Griff. "We haven't got anyplace else to go."

The dog barks again.

"That Karl's still a good dog." Einar turns toward the house. "He's never offered to bite anybody."

"Does that mean yes?"

"There's the room at the top of the stairs. It's got two beds in it." He keeps walking. "I guess you remember how to find it."

JEAN CUPS a hand under the faucet at the sink at the back of the loft and drinks. She washes her face and rubs it dry with a towel, then takes a deep breath. The water helps.

There's a toilet and a shower stall next to the sink, but no wall to separate any of it from the rest of the room. She looks at Griff sitting on the edge of a bed and sniffs an underarm and reaches under her shirt with a roll-on deodorant and swipes under both arms.

They listen to Einar in the kitchen, then hear him go out through the side door.

"He won't hurt you," she says.

"Will he hurt you?"

Jean combs her hair away from her face. "He already has."

"He hit you?" Griff sits up straighter on the bed, and for the first time all morning she looks like she might want to run.

Jean kneels in front of her. "No, he's not a hitter," she says. "You'll be lucky if he looks at you. And I hurt him too." She pats Griff's knee and stands. "I'm going to walk back to town. The stores'll be open now, and I want to see if I can find a job."

"But you're coming back?"

"Of course I am." She kisses Griff on the forehead. "You should get some sleep."

"I don't think I can."

"I was looking forward to it." Jean looks at the other bed. "But now I'm too wired."

She walks to the railing. The room below has a fireplace, two cloth-covered chairs and a tattered couch with a saddle turned up on the cushions. The end tables are stacked with magazines and newspapers are scattered across the floor. It's exactly how she remembers it, only now there's all this clutter.

"These are too stiff to wear."

She turns back. Griff has pulled her new jeans from the shopping bag and she stabs at the floor with their rigid blue legs.

"They need to be washed. They're just stiff because of the sizing."

"Do you think he has a washer and dryer?" Griff lays the jeans on her bed.

"You should ask him. I'm sure he does."

Griff nods. "Maybe we should've called first so he wouldn't be so surprised to see us."

"Maybe we should have." Jean starts down the stairs and stops. "You don't have to stay up here if you don't want to."

"I will for awhile."

Griff moves to the railing and sits with her feet dangling over the edge of the loft. She grips a spooled upright in each hand as though they're wooden jail bars and stares through them into the living room. She says, "I'll just wait a little bit." She points her chin down. "Until there's somebody there."

NINE

———

E INAR CAPS the syringe and tosses it in the trash can. He gets Mitch propped up against the pillows at the head of his bed and lets him rest there with his eyes closed, breathing through his open mouth.

"You want a shave?"

Mitch shakes his head. "It can wait until later."

Einar walks to a window and stands looking back at his house. He guesses the girl's inside, gone to sleep. He hopes she has. She seemed nervous. He's forgotten how nervous kids can get. He thinks it's because they notice too much and don't know enough not to care.

"Who were you talking to outside?" Mitch has his eyes open. He still breathes through his mouth.

"When?"

"A little while ago. What'd you think I meant?"

Einar shifts at the window. He looks at the extra chair against the wall but doesn't sit. "Jean came back."

"Jean Gilkyson?"

"I don't remember knowing a whole hell of a lot of other Jeans." Einar brushes the dust off the seat of the empty chair. "I'm sorry if Karl's barking woke you."

Mitch shifts himself higher against the pillows.

"She brought a kid with her. She claims it's Griffin's." When Mitch doesn't say anything Einar looks over to make sure he hasn't fallen back asleep. "Aren't you going to say something?"

Mitch shakes his finger at him like he's glad there's just the two of them in the room, like this is something he's thought about a lot and Einar's the only man alive who would understand. "Maybe Jean's dying," he says, arching his right eyebrow. The left one's just a smear of scar tissue. "I'll bet she's only got a month or two left and couldn't imagine how to screw you over, so she went out and rented a kid to inherit your vast estate." He's leaning forward now, away from the pillows, enjoying himself. He looks better than he has in a week. "Nowadays a woman wouldn't have to go to Gypsies for a black-market kid." He nods conspiratorially. "I'll bet if you check it out, it's something they can get done over the Internet."

"Fuck you."

Mitch smiles the half-smile his scarred face allows. "Is it a boy or a girl?"

"She's a girl. Are you hungry?"

"Yes, I am. If she brings me something I'll eat it."

"If who brings you something?"

"Your granddaughter."

"I'll bring you whatever you want."

"I want her to. I want to meet her."

Einar moves to the door and opens it to let Karl in. The old dog lies down on the carpet scrap, groans and curls up tight.

"The Fish and Game trapped a bear at that campground up Post Creek."

Mitch swings his legs over the side of the bed. "When did they do that?"

"Yesterday, late. Curtis told me. They caught him in one of those traps they've got rigged out like a trailer. They put some meat in the bottom and he walked right in."

Mitch's pants lie in a wad, waist up on a footstool beside the bed. He steps into the legholes, works his feet clear through, and bends over his knees and pulls the pants up as far as his thighs. He kicks the stool away and stands just long enough to get them over his butt and then sits back down, waiting to catch his breath.

"You think it was our bear?" He zips the pants and buckles the belt at his thin waist.

"It'd be easier if you'd let me help you get dressed."

"Was it a grizzly?" He looks up at Einar.

Einar nods and looks back out the window, toward the pastures. "He's sure as hell not my bear," he says. "If you want to claim him, I guess you've got the right."

"Did they kill him?" Mitch takes a shirt from the bedpost.

"He's in that little zoo Angie has. They put him in the pit she dug for her mountain lion. I guess they don't know what to do with him."

Mitch gets up on his canes and shuffles to the workbench. He lowers himself into the chair, and when Einar reaches out a hand he lifts a cane to warn him away.

"I want you to have a look at him for me."

"All right." Einar leans into the doorjamb. "If

you want, I'll wait until tonight and kill the son of a bitch for you. I wish I'd made a better shot the first time."

"That's not what I want. I just want him looked at. I want you to tell me how he seems." Mitch turns on the light over the workbench. "Do you think you'd recognize him?"

"I've only heard of one other grizzly in the Bighorns, and that was before either one of us was born."

Mitch stares through the magnifying glass at the antler clamped in the vise, but Einar can tell he's not really looking at anything at all.

"If you're getting ready to leave, will you pull the covers up on my bed?"

Einar steps to the bed and straightens the flannel sheet, evens the quilt and squares the pillows.

"I don't want her to think I keep a poor house," Mitch says, slumping back in his chair.

Einar stands by the bed and watches him tap a finger at the hole in his head where his ear used to be. It's just a habit. Like his hand wishes the ear was still there.

"Do you know who you're talking about?"

Mitch drops his hand in his lap. "I'm talking about your granddaughter. I don't want her to think I'm a slob."

"I thought maybe you were losing your mind. I forgot about her for a minute."

"You won't forget to look at my bear."

"No." Einar scoops a cup of kibble from the bag and spills it into a bowl that he sets by the old dog's head. "I won't forget."

TEN

WHEN GRIFF hears Einar in the kitchen she starts down the stairs. She's careful not to trip, but wants to make enough noise that he'll know she's coming. She thinks she's probably surprised him enough already. Each step's only a log cut in half lengthwise. The whole house is made of logs. She thinks it's like being inside a forest that's fallen down and been stacked up on its sides. It's not only a lot better than a trailer house, it's better than anyplace she's ever seen. It's a real house, the kind that isn't going to wear out before the people who live in it do.

She stands at the entryway to the kitchen and watches him running water into the shiny metal pail at the sink. He's put on jeans and a shirt, and he doesn't have his hat on anymore. Steam rises up from the pail and fogs the window over the sink. The countertops at his sides are stacked with dirty dishes and boxes of crackers, and quick-cook rice and elbow macaroni. She thinks her grandfather's maybe like the old dog, Karl. Just bark, and a little bit messy. She hopes she's right. She doesn't want to do anything that'll make her find out she's wrong.

"I used the bathroom," she says.

The water's still running. "I heard you," he says.

"Can I have a glass of water?"

"There's glasses in that cupboard there." He pokes out his right elbow toward the cupboard above the counter.

She drags a chair from the round wooden table at the far end of the kitchen. There's something on the table that looks like it came out of a car, from under the hood. It sits on newspapers that are stained with oil, beside a screwdriver, a wrench, and a can with WD-40 printed on it. The chair's heavier than she thought it would be. It feels real, like the rest of the house feels real. She stands on the chair and reaches to the back of the second shelf. There's only one glass in the cupboard and she steps down with it. While she's waiting for him to get done at the sink, she replaces the chair.

He turns the water off and sets the pail in the dishrack to drain, then dries his hands on a towel. He looks at her standing there holding the glass. "We drink a lot of milk around here."

She says, "I like milk."

He opens the refrigerator and sets out a jar. She's never seen milk in a jar, but she doesn't say so.

"Your mother send you down here all by yourself?"

She fills her glass and screws the lid back on the jar. "She went to town. She said she needs to find a job." She thinks her grandfather's as tall as Marvin, just not as wide. If she doesn't tilt her head back when she talks to him she's staring right into the belly part of his plaid shirt.

"I suppose you're hungry?"

"I am a little bit." She sips the milk. It's like it has lumps of sour butter stirred in it, but she likes the taste.

He opens the refrigerator again. There's another jar of milk and a loaf of white bread and something wrapped in white butcher's paper. There's a brick of yellow cheese, a carton of eggs, and the shelves on the door are lined with different bottles and jars. He sets out the bread and cheese and the butcher paper on the only clear space on the counter.

"You weren't gone very long," she says.

"When was that?"

"While I was upstairs."

He takes a jar of mayonnaise from the shelf on the door. He unscrews the lid and sniffs and holds the jar up. "Do you like this?"

"Yes, sir," she says. "I always liked mayonnaise. Even when I was little."

He lays four slices of bread on the counter. "I went out to give a man his medicine. He needs a shot every morning."

She watches him spread the mayonnaise on the bread. His hands are big and rough and dark, and there's darker spots on the backs like old people have. She says, "I knew a girl who had diabetes. She had to get shots at school every day."

"He's not sugary enough for diabetes. That's not what's wrong with him." He folds back the butcher paper, and there's a stack of sliced cold meat. "This all right with you too?"

"Yes, sir. If it's baloney."

He stops, holding a slice of baloney, looking down at her. "Are you going to stand there the whole time?"

She steps back. "Not if you don't want me to. Does it bother you?"

"I'm not accustomed to being watched."

She nods and steps farther away, and when he keeps looking, she walks into the big room where she saw the couch and the saddle. She sips her milk. She wishes she had known before now that milk this good came in jars.

On the mantel above the fireplace there's a football helmet with the word BOBCATS stenciled over a pawprint. There are framed pictures of a man in a wrestling tunic, the same man holding a length of cord with dead fish on it, the man on a horse and then standing in a corral with a rope. He isn't her grandfather.

She hears him behind her. He's standing at the end of the couch holding a tray.

"What do you think of that milk?" he asks. "It's the real McCoy, isn't it?"

"I don't know what that means."

"Do you like it?"

"I like it a lot."

He lowers the tray. There's another glass of milk and two plates with a sandwich on each. "Set your glass up here."

She sets her milk on the tray and points at the mantel.

"Are those pictures of my dad?"

"Yeah, they are. The football helmet was his in high school."

"Where does he live now?"

Einar sits in a chair. There's already a heap of clothes on the seat, but he just sits on top of them.

"He's dead. Didn't your mother tell you that?"

"She said you were dead too."

He holds the tray on his knees. "Could you take this out to the man who lives in the little house for me?"

Griff looks toward the room off the kitchen. "Through there?"

"Yeah."

"Is it where the dog lives?"

"It's the same place."

She looks at the sandwiches on the tray. "Do you want me to take it out there now? It isn't lunchtime yet."

"It doesn't matter what time it is. He's hungry now, and this is what we've got."

She looks at the table with the car parts on it. "How come he doesn't eat in here with you?"

"He used to. Now it's easier for him out there."

She likes being asked to do something different. It's like he trusts her. All Roy ever asked her to do was get out of the way. "Are you the one who usually takes the man something to eat?"

"It's always me, but this morning it's you. I've got an errand to run."

She wants to ask him what the errand is. She thinks it might be interesting, but she takes the tray from his knees instead. She wants to do this right. She wants him to ask her to do other things.

She follows him to the little room off the kitchen, and there's a freezer with shelves above it and across from it a washer and dryer with shelves above them too. Hanging near the outside door is a row of coats and caps, and a cowboy hat like the one her grandfather had on earlier, but this one's older and stained. Below the coats are more shelves lined with boots.

He opens the back door and stands with his hand on the screen door's handle. She leans against the freezer to get a better grip on the tray. Her hands are sticky with sweat.

"Can I use your washing machine?"

He watches her with the tray. She's spilled a little milk from the full glass, but he doesn't say anything about it. "Do you know how?" he asks.

"I used the one in Iowa."

He looks at the washer like he's trying to remember what it is. "I don't want it broken."

She isn't sure what to say. She finally says, "My new jeans are too stiff to wear."

He looks out through the screen door. She wants to tell him it's only a washer, and that she's been doing her own laundry since she was seven, and that on her next birthday she'll be ten. "You don't have to be so grouchy," she says. "I didn't know about you either until the day before yesterday."

He doesn't say anything at all, and he doesn't turn, and she wishes she'd just kept her mouth shut. That's what Roy always told her mother, and she knows saying he's grouchy is backtalk. Her neck and shoulders feel hot.

He turns and nods toward the washer. He still looks pretty much the same, sort of between mad and thinking about something else. "The detergent's there above it," he says. "You'll have to get a chair like you did for your glass."

She's proud of the things she can do, and wants him to be proud of her too. "I'll carry the chair all the way in," she says. "I'll pick it up. I won't scrape the legs on the floor."

"All right then." He pushes through the screen door and she follows him out. He nods toward the smaller cabin. It has a porch, and it's made of logs too.

She steps down onto a trail worn in the lawn right to the cabin. "What do I call him?"

"His name's Mr. Bradley."

"Okay," she says. She smiles. "I'm good at meeting new people."

He doesn't smile back, and she can feel him watching her cross to the smaller cabin and step up on the porch. She stops at the door and looks back at him, and he nods that she should go ahead. She balances the tray against her knee and knocks on the door. She bets he thinks she'll drop the tray, but she won't. She knows she'll do this exactly right.

ELEVEN

———

Mitch hears her steps on the porch-boards, hears her pause, hears her knock. "You're going to have to let yourself in," he calls.

There's another pause. Longer this time.

"There's no doorknob." Her voice sounds puzzled, almost lost, and he thinks he should have remembered the door. He's allowed himself to get excited, that's why he didn't.

"Pull the leather thong," he shouts, and wonders just how strange he'll seem to her—certainly a sight more incomprehensible than a door without a knob. He's worried he'll frighten her, that his appearance might somehow damage her.

He buttons his shirt at his throat and feels around the collar to make sure it's not crimped, that the points of the collar aren't sticking up. "There's just a latch on the inside. The leather thong lifts the latch."

The door swings open, and Karl stands up wagging his tail, thumping an even rhythm against the log wall. Mitch tucks his feet back under his chair. He's gotten his boots on but not laced and doesn't want her to notice.

She stands blinking in the doorway, letting her eyes adjust. She takes a step into the room, and he thinks this—like the latchstring—is something else he should have considered. He's not prepared for how much she resembles her father. She has her father's chin and the same upswell in her lower lip. She holds her shoulders squared with her hips, fallen back on her frame, just as Griffin faced the world. It's her father's body she's in, he thinks, her inheritance.

"My name's Griff Gilkyson," she says.

"I'm over here."

She turns to the sound of his voice. The light from the open door falls across to where he sits on the far side of the table at the foot of the bed, shadowed. He's where he planned to be sitting, not wanting to be the first thing she saw.

She walks out of the glare and stops, wincing at the sight of him as though she's been slapped. She stares down at the tray, and he leans back in his chair. He saw the flash of panic in her eyes and imagines her counting the objects on the tray, the glasses, plates, the paper napkins, counting them twice, wishing there were more things to count.

He asks, "Are you feeling dizzy?"

She nods. She actually widens her stance as if she's afraid she might fall.

"Why don't you slide the tray on the table if you think you're going to drop it."

She steps forward and sets the tray just on the table's edge, then folds her arms across her chest with her hands hidden under her arms. She tilts her head to sneak another look.

"I thought I might throw up the first time I had a look at it," he says.

She nods with her head still tilted and clears her throat like an uncomfortable adult might. "I've puked lots of times," she says. "My mom says it's why I never stay sick very long, because I get it out of my system." She clears her throat again but doesn't step away. The door's still open and she hasn't moved toward it. He'd hoped she'd be a brave girl, that she'd stand her ground. He thinks that's another aspect of her father she owns.

"When I was still in the hospital," he says, "a nurse brought me a mirror after they took the bandages off. I got light-headed and couldn't look in a mirror again for awhile." He sets the plates on the table and props the tray up against the foot of the bed. He says, "There's two whole sandwiches here."

"One of them's mine." She takes a deep breath. Like she's been asked to swim the length of a pool underwater, from one end to the other. She levels her head and makes her face appear like everything's just right, and he wonders how much practice she's had at it, how many times she's been required to stare at something horrible and act as though it's nothing at all.

She takes another step toward the table and still hasn't looked away from him. "When the nurse brought you the mirror, did you puke then, or were you just dizzy?"

"Just dizzy." He takes a bite of his sandwich. "The only time I ever threw up was when I saw a man eat a snail."

She raises an eyebrow. "People don't eat snails."

"Yes they do. I didn't believe it either until I saw it." He sips his milk and wipes his lip with the back of his hand, and when he doesn't say anything else she slips into the chair where he put her plate. She's so slight she doesn't have to pull the chair away from the table. She looks like she's still thinking about snails. She picks up her sandwich in both hands and stares right at him before she takes a bite.

"Does it hurt a lot?"

"It itches sometimes." He traces a finger over the slick pad of scar tissue on his cheek, the part that drags the corner of his mouth down. "This part here looks sort of like a map of India."

She takes another bite of her sandwich. She says, "I don't know what India looks like," and then, "I'm sorry I talked with my mouth full." She holds a paper napkin in front of her mouth while she chews. After she swallows she lowers the napkin. "What happened to you?"

"I got mauled by a bear."

"A real bear?" She can't hide the astonishment on her face.

"It wasn't the bear's fault. He was eating one of your granddad's calves, and we interrupted his dinner. We were kind of like uninvited guests."

The dog circles and lies down again. She watches him until he's settled.

"Why didn't the bear bite Einar?"

"I was closer. I was out of the truck."

She puts the sandwich back on her plate. "But he saved you, right?"

"Yes, he did. He shot the bear."

She nods and leans a little to the side as though to look behind him, but he knows there's nothing there worth seeing. He turns his head so she can see the whole side of his face, where his left ear should be.

Her cheek ticks before she makes her face plain again. She touches her own ear. "You're making up the part about the bear. Right?"

"Do I look made-up to you?"

She shakes her head without seeming aware of it. "Can I touch it?" she asks.

He puts his sandwich down and pushes the plate away. He didn't think she'd be this brave, and he's not sure her father would've been. He says, "No one's ever asked that before."

She slips out of the chair and stands by his side, raising a hand and then wiping it against her pants and raising it again. When he closes his eyes he feels the small pad of a single finger move tenderly over the side of his face.

She says, "It's smoother than I thought it would be."

He opens his eyes when he hears her move. He watches her carry her sandwich to Karl and kneel down by the dog. She feeds him the meat, then sniffs at the bread and lets him eat that too. "This sandwich isn't very good," she says.

"Einar's not much of a cook."

She's still holding the napkin when she stands up, looking around the room. He doesn't realize she's looking for a trash can until she wads the napkin into her pants pocket. Then she steps to the workbench and bends over the antler clamped in the vise. "They're little dogs," she says.

"Wolves."

She looks at him and then back at the antler. She nods, taking his word for it.

"Did you make this?"

"I made all of them."

She studies the antlers hung against the log walls, spinning slowly in a circle. "Did you bury the bear?"

"Your grandfather didn't kill the bear," he tells her. "He just wounded it."

She stares at the floor, perhaps thinking of how a bear might heal itself, then walks to the window and puts her hands up against the sill. He watches her study the mountains. "Was it a mother bear?" she asks.

"You mean was it a bear trying to protect her cubs?"

She nods without turning.

"No, it wasn't. It was just an old bear who was having trouble making a living. They don't usually come down this close to people."

She turns. "Then it doesn't happen all the time? You don't always have to watch where you go?"

"No," he tells her. "It happens sometimes in Yellowstone, but not for a long time here."

"My mother told me which way Yellowstone is," she says and comes back to the table. "Where did you see the man eat the snail?"

"In a fancy restaurant in Denver."

His left hand rests on the table in front of his plate, and she touches the back of it, skidding her finger toward his wrist to pull the creases away from his knuckles. Scar tissue shows just under his cuff, and she touches there too—so lightly, he thinks, that if his eyes were closed he could mistake it for a slight breeze. But his eyes aren't closed, and when she blinks, the light through the window flickers in her long lashes. She doesn't look up from his hand.

"Once I saw this kid eat a miller moth," she says.

TWELVE

———

EINAR DRIVES the one-ton flatbed to town. He parks in Angie's graveled lot and stands out of the truck, leaning into the door panel and rubbing his thighs. His ass aches too, but his thighs are worse. He hasn't given up altogether on the tricycle, just decided to take a day or two off. He doesn't want to get so puny he can't take care of Mitch, and there's not enough work left on the ranch to keep him fit, keep his wind up, so he'll try it again when his legs feel better. He starts across the lot.

Angie's built an arch over the zoo's entrance with two bent poles a foot apart and mounted on uprights, and the name's spelled out with sticks nailed to the poles: ANIMALS OF THE ROCKY MOUNTAINS.

Angie sits slumped under the archway selling tickets, in a booth sided with rounded slabs with the bark left on. They're just lengths of pine—

the first cuts the lumber mill makes to size a log, and usually chipped into pulp. Einar thinks Angie must've begged a truckload for fire-starter and used them here instead.

When she sees him she waves. "I've been expecting you," she says. "You here to see the bear?"

"You're reading my mind," he says.

Angie sets a brown paper sack on the shelf atop the booth's half-door and leans on her folded arms behind the sack. She wears a blue T-shirt with a wolf on the front, and the backs of her arms sag out of its sleeves to her elbows, her forearms puddling white against the amber varnish of the shelf.

"I won't charge you if you'll feed him these."

"What's in there?"

"Apples."

"What do you usually charge?"

"Kids two dollars, adults five, old guys like you get in free if they help with the feeding."

Angie wears a straw cowboy hat with a rattlesnake hatband. The snake's mouth is open, striking into the air with its fangs bared. Einar takes the sack off the shelf.

"I had the Fish and Game put him in that pit I built for Meryl. That's what I called my mountain lion." She stares down the chipped pathway like she expects to see Meryl coming toward her. "I had her since she was just six months old."

"I heard she died."

Angie turns back to him. "She woke up sick one morning and died two days later."

"What of?"

"I don't know." She takes the hat off, turns it to have a look at the snake and puts it back on. "She just got sick and didn't get better. I named her Meryl for Meryl Streep." She seems like she's about to cry. "I had the vet out here three times."

"I'm sorry."

"Ted and I buried her under the water tower."

"The one for the city?"

"Yeah. You won't tell anyone, will you? I thought it'd be nice to think about her every time I looked at the tower."

"I won't say a word."

Einar follows the curving path along a chain-link fence that's got a moose behind it. A sign on the fence says its name is Barney. All the animals in Angie's zoo have names and sad stories. According to the sign, Barney's mom was killed when he was only a day old and a lineman for the rural electric company found him in the willows beside Owl Creek and brought him in, twelve years ago. Angie had him gelded when he was old enough to stand it, and he hasn't shed his antlers even once, and they never lose their velvet. The sign doesn't say that Angie feels her animals are happier and a whole lot less trouble once they're fixed.

She also has sandhill cranes, three antelope, a fox, a pair of bobcats, four coyotes, a raven with a bad wing and a golden eagle. Every one of them's been orphaned or abandoned, or damaged and ready to die. Angie and her husband, Ted, started the zoo because they couldn't keep them all at home. Ted drives around all day in an ATV, feeding and watering and scooping shit. The animals are like their children.

Einar looks in at the bobcats, Tom and Jerry. They're both asleep on top of the flat-roofed shelter Ted built for them. Their enclosure is fifty-by-fifty and fenced up twenty feet high with hogwire, and Ted suspended a whole set of truck tires from ropes so they can bat them around, and he even dug a den.

Across from the bobcats there's the snake-pit. It's Angie's moneymaker. She doesn't think rattlesnakes deserve shelter or rehabilitation. They're in the pit just because she caught them and threw them in. Last winter at the post office, she told Einar she had more than a hundred and thirty. Kids pay two dollars year-round just to take a look.

She had Ted dig a hole ten feet deep and build a waist-high circular brick wall around the top. It looks like a well you'd see in a storybook, and there's metal mesh over the top so nobody falls in. Today five kids are pressed up against the wall, peering down through the mesh and whispering, the smallest one up on his toes.

Angie pays three boys to capture mice in live traps. She doesn't care for mice any more than she cares for rattlers, and on Saturdays when the boys bring in the mice, she swings the metal mesh back on its hinges and they drop them in. She gets a good crowd on Saturdays, and if any of the kids seem to enjoy it too much she won't let them back in. It's one of the reasons Einar likes Angie. She's got limits to what she'll do to make a living.

The big pit still says MOUNTAIN LION on its sign. It's the size of an Olympic swimming pool with a chainlink fence around the edge, a shelter along one side and a cave burrowed into another. A concrete ramp allows Ted to lay the fence down and back a truck in. There's a tank with fresh water, and rocks and logs scattered across the dirt floor, but it still looks like a ruined pool.

AN UNFINISHED LIFE

The bear's standing in the far corner with his head held low in front of him. He rocks back and forth, keeping his eyes unfocused. He looks gaunt, numbed, his sides matted with mud and with his own shit. He scoops at the air, back and forth, with his big dish-shaped face.

This isn't what Einar expected. He expected to hate the bear, maybe even fear it, but the sight of the animal disgusts him. He circles the pit. He stops and stares through the chainlink every few feet, but the bear doesn't care, doesn't turn or even raise his head to look at the man who once wounded him.

Einar thinks it's the snakes that don't belong, and now this bear. Everything else has been brought in as a cub or kit or fawn or calf and never known anything better, having never experienced a wilder, natural life. They've been nursed, healed, fed and watered, and grown accustomed to being watched. Maybe they feel grateful, he thinks, or at least resolute. This bear doesn't.

He takes an apple out of the sack and tosses it over the fence. It rolls into the middle of the pit, and the bear starts toward it, stops and rocks, then moves forward again.

"Do you work here?"

Einar looks down at the small boy standing at his side, his small fingers clutching the fencing, and then throws in another apple.

"You shouldn't feed the animals if you don't work here."

"I was asked to, son. I'm like a volunteer."

The boy nods and pushes away from the fence. "I'm Joey Bloom. I just moved here from Memphis, Tennessee. I don't know anybody yet, but there's people who know me in Tennessee."

"I'm Mr. Gilkyson. You move here all by yourself?"

The boy points at the snakepit, where a tall man waves back at him. "I'm with my dad. He said I could come over here if I stood by you. He read me a book about bears. In the car when Mom was driving."

The bear mouths up the first apple and tilts his head back, chewing carefully and drooling.

The boy's staring at the bear. "Did you know grizzly bears weigh just a pound when they're born?"

"I know some of those cubs get eaten by their fathers."

Joey gapes up at Einar, his eyes blinking slowly behind the thick lenses of his glasses. "I didn't know that."

"A friend of mine had part of his leg, most of his butt and a kidney eaten off by a bear."

Joey makes a face. He turns and grips his side above his belt. "This is where your kidney is, right?"

"That's right."

The boy shudders and watches the bear eat the second apple. "Can I throw him one?"

Einar holds the sack down, and Joey reaches in. He steps back and throws the apple into the fence. It bounces at his feet and he picks it up and throws harder this time. The apple clears the fence, and the bear lumbers toward it.

"Did the man die?"

"No, he didn't. But it kills you to look at him."

Einar watches the boy grip his side again and squeeze harder and drop his hand.

Joey turns to him. "My mom wanted to stay in Tennessee. She thinks Wyoming's depressing. She says there's not enough water in the whole state to grow a good garden."

"Your mom's probably right. You want to feed him the rest?" Einar hands him the sack, and he looks in.

"There's only three left."

"I didn't say it was an all-day job."

"Okay." He pulls out an apple and throws it over the fence on his first try, then moves up against the wire mesh again.

"Try to make sure you don't turn out like that."

Joey pushes his glasses higher on the bridge of his nose, obviously unsure of how to respond. "Okay. I won't."

Einar watches the boy watch the bear. "What do you like to eat?"

"What?"

"I want to know what you like."

Joey looks into the sack. "I won't eat these apples. You said they were for the bear."

"That's not what I meant. If your mother asked what you wanted for lunch, what would you say?"

Joey takes an apple out of the sack and turns it, considering. "PBJ."

"What's that stand for?"

"Peanut butter and jelly. It's a sandwich with peanut butter and jelly on it."

"I know what the sandwich is. I just never heard it called a PBJ."

Joey nods and hurls the apple over the fence.

"All right then," Einar says. "It was nice meeting you, Joey Bloom."

"Yes, sir. I'm sorry about your friend who got hurt by the bear." Joey glances quickly at his father. "Can anybody buy a hat like you have?"

"I don't know why not. They sell them right here in town."

Einar tilts his hat off and holds it down for Joey to look at, squinting through his glasses. Then he nods, pivots and throws the last apple over the fence.

THIRTEEN

———

GRIFF SETS THE LUNCH tray on the table on Mr. Bradley's porch. Three chairs line the wall next to the table, and she sits in the middle one. She can hear Mr. Bradley inside at his workbench. He showed her how he carves the wolves out of the antler with the dental drill, but the sound made her mouth water, like she really was at the dentist's, and just watching wasn't much fun.

She doesn't feel like going back to her grandfather's house yet. She looks toward the mountains and sees a horse standing in the corrals next to a barn and two sheds. She thinks she should wait until her grandfather gets home before she looks at the horse. She should ask. The horse might be special, like Roy's father's pocket watch. It's better to ask before you look at something special.

Away from the mountains there's a line of

trees, and just where the trees start there's a little building made of old boards. The building doesn't look very special, so she doesn't think anybody'd mind if she looked at it. Her mother didn't tell her she couldn't explore, and it's almost like they live here now. For a month, anyway.

She jumps down from the porch and starts toward the little building holding her arms straight out from her shoulders, like she's walking on a tightrope. She places the heel of her front foot against the toe of her back foot, one careful step at a time. She wants the morning to last.

Halfway there she hears a sound and drops her arms and turns her head. She thinks it's the wind, but when she looks up at the trees the leaves aren't moving at all. Her heart starts to beat faster. For a minute she thinks God's answered her prayers and sent a tornado, but the horizon's blue all around her, with no clouds squeezed into funnels. It's just a ghost sound, she thinks. Goose bumps prickle her forearms, and she rubs her arms until they go down. She looks up again into the gray-green leaves and wishes she hadn't thought of ghosts but it's too late now. She starts back to Mr. Bradley's cabin but doesn't run. Ghosts won't usually chase you unless you act like you're afraid. She stands waiting at the open door, careful not to act like she's afraid.

He still sits at his workbench. The light's on over his head and he stares through the magnifying glass, holding the drill like a fat pencil and running it in short bursts by stepping on a pedal on the floor. The drill's not the sound she heard, she's sure of that. She thinks Mr. Bradley doesn't look so scary once you get used to him, like a scary movie you've seen three or four times in a row. After you know where the awful parts are you start to notice the regular stuff.

She knocks lightly on the doorframe, and when he looks up she asks, "Can Karl come with me?"

"He can if he wants." He asks Karl, "You want to go with Griff?"

The dog gets to his feet and stands staring under the bed.

"You better call him yourself."

Griff claps her hands and says, "Come on, Karl."

Mr. Bradley tells him, "It's all right," and the dog shuffles toward her, his nails clicking against the pine floorboards, his head low and shoulders hunched. She thinks he must feel embarrassed, like he just understood this was what he was supposed to do all along. In the doorway he looks back at Mr. Bradley like he's sorry he got confused.

Griff heads toward the little building again, with Karl at her heels. It makes her feel safer just to hear him panting behind her, and when the ghost sound gets louder she steps to the side and lets Karl come up beside her. He doesn't seem too worried, but she thinks if she hadn't clapped her hands he'd still be in the cabin staring under the bed. If it's something really scary, she thinks, at least she'll be able to outrun the old dog. But then how would she explain that to Mr. Bradley? That she let the ghost get his dog?

She walks into the high brown grass under the trees. She's just tall enough to look over the top of the grass, and she's careful where she steps. The sound keeps getting louder, and when it's so loud she can't hear Karl panting or her own heart pounding, she squats down and parts the grass in front of her.

Beyond a bank of rounded stones there's a creek. She holds her breath and listens. "It's the water," she whispers. Karl stands beside her, with what looks like a smile on his old white muzzle. "It sounded like the wind," she tells him, and he cocks his head and then wobbles out over the stones and stands in the creek up to his belly and laps at the water. She calls to him that she didn't really think it was a ghost, and then closes her eyes and listens harder.

The sound seems to lift and hold her, the way you feel at the top of a roller coaster just before the screaming starts, in that second when you've lost control but nothing's happened to you yet. Like something bigger's got you and doesn't care what you think about it. When she opens her eyes, Karl's not in the water anymore, and she calls his name but he doesn't come. She starts back through the tall grass, eager to tell Mr. Bradley how the sound of the water got inside her and lifted her up. She's wondering if he's ever been on a roller coaster, because that's the way she wants to describe the feeling, when she sees Karl lying on the porch of the little building she wanted to explore.

She kneels down and loops an arm over his shoulders and kisses the top of his head and tells him he's a good dog. He's got his nose pressed to a small window and she lies on her belly, with her face right beside his, and tries to look through the window too. She can't see much, and Karl's wet and his breath's bad. She stands and pulls the latchstring, knowing how these doors work now.

Inside there's a woodstove across from two lawn chairs on a platform. She steps onto the platform, then looks down at the little window and waves to Karl.

On a wall there's a picture of a man with a beard and a hat with horns, and she wonders if he's famous. There's also a picture of a tall man with very black skin. He's wearing a sort of animal-skin skirt and holding a spear. She looks at maps of countries she doesn't recognize, then sits in a chair and tilts her head back and gazes through the window in the ceiling. She watches a white cloud move across the blue sky and feels as though she's falling backward. It's the same kind of feeling she had at the creek, but smaller. Like on a smaller roller coaster, she thinks.

She makes sure the door's latched tight when she leaves and walks back to Mr. Bradley's cabin with Karl at her side. He sniffs the lunch tray she left on the porch table and then lies down in the sun next to the door. Mr. Bradley's still working with the drill, so she decides to tell him about the roller coaster later.

She carries the tray into her grandfather's house and sets it on the counter by the sink and walks into the living room. She turns in a circle and can't find a television. No CD or tape player either. There isn't even the sound of the creek. She thinks he might keep a television in his bedroom and walks next to the wall in the hallway so the floorboards won't creak. But there's only a double bed, a dresser, a straight-backed chair and a low table beside the bed with a lamp and a clock radio. No television.

The bedcovers are folded down on the side nearest to her. She pulls them up under the pillow and smooths the blanket and fluffs the pillow. It smells like hair oil and sagebrush, a little bit sour like the milk. She sits on the edge of the bed. The room's warm with sunlight, and there're tiny dust specks turning in circles through the light.

She starts to cry and doesn't know why. She just doesn't want to pack anymore. Doesn't want to have to be careful all the time, walking next to walls and listening hard to the words people say to tell if they're mad.

She's still crying when she figures out that it feels good when you're at the top of a roller coaster, right before rocketing down the other side, because your body thinks it doesn't have to pay attention to the rules anymore. The roller coaster tricks your body into believing you can drop forever and never hit anything at the bottom.

She stands and wipes her eyes and turns the covers down on her grandfather's bed so he won't know she was in here.

She walks up the stairs to the loft and gathers her dirty clothes and her mother's clothes and the Wal-Mart bag, then carries everything to the little room with the washer and dryer and sorts the clothes into a white pile and a dark. She carries in a kitchen chair and gets the laundry detergent down from the cupboard and strips out of her shirt and jeans. She puts on one of her mother's T-shirts and it falls below her knees. After starting the dark load she opens the freezer and sees that it's half-filled with packages wrapped in white paper. On the shelves above the freezer are cans of green beans and corn, and a few cans each of peaches and pears and plums. She thinks this must be what her grandfather and Mr. Bradley eat when they run out of baloney.

When she's back in the kitchen she starts washing dishes because she knows how and there isn't anything else to do, and she doesn't want to start crying again. She fills the dishrack and dries those dishes and puts them away where she thinks they go. She already knows where he puts the glasses. She finds some saltines left in a box on the counter and eats them all. Then she washes a whole other rack of dishes.

She has all the dishes done and the counter-tops wiped when she hears the clothes washer finish. She puts the dark load in the dryer and starts the white load. She pulls her mother's T-shirt off and throws that in the washer too. She stands for a minute in her socks and panties and chemise and decides they can wait to be washed.

She stands below the row of coats and jackets hanging from pegs by the back door and pulls down a gray hooded sweatshirt. She has to roll the sleeves up to see her hands. The front's stained brown, and when she sniffs it smells just like Karl. She steps into a pair of boots because they're there and it might be funny to try them on. They have high blocky heels and pointed toes, and the tops are stitched to look like leaves growing on vines. When she takes a step her foot slides down toward the toe and it makes her laugh out loud.

She clomps out to the living room in the boots. The sweatshirt's so long she has to lift it up to watch herself walk. She climbs onto the rolled arm of the couch and is balancing there, trying to see herself in the framed mirror at the far end of the room, when her grandfather walks in the front door carrying a bag of groceries.

He looks into the kitchen, and then again, longer, like there's something in there he hasn't seen for a long time. He takes off his cowboy hat and sets it upside down on the chair by the door and walks into the kitchen, and she slides down real fast. She can't tell if he saw her or not.

When he comes into the living room she's standing away from the couch, maybe far enough away that he won't think she's hurt anything. She tries to remember if she moved anything in his bedroom or played with the dials on the clock radio.

He just says, "Sounds like you got the laundry detergent down all right."

"You said I could." She's worried she's in trouble for wearing the sweatshirt and boots, or because she was up on the couch. Everybody gets mad about different things, and she knows she can't always guess right. His face looks regular, just wrinkled and whiskery, but he could be real mad inside. Sometimes Roy looked fine when he wasn't.

Einar walks up the stairs to the loft. She thinks he's probably going to pack up all their things and make them leave, but he comes down carrying a trunk that was at the foot of her bed. It's made of wood and has little pieces of metal on the corners, and she hopes she hadn't piled anything on top of it. She can't tell if he's mad or really mad.

He sets the trunk on the living room floor and kneels in front of it. He lifts the lid and takes out a folded shirt and shakes it, and then a pair of jeans. He holds them out to her. "You ought to see if this stuff fits."

She takes the clothes from him. His face still looks okay, like he's not mad at all. The shirt has snaps instead of buttons and the snaps look like pearl, but she thinks that would be silly. He's still kneeling in front of the trunk.

She says, "I need you to turn around."

He grunts when he gets up, then walks to the fireplace and acts like he'd never seen the stuff on the mantel.

She kicks off the boots and pulls the sweatshirt over her head. She checks to see if he's turned around, but he's still staring at the mantel. She pulls on the jeans. They're faded at the knees but they aren't ripped anywhere, and they aren't too big.

"Thanks for doing those dishes," he says. "It take you very long?"

She's snapping the fake pearl snaps. "I don't know how long it took. I don't have a watch." She tucks in the shirt and holds her arms away from her sides to see if the sleeves are too long, and they're not. She won't even have to roll them up. She jumps up to see herself in the mirror, but it makes too much noise and she can only see her face and shoulders for a second at the top of her jump. "Okay," she says. "You can turn around now."

He just looks at her and says, "All right, then." He walks to the trunk and lifts out a stack of jeans and shirts that he sets down on the floor.

"Where did you get all this stuff?"

He closes the trunk and lifts it. "They were your dad's."

She follows him up the stairs because she thinks he might want her to. "Was he a midget?"

"Of course he wasn't. I kept the clothes from when he was a boy."

"That's a long time." She isn't trying to be funny. She's just never heard of anybody keeping stuff for so long.

He stops on the stairs and looks back at her. "I'm careful about what I throw away."

As he puts the trunk back by her bed

he says, "Do you like PBJs? I think I might have one."

She raises an arm into the light from the window. "What kind of jelly?" There's a silver thread in the material that sparkles in the light.

"I got grape."

She slips her hands into the back pockets of the jeans to stop looking at the silver threads. So he'll see she's paying attention. "Is grape your favorite?"

He stares at her like he sort of recognizes her. "The grape was on sale," he says.

He starts back down the stairs, and she follows.

"Have you ever been on a roller coaster?"

"You ask a lot of questions."

"I don't mean to."

He stops. He's far enough below her that his head's level with hers. His hair is pressed down on the sides from wearing a hat, and his face doesn't look so old up close.

"It's not a bad thing," he says, "asking questions." And then, "No. I've never been on a roller coaster, and I doubt I ever will."

When he starts down the stairs again she tells him, "I went in your little building."

"There's more than one. What was it like inside?"

He still doesn't sound like he's mad. "There were chairs and a stove to burn wood. And maps. But there wasn't a bathroom."

In the kitchen he takes a jar of peanut butter and one of grape jelly out of the grocery bag. She wonders what else he bought.

"That was the sauna you were in."

"I don't know what a sauna is."

He takes the loaf of bread out of the refrigerator. "You build a fire in the stove and you sit in there naked and sweat." He stands holding the bread. "It's not a building that really needs a bathroom."

Her feet are cold, and she wishes she had a pair of fancy stitched boots of her own. "How long do you usually sit in there for?"

"Until you're tired of it. Vikings used to do it."

"Am I part Viking?"

"You're half." He looks at where she shifts from one foot to the other. "My half."

She hopes her socks aren't dirty, but she doesn't want to check. She wants to ask if she's related to the man in the picture with the horns on his hat but decides to wait till later. "Are these clothes mine now? Or do I have to give them back?"

"I guess they're yours. They won't fit anybody else."

She expects him to say more, but he doesn't.

"You left your hat upside down."

He looks at the chair by the door. "That's because it's not on my head." When she looks over at the hat he says, "You set it down like that so the brim won't curl."

FOURTEEN

————

THE SECRETARY looks up from the computer keyboard and smiles when Jean comes in. "Howdy, howdy," she says, but she doesn't stop typing. Her fingers are long and tapered, and her nails filed and buffed glossy. Her wrists are slender, but that's it. Everything else goes lumpy. She wears a loose print dress to hide everything that's not hands and wrists, and some gal on the radio's singing about living on dreams and SpaghettiOs. The secretary hums along. Her hair's more gray than brown and it's cut short.

Jean looks at her own hands, at the nails bitten ragged. Everybody's got something, she thinks. This woman sitting behind the desk has the hands and wrists she wants. Jean slips hers into her pockets. "Can I see the sheriff?"

The secretary still types. "You bet you can." She smiles again. She's got those sexy half-circles at the sides of her mouth, and when she smiles the creases deepen and fan away from her mouth. Jean remembers Roy telling her this was a sure sign of being good in bed. Jean's cheeks are smooth, and so are Roy's, but she adds the half-circles to the list of things she wouldn't mind having.

"It's none of my business, but how much trouble are you in?" The secretary's quit typing.

"I'm not in any trouble." Jean laughs like she's killing time before an afternoon matinee. "I just thought I should talk to the sheriff. That's all."

The secretary scoots her wheeled chair back from the keyboard, folds her hands in her lap and tilts her head. Her neck's as slender as her wrists are. "Darling, there's one whole side of your face swollen up with trouble. So why don't you make my day and tell me you shot the son of a bitch who worked you over. My name's Starla."

"Starla?"

"Starla Reese, and I can help you a whole lot more than any sheriff can."

"I didn't shoot anybody, Starla."

Starla looks at Jean like she's truly shocked, then rolls her chair over to a file cabinet and leans into the bottom drawer. "This isn't something I do five times a day for any Jane, Sue or Nancy." She stops rummaging in the drawer and turns her head to wink at Jean. She clucks her cheek and winks again. "What I'm going to show you now is absolutely a girl's best friend."

She sits up fast in her chair, and she's got a pistol in her right hand. It's shiny and short-barreled, and she handles the thing like she uses it every day of her life. She places it on the desktop between them and says, "My name used to be Susan, but Susan didn't care much for firearms."

Jean feels herself start to go numb. It's the feeling she used to get when Roy raised his voice, working himself away from disagreement into something dangerous.

Starla taps the desk beside the pistol. "Anytime you think you'd like to borrow her, all you have to do is ask." She swivels her chair closer to the desk and leans over the pistol. "When I was Susan," she says, "I used to be a librarian." She licks the pad of one of her perfect fingers and wipes a smudge from the pistol's barrel. "Susan had a rich internal life." She winks again. "Starla lives it."

Jean tries to smile. She's used to smiling at crazy people. She'd smiled at Roy, hadn't she? "I'm really just here to see the sheriff," she says.

Starla picks up the pistol and nods toward an open doorway to her right. "Suit yourself. He's through that door right there."

Jean turns away.

"And hey."

She stops.

"Wyoming's the best state there is to shoot a man. There isn't a good-old-boy judge in this county or any other that'd take a look at your face right now and not say, 'Well done, girl. Where do we go to find the body?' If you don't believe me, just stop by the library. It's all a matter of record."

Jean stares at the woman, sexy half-circles and all. "You're so goddamn clueless," she says. She doesn't raise her voice, but it feels just as good to say it as she thought it would.

Starla settles the pistol on her lap.

"Have you ever been hit?" Jean asks.

Starla shakes her head.

"How about Susan?"

Starla shakes her head again.

Jean steps closer to the desk. "I didn't get the shit slapped out of me because I didn't have a gun," she says. "I got hit because I fell in love with the wrong man and was too stupid and scared to stop pretending I hadn't made a mistake. I wanted him to be the man he said he wanted to be. None of it happens all at once, Starla. So think about it."

She wants to tell Starla all of it, how it happens so slow you believe the lies you've told yourself, but the woman looks like she wants to start bawling. Jean hopes she will.

She turns and walks to the open door and looks in. Her insides feel dry and cracked, like she might be coming down with the flu.

The sheriff's office is a twin to Starla's: cinder block walls painted too white, a gray gas wall heater, a gray metal desk. The sheriff sits behind his desk, bent over a paperback novel, spooning what looks like tuna-fish salad from a brown Tupperware container, chewing while he reads. He's younger than she thought he'd be. Brown hair, parted on the right, clean-shaven, just the start of the hunched shoulders men get from working at a desk, but still thick from something more than deskwork.

He looks up. "I'm sorry." He sets the Tupperware aside and wipes his mouth. "Have you been standing there long?"

She steps into the office. "I'm Einar Gilkyson's daughter-in-law."

"Yeah. I know." He folds a corner of the page he was reading and closes the book.

"I've only been in town eight hours."

He stands. His pants match his shirt, both county-brown, but his clothes hang on him like they should. No paunch. "I ran into Nina Haaland this morning. She said she'd hired you to waitress at the café." He extends his hand. "My name's Crane Carlson."

Jean shakes his hand, and he motions toward a metal chair with a pea-green plastic seat. The same color as the curtains and carpet. She sits in the chair and takes the sheaf of papers from her purse and holds it out. Her arm quivers, and the young sheriff stands and takes the papers from her, then sits again and turns to the first page.

"It's a police report," she explains. She squeezes the arm she'd reached out, the muscles above the elbow ache as though she'd strained it lifting something heavy.

Crane looks up. "I can see that." His face looks calm and there's no judgment in his voice. "Did you file it on the guy?" He lifts his chin toward her face. "The man who hit you?"

She's looking at the bighorn sheep's head mounted on the wall behind him, next to a set of mule deer antlers where he's hung his sheriff's jacket and three caps. She can hear Starla in the outer office, the squeak of a file cabinet drawer. "I'm sorry?" she says. "When I'm upset I don't pay attention."

Crane lifts the report up between them. "Is this about your injuries?"

"Not for this time. For another time." She knows exactly how many times Roy hit her, but this is the first time she's admitted out loud that it was more than once. It makes her mouth taste sour. She wonders what this man must think of her.

Crane looks at the ring finger of her left hand. "Is he your boyfriend or your husband?"

She covers her hand. "What makes you think he's either one?"

He lays the report beside the Tupperware. "Because people aren't usually assaulted more than once by a stranger."

She closes her hands into fists. Fuck this hick, she thinks, and his secretary too. She stands out of the chair and points at the sheep's head. "Did you kill that animal?"

"The guy who had the job before me did." He leans back in his chair. "He hasn't come back yet to haul it away."

They hear Starla tapping at her keyboard.

"She show you her pistol?" he asks.

"What do you think? Of course she did."

"I'm sorry. She watches too much TV. I'll say something to her."

"She's crazier than shit."

Crane nods. He lowers his voice. "I think she wants to be a writer."

Jean doesn't want to laugh, but she can't help it. "Like true-crime novels?"

He rolls his eyes toward the doorway. "Actually, I think that's why she took the job here. Firsthand experience." He taps the police report. He wants an answer.

"He was my boyfriend," Jean says. "I was embarrassed to tell you because I thought you'd think I was one of those women this happens to all the time."

"That's not what I was thinking, but are you?"

"I guess I was."

"And you're worried your boyfriend"—he looks back at the report—"you're worried this Roy'll follow you here?"

"I don't know for sure." Her mouth fills like she's bitten into a lemon wedge, and she swallows. "I have a daughter."

"Is she his?"

"No."

"But you think he might follow you anyway?"

"Yes."

Crane starts around the desk. "I'll make a photocopy." He stops in the doorway. "Is he crazy?"

There isn't a hint of anything in his expression except wanting to know, and she wonders if that's something he learned on the job.

"Roy thinks he's in love," she says.

"That'll do it."

"I guess it will."

She hears the photocopy machine warming up in the secretary's office. Shit, she thinks. She feels like she's in the principal's office for getting in a fight on the goddamn playground. There's an open can of root beer on the sheriff's desk, and she stands and sneaks a sip. The bitter taste goes away.

His desk is heaped with papers. There's a radio on top of the computer, but the dials are broken off, and an upright vacuum is pushed into the corner. Filing cabinets line one whole wall, and another's covered with three-by-six sheets of corkboard tacked full of maps and ten-most-wanted posters.

She bends at a shelf below the corkboards to look at a row of framed photographs. Crane Carlson with a black Lab in a duck blind. On a horse. A high-school Crane in a basketball team photo; the jerseys read ISHAWOOA BOBCATS, and written at the bottom in gold lettering is 1988 CHAMPIONSHIP. She turns the photograph to shift the glare from the overhead light. He looks just like any boy. A regular boy. Maybe a little bit goofy, as if he'd been told to sit still or get benched the next game. She hears him come back in and taps the glass over the photograph as she turns around. "You're Crane Carlson."

"And you used to be Jean Evans."

She doesn't feel like she's in the principal's office anymore. She shakes the photograph toward him. "You were the guy who streaked the homecoming game when I was a sophomore."

Crane hands her back the police report. "My single claim to fame."

She replaces the photograph, then folds the papers back into her purse. "This is exactly what I hate about small towns."

"That everybody knows everybody else's business?"

"Yeah."

He sits behind his desk again. "It's what I like about them."

She stops at the door. She can see Starla in the outer room, still typing. She turns and pats her purse. "Everybody in town doesn't have to know about this, do they?"

"What happens in this office stays right here."

She looks again toward Starla.

"Starla keeps both her opinions and that pistol at the office. Does Roy know you're in Ishawooa?"

"He knows where I'm from."

He picks up the Tupperware like he might start eating again, then sets it back down. "If you get worried, will you let me know?"

She looks down at the pea-green carpet. She can hear the buzz of the fluorescent lights, can smell the tuna fish and mayonnaise. "I'll let you know."

Crane smiles and holds it, meaning to show her that he's listened, that he cares, that he's a man who can handle whatever life throws at him, or at her. She smiles back, and wishes he didn't have those half-circles at the sides of his mouth.

FIFTEEN

———

MITCH IS AT HIS WORKBENCH when he looks up through the open door and sees Jean crossing from the house. The sun's gone down, and the mercury light just came on above the workyard.

Einar's told him that she's been beaten, but her hair's fallen over her face, and he can't tell how badly she's been hurt. She holds his dinner plate in front of her in the soft yellow light.

He looks to where his hands rest on his thighs. He imagines her still beautiful because she always was, even as a kid. He doesn't believe there's a man alive who could knock the beauty out of her. He hopes he's not wrong.

He squares his chair to the doorway and turns the light above the workbench so it shines on his face. He wants to be the first thing she sees. She's whistling when she steps onto the porch. It's not a tune he recognizes, and he thinks he ought to buy a radio, that it wouldn't hurt to learn some new music. He straightens himself in the chair.

He's heard it said that a man can't choose his family, but that's what he did. He chose Einar Gilkyson, and Griffin and Ella, and this woman too. It doesn't matter that he hasn't seen her for ten years, and he knows he'll choose the slight girl he met just this morning. Not because she's Griffin and Jean's, but because he liked what he saw. It's the way he's always made his choice of family.

She steps in smiling without even breaking her stride. She stares right at the mutilated side of his face as she sets the plate on the workbench. Her eyes don't flicker and her smile doesn't wilt.

She cups his face in her hands and kisses him on the forehead, then turns his face up and kisses him on the lips. She says, "Goddamn, I've missed you, old man." And then she holds her cheek against the side of his face and breathes in deeply and holds her breath. When she exhales she whispers, "I didn't know it until now, but I've even missed the smell of you."

He watches as she pulls the extra chair out and sits down. Her left cheek and jaw are swollen and bruised, but on the inside she seems just right.

"That food'll get cold unless you start eating," she says.

She's fried him a steak, and there's a potato and green beans with bacon bits stirred in the way he likes.

"When I'm in town tomorrow," she says, "I'll get us a better choice of groceries."

She gets up and bends over the antler clamped in the vise, her hair hanging almost in his plate as he cuts a bite of steak.

"Jesus Christ, when did you start these carvings?"

"After I laid up in here," he says. "I bought the drill from Ray Dawson. They made him quit dentistry even before he died. It's easy with the drill."

She walks to an antler of carved horses mounted above the front window and stands under it, looking up.

"It can't be that easy. Nothing as beautiful as these can be easy."

He chews the steak and watches as she sits again.

"I wish Ella had lived," she says. "I wish I could've met her."

Of all the things he thought she might say, Ella hadn't occurred to him. "What made you think of her?"

"I don't know. I guess I thought she might like these carvings."

He sits back with another bite of steak. "Ella was easy to be around. She treated me fine." Karl sits by his knee, begging, his nose working the air. "Like I was more than just useful. Sort of like a spare husband." He feeds Karl a piece of fat.

"What did you think of my kid?"

"I thought the world of her," he says. "I think a good mother makes all the difference."

He watches the compliment register in her eyes.

"I wanted Griff to meet you all by herself." She leans forward and rubs the dog's shoulders, but he won't look away from Mitch. "There shouldn't be a crowd for the best things in life."

She sits back in her chair and starts whistling again. He knows the light's still on the side of his face.

She shakes her head and says, "Fucking-A, Mitchell."

It's the third time she's cussed, and it pleases him. Not as much as her kiss pleased him, but he remembers her cussing up a storm when she was a kid, dragging out the worst language she could think of to hide her nervousness.

"When Einar said you got mauled I thought I knew what that meant," she says.

"It's not so bad." He waves his fork at her. "I never was what you'd call handsome."

"Where else did he bite you?"

He looks down at the dog. "I guess my head's the good part," he says.

She shudders and hooks her hair away from her face and tucks it behind her ears.

"It looks like you got into it with your own bear," he says.

She juts her bruised jaw out. That's something else she used to do. She's never been coy. "You mean this little thing?" She touches her jaw. "This was my fault. I stayed somewhere I shouldn't have been in the first place."

"That's what I say about my bear too."

"Are you in a lot of pain?"

He cuts his potato open and slips the pat of butter from the edge of the plate with the flat of his knife. "I don't seem to be able to get away from it." He slots the butter into the potato. "But it's not too bad right now."

"Then hell," she says. "I'm the lucky one."

She works her jaw around like a dog chewing a bone that's too big. "My face only hurts when I think about it."

He puts down the knife and fork. Having her here's even better than he imagined. It's like she never left. She could be fourteen and he'd just be a middle-aged man, but a whole man, taking pleasure in his work and the family of his choosing.

She points at the canes hanging on the back of his chair. "Do you need those everywhere you go?"

He nods. "And Einar gives me a shot of morphine in the mornings."

"Well," she says. "Fucking-A."

SIXTEEN

———

EINAR SETS the bottle of whiskey on Mitch's workbench and steps back out onto the porch. He strips his jacket off and shakes it under the porch light and beats his hat against his leg to get the water off that too. He hangs them both on the rack inside the door. "I hope this lasts all night," he says.

He takes the cribbage board and a deck of cards from a shelf above the bench and pulls a chair to Mitch's bed. He doesn't have to look up from shuffling the cards against his thigh to know Mitch is staring at the bottle. "I keep it in the granary." He sets the deck on the edge of the bed. "You want to cut for the deal?"

Mitch cuts an eight. "How many bottles of booze've you got stashed around this place?"

"Just that one." Einar holds up a four, shuffles again and deals out their hands. They fan their cards and discard two apiece into the crib. "I like to look at it sometimes."

Mitch plays a ten. "You keep a full bottle of whiskey in the granary just to look at? For what, two years?"

"I guess it's been that long." He snaps down a queen.

A burst of wind slaps the rain harder against the roof, and they stop and listen, and Mitch plays a jack. "That's a run of three." He pegs three points on the board. "Why'd you bring it in here?"

Einar shrugs. "Because I had it with me when it started to rain." He looks down at the cards. "That's a go."

"You don't have to mope, for Christ's sake." Mitch plays an ace and says, "Thirty-one for two," and pegs the points. "I just asked why that bottle's sitting on my workbench all of a sudden."

"It's here because it wasn't safe in the granary anymore."

When Einar plays a seven, Mitch lays another on top of it. "That's a pair for two," he says.

Einar keeps his head down. He's getting beat and doesn't think he can do anything with what he's likely to find in the crib. That's the kind of day it's been.

He let Jean fix dinner, and he ate it and walked to the barn. He was fine in the barn. He sat in the chair in the granary and talked to the raccoons until they got tired of him, and then he walked out to check the headgate in the west pasture. That was when it started to rain.

He's only playing cards to wait out the rain, and for Jean and the girl to go to bed, but he won't tell Mitch that. He wishes Curtis had been at the headgate. He'd've asked Curtis to keep the bottle for him.

Mitch says, "Jean's kept her looks, don't you think?"

Einar plays his last two cards and pegs a point for a go, and while Mitch counts his hand he stands and walks to the window, staring at the rain blowing eastward in the yardlight. He says, "That's the trouble with the wicked: We look fit when we arrive in Hell."

"You don't look all that fit. You going to count your cards or not?"

"You count them." He can hear the scrape of the cards and the rustling of Mitch's bedcover.

"You got nothing in your hand and a pair in your crib," Mitch tells him. "Is it going to ruin you having her here?"

Einar turns faster than he means to. He doesn't know what he expected to see except a man he's known for most of his life propped up in bed. "That woman killed my son," he says.

Mitch taps the deck against the cribbage board to even the cards and sets it by the board. "It was a car accident, Einar. They call them accidents because it's nobody's fault."

"They call them accidents to make the guilty feel better."

"That's just bullshit and you know it."

"I know Griffin's still dead." He looks down at his boots. They're dark with water and mud and horseshit, and he looks to see if he's tracked the floor.

Mitch says, "That'll be easier to sweep up when it dries." He swings his legs over the side of the bed and sits there in his undershirt and shorts. "Is it cold in here?"

"Yeah, it is."

Mitch pulls his blanket over his shoulders.

"You better have a pair of socks on," Einar says. He steps to where Mitch's boots stand at the foot of the bed, the socks laid over the boot tops. He kneels in front of him and rolls a sock back to its toe. Mitch cocks a heel against his thigh and Einar rolls the sock down over the instep and up over the ankle.

Mitch asks, "How'd the bear look?"

"Better than you."

"A little or a lot?" Mitch sets the heel of his other foot up.

"Not much. Angie had me feed him a sack of apples."

"I didn't know bears ate apples."

Einar rocks back on his heels. "Well, I guess they do. He wasn't too shy about it."

Mitch sits above him holding the blanket tight at his throat. "I'd like you to keep feeding him. Would you do that for me?"

"All right."

"I mean every day. I don't think he'll hibernate in there at Angie's, and if he can't go to sleep I don't think he'll last very long."

"I said all right." Einar stands. "I'm sorry, I don't feel like cards tonight."

"We can finish another night. I'm only about a street ahead of you."

Einar motions toward the bottle. "Will you put that someplace for me? I'll need it somewhere where I don't have to look at it."

"Why don't you march in and flush it down my toilet right now?"

"Because I need to know I've got it somewhere. Unopened."

Mitch looks around the room. "I'm probably not the king of hiding things right now."

"Just put it out of sight." Einar turns back to

the window. The lights downstairs are out now. Without moving he says, "How about that kid?"

"You mean your granddaughter?"

"Who else would I mean?"

The wind throws the rain hard against the cabin's west wall.

"I believe she's a good get," Mitch says.

Einar turns toward the door. "I'll see you in the morning, then."

SEVENTEEN

———

GRIFF OPENS the window at the end of the loft. She can hear the creek, and once the window's all the way open there's the sound of the wind too. The screen's beaded with water, and she stands in the dark and breathes the wet air. It makes her shiver, but she feels a little bit like this place belongs to her. Knowing the different sounds helps, the rain and the wind and the creek. It's like she's already lived here, or it's a place she needed to find. Like home.

Her mother and grandfather didn't speak while Jean made dinner and then her grandfather took his plate out on the porch to eat, and after her mother was done she carried some dinner out to Mr. Bradley's cabin. It was stupid and weird, but they both acted like it's what regular people do. It made her want to scream.

She thinks it's too early to ask why they don't

like each other. She wants to stay here even more than she wanted to stay at Mary's house in Sioux Falls, a lot more, but when her mother's around her grandfather the air feels all staticky, like if you touched either one of them you'd get a shock. She knows she'll have to ask her mother why, because she doesn't want to do whatever her mother's done. She adds the question to the list of ones she'll ask later, when the air's less staticky and the answers won't be so dangerous.

She slips her diary out from under her mattress and turns on the lamp by her bed. She prints carefully at the top of a new white page: THINGS I LIKE ABOUT OLD MEN.

1. They don't hurry. They don't act too busy to listen to you even if they don't want to.

She can't think what to write next, and then she sees her jeans and shirt folded on top of the chest by her bed.

2. They keep things like clothes and pictures. Even though they didn't even know you were alive and would like to see them. And even though they didn't know they'd fit you.

She hears her mother come in through the mudroom and slips her diary back under the mattress and turns off the light and gets into bed. She thinks of all the questions she has and decides it's safe to ask about Mr. Bradley. That shouldn't start a fight. She hears her mother on the stairs and then sitting down on her bed.

"Do you want me to turn on the light?" she asks.

"I thought you were asleep."

"I was listening to the rain. Do you know the creek sounds like wind?"

Her mother smells real fresh, like the air coming in the window.

"Yeah, I knew that," she says.

She can hear her mother taking her jeans off. "Have you been with Mr. Bradley the whole time?" she asks.

"I took a walk."

"In the rain?"

"I like to walk in the rain."

She hears her mother get a sleeping T-shirt out of the dresser and a towel from the shelves beside the sink. Her mother dries her hair and spreads the towel over her pillow and climbs into bed.

"Were you afraid?"

"You aren't sleepy yet, are you?"

Griff shakes her head, then realizes her mother can't see her and says, "Not yet." And then, "Weren't you afraid a bear might get you?"

"I'm sorry I brought you here," her mother says.

She wants to be on her mother's side, so she can't say that the sound of the creek and a whole forest of logs stacked into a house make her feel safe. That's something that can wait too. "It's okay," she says. "Has Mr. Bradley always been here?"

"Not always."

She can hear her mother turn in her bed. "Was he here when you were a girl?"

Her mother gets up and goes to the window and Griff thinks she'll close it, but she gets another blanket and goes back to bed.

"Mitch and Einar met in the army. I think they got along because they were both from Wyoming and no one else was. Mitch's grandfather homesteaded a ranch on the Green River, but Mitch's dad couldn't keep it together. After the war, Mitch didn't have anyplace else to go."

"Was Mr. Bradley nice to you when you were little?"

"Yes, he was. He's still nice to me."

It makes her happy to find out that it didn't

take a bear to make Mr. Bradley nice. She thinks it might take two bears to make somebody like Roy nice. She waits a little bit, the way people do when they want to change the subject, and then says, "Einar says I'm half Viking." She's careful not to say "grandfather" right now.

"How'd that come up?" her mother asks.

"I was in his sauna, and there's a picture on the wall of a man with horns. I think that's how it came up."

She hears her mother turn in bed and wonders if she's looking at her, trying to make her out in the dark.

"Einar didn't lie to you."

"What else am I?" she asks.

"You mean my half of you?"

"Yeah."

"My mom was Irish. My dad was a Welshman."

"Were the Welshmen Vikings?"

"No. They mostly mined coal and prayed a lot."

She tries to picture a man praying. It's not something she's ever thought a grown-up would do. "What did they pray for?"

"That the Vikings wouldn't get them."

She wonders if her grandfathers knew each other, and maybe if Einar didn't like Welshmen, then that could be why he doesn't like her mother. She decides to believe this, even if it's not true. It was like a feud. It wasn't anything somebody did wrong.

"Your grandfather—" her mother says.

"You mean Einar?"

"Yeah, Einar. You should know he's lost just about everything he cares for. He really loved your dad. That's something else you should know."

"Then it's okay I'm part Viking?"

"You'll get used to it," her mother says. "You probably already are."

She hears her mother turn in bed again, and she listens to the rain and wind for a while. "Is there a school here?" she asks. She can't keep everything inside. If she tries to, she might forget one of her questions. Her mother doesn't say anything. "Mom?"

"I heard you," she says. "We aren't going to stay long enough for you to go to school."

"I don't want to get behind."

"You aren't going to get behind."

There's an edge in her mother's voice, but she doesn't care. "You should've told me about my grandfather and Mr. Bradley," she says. "You should've told me I had someplace to go."

She holds her breath. She thinks she

should have remembered to say "Einar" instead of "grandfather." She listens for her mother's breath, and when she can't hear it she thinks of all the bad things Roy said to her mother. She was careful not to use a mean voice like that. She didn't want to be mean. She just couldn't keep everything inside.

She pictures her mother's face the way it is now, bruised, still swollen, and wishes she could take back what she said. She thinks if Jean wasn't her mother she'd just be a woman with a beat-up face and wet hair. If she saw that woman on the street, she wouldn't be mean or ask her anything that made her feel worse. But she still wants to know why Einar was a secret, and why she didn't know she was half Viking. Why they can't stay.

"You're right," her mother says. "I should have told you."

Her voice is real small, and Griff can tell she's turned toward the wall.

EIGHTEEN

T HERE'S THE ELECTRIC whine of the
alarm, and Einar sits on the edge of his bed
and thumbs the buzzer off. He'd been lying
awake waiting for it. It's still dark.

He's set the alarm ten minutes earlier every
morning for a week, and every morning she's already up and dressed, waiting for him. He takes
his jeans and shirt from where he'd draped them
over the chair the night before, gets into them
and then sits on the chair and stomps his boots
on. He wonders if she can hear him thumping
around his room, and then wonders what the
cow must think of this nonsense. This morning
he'll be over an hour early to milk her. If the girl's
down there this morning, he'll get up tomorrow
at his regular time and give them all a break. He
tells himself he started setting the alarm earlier
only to see if the first morning was a fluke. But
the truth is he wants to see what she's made of,

whether she'll weaken. Mitch has always claimed most people die in bed. If the last week is any indication, this kid ought to live forever.

The very first morning he found her sitting at the kitchen table with her back to him. She was dressed in Griffin's clothes—the snap shirt and Wrangler jeans he'd given her—and when he saw her out of the corner of his eye it staggered him. He felt so dislocated that he had to turn away. He walked into the living room and stared in the mirror to make sure he was still an old man. He looked at the pictures of Griffin all grown up, where they sat on the mantel, then walked to the window to have a look at his son's grave marker on top of the sage rise west of the house.

He got his hat and walked to the barn. She followed him as far as the big doors, and when he rolled them back on their tracks she stood away. She watched from the corrals as he haltered the milkcow and led her into the barn.

He was sitting on the milkstool when she said, "What's the cow's name?" He looked around but couldn't see her anywhere.

He dropped his hands away from the warm teats. "Where are you?"

"Here," she'd said. He could hear her shuffling in the cold, and he squinted in the direction of the sound. She was standing out on the north side of the barn, looking in through a crack in the weathered siding.

"Well, I call the cow a cow."

"What about the cats?" she'd asked. "So you can tell them apart."

He looked back at the mob of gray and black and mottled cats wrestling in the shadows. "I call them what they are," he'd said. "They're all just cats."

"Mr. Bradley's dog has his own name."

He could see her breath where it entered between the boards, rising in the gray light. "Dogs are different."

"What about horses?"

"Horses are in a league of their own," he'd said. "My horse's name is Jimmy."

She didn't ask about anything else, and he waited until the milking was done and she still hadn't come in. He called, "Isn't it cold out there?"

"It's not so bad," she said. "It always warms up real fast."

When he led the cow back to the pasture, the girl moved away from the barn, and then later followed him to the house, but at a distance.

THIS MORNING he takes the flashlight from where he stands it on his dresser and checks the thermometer outside the bedroom window. It's still above freezing, if not by much. The nights are getting colder.

In the kitchen the light's on over the sink, and she's sitting at the table with a glass of milk. Her coat's folded across her lap, and she looks up when he steps to the sink for the milk pail.

"You're up early," he says. It's what he's said every morning after the first.

"Yes, sir," she says. "I'm not a good sleeper."

She stands out of the chair and gets into her coat, then takes the bright red wool gloves from the pockets and pulls them on. He likes the red gloves but thinks he might get her something stiffer at the hardware store. Leather, or maybe canvas. What the hell, he thinks. It's been like this every morning for a week. She's a kid who might be good help.

She walks beside him now and helps push the barn doors open, and for the past two days she's haltered the cow and led it into a stall while he scoops a coffee can of grain for the cow's feed-box. This morning he has to turn on the barn lights.

Some mornings she stands near the cow's face, holding its halter rope while he milks, and on other mornings she squats among the cats. He's told her to stay away from the business end of the cow, that he doesn't want her getting kicked.

A smallish gray tom with a kinked tail allows her to hold him, and she's named it Jack. This morning she whispers, "Jack, Jack, Jack the Cat," and cradles the thing up high against her chest, putting it down carefully when Einar carries the pail into the granary.

She hasn't yet gotten used to the raccoons. She edges past them and stands by the oak rocking chair, watching them at their bowl of milk with real suspicion. The single bulb hanging into the middle of the room makes her face appear paler than he knows it is, but her lips are as red as her woolen gloves.

"Do they hurt?" he asks.

She looks up from the raccoons and wrinkles her brow. He was vague on purpose, because he likes what she does with her eyebrows when she's confused, the way her soft face puckers around a question.

"Your lips. They're red as a baboon's ass."

She works them back and forth, the top lip against the bottom, and it reminds him of how a horse takes a feed cube from his palm.

"I can't remember not to lick them," she says. "They get real dry."

He sets the pail on the grain bin. "I could

dab a little fresh cowshit on there," he tells her. "You wouldn't lick 'em then."

She backs toward the window, but she's only acting like she's frightened and he smiles so he can watch her relax completely. He doesn't smile at her much, but every time he does it reminds him of how tensely she holds herself against the world. He takes a tube of ChapStick from a pocket in his canvas jacket and hands it to her.

She turns to look at her reflection in the window while she smears the ChapStick on her lips, and when she hands it back she asks, "Do I have a grandmother?"

Her shoulders have risen toward her ears again.

"What did your mother tell you?"

"I never asked." She pulls off a glove and dabs at her lips with a fingertip, then sniffs the finger and puts the glove back on.

He takes up the pail of milk and she grips the bail with him, and they start back through the barn, the pail swinging between them.

"You better get used to having me first," he says.

Outside the barn the eastern sky's brightened to steel and mauve, and he can make out Curtis riding the west pasture. In this light the colt looks nearly black.

"Do you see that man?" he asks.

"I've seen him before," she says.

"His name's Mr. Hanson. I lease him my land, and if anything ever happens to me and you need help, he's the one you should ask."

She doesn't say anything.

"Nothing's going to happen to me, but if it does he's right there."

"He doesn't know me."

"Yes he does. He knows you're my grand-daughter. That's all he'd need to know."

He watches her looking at Curtis and the colt.

"Tomorrow morning," he says, "I'm getting up at the normal time."

She shrugs, and when her shoulders drop they're level. "Okay by me," she says.

HE DOESN'T SEE Jean until they're across the workyard. She's on a ladder leaned against the side of his house, and he might not have seen her at all except for the racket she's making.

Griff stops when he does, and he sets the pail on the ground. "Can you lift that by yourself?" he asks. When she doesn't answer he looks down and sees that she's nodding. He thinks that's an-other thing he's learned about her. That when she's worried she doesn't speak. "It's all right," he says.

He watches her lift the pail and carry it, hunched and spraddle-legged, to the steps. She hefts it up one step at a time, and once she's on the porch he walks over to the ladder and stands looking up at her mother.

Jean's got a smooth wire fed through an eye-hook she's screwed under the eaves. The other end of the wire's already attached to Mitch's cabin at the same height. She ratchets out the sag with a come-along, and when she's got the wire taut she twists it off and unclips the come-along and drops it to the ground. Then she sees him. "I wanted to get this done before I left for work," she says, starting down the ladder. "Why doesn't Mitch have a wheelchair?"

He pushes his hat back so he can see her without tilting his head. She's above him, two rungs off the ground.

"He wouldn't get in one." He looks toward the cabin and can hear Mitch's canes tapping against the floorboards, the soft scrape of the bad foot dragging behind the other. "I tried."

Jean steps to the ground. "He's dying, isn't he?" She's skinned a knuckle, and she sucks at it.

They hear Griff come out on the porch and watch her walk to the big Russian olive tree in front of the house. She climbs up the boards nailed into the trunk and sits at the edge of the platform built through its limbs.

Jean takes her knuckle out of her mouth. "I remember when you built that," she says. "I remember the thorns."

"Mitch and Griffin built it. I just paid for the lumber, and hell yes he's dying. He always had high blood pressure, and now he's only got one kidney left and it isn't working like it should." He can hear Mitch at his workbench.

They watch Griff climb down and pick up the gray cat that's mewling at the base of the trunk. She unsnaps her shirt and stuffs it inside and starts back up to the treehouse.

"What about dialysis? You could take him into Sheridan."

"I already told you I couldn't even get him in a wheelchair." He looks at the wire and realizes he's been whispering. He clears his throat. "You got any more improvements you want to make around here?"

"I thought Mitch might like to get outside, but the ground's too soft and uneven. This way, if he wants to, he can hook a cane over the wire and it'll steady him." She picks up the come-along. "I'll pay you back for the wire. I found a spool of it in your toolshed."

He hears Mitch's door open. "I suppose you talked to him about it?" He's not whispering anymore.

"Yes, she did." Mitch hooks his cane over the wire and steps off the porch. He stands steady, holding the bottom end of the cane and grinning. "Since we've got some interesting people around here, I thought I might like to get out a little." He takes a step and winks at Jean.

"I already gave him his shot this morning," she says.

Jean's knuckle is still bleeding. Einar looks down at the ground. "Don't worry about the wire," he says, and takes the come-along from her. "I'll put this back with the rest of it."

He straightens the ropes in the pulleys, knowing she's watching and that it's not something that needs to be done.

"Why don't you just tell me, Einar." She presses down on the knuckle with her thumb. "What is it you hate most about me?"

He studies her face and tries to think of it as a new thing, but it's not. The bruise on her cheek and jaw is largely healed, just puffy and yellowed, but her eyes are still as dark as they always were. He looks up at Griff in the olive tree. Jack's curled in her lap. He speaks without turning back to Jean, and loud enough for Mitch to hear. "That I have to breathe the same air as you."

Then he walks away with the come-along and the spool of smooth wire.

IN THE MORNING he took a roast and half a dozen packages of hamburger out of the freezer. They've thawed now, and he unwraps the roast first and centers it on a cutting board. It's not his beef, but it was raised on his grass. He buys half a butchered cow from Curtis each fall. He's cutting the roast into cubes when Griff comes in, breathing hard.

"Is that for dinner?" she asks.

Her face is flushed from the wind and sun. Her hair's falling out of its ponytail and mostly hangs about her face.

"What happened to you?" he asks.

She leans into the counter and looks at the unwrapped packages of hamburger in the sink. "I ran."

"From where?"

"From the end of the pasture." She pulls the cloth-covered elastic band out of her hair and starts to gather all the loose ends at the back of her head. "I got afraid."

He scoops a handful of the cubed roast into the big mixing bowl. "What spooked you?"

"I don't know. I just get scared sometimes." Her hands are behind her head, and her elbows wing up and away from her shoulders. "I went up to look at your horse."

"You weren't afraid of Jimmy, were you?"

"Do you ever ride him?"

"Sure I do. But I don't need to every day." He waves the butcher knife over the cutting board and sink. "And this isn't for us," he says. "It's for a bear."

"The bear in the zoo?"

"How do you know about that?"

"Mr. Bradley told me. He said that's where you go every day." She watches him cut up the last of the roast. "Winnie the Pooh likes honey."

"Did Mr. Bradley tell you that too?"

"It was in a story my mom read me when I was little."

He juts an elbow toward the cupboard by the refrigerator. "The honey's up there."

She carries a chair to the counter and steps up on it to get the jar of honey.

"There's a bottle of vitamins I just bought on the lower shelf," he says. "Reach it down when you find the honey."

She sets the vitamins and the honey on the countertop and steps down from the chair holding an empty pint of Ancient Age against her right eye, staring at him through the clear glass.

He wonders what he must look like to her. "I didn't drink it today," he tells her.

She screws the cap off and holds the bottle up to her nose, and sniffs and grimaces. "But you drank it sometime?"

"You might find more of them around here if you look. You can put that one in the trash."

She drops the pint in the trash can under the sink. "Was it whiskey?"

"Yes, it was."

She carries the chair back to the table and leans into the counter and watches him unwrap the hamburger and knead it into the cubed roast. That's all she does, but he thinks how quiet the house was before she came indoors. Just the snick of his knife against the board, the sound of a magpie in the yard.

"Do you want me to pour the honey in?"

He lifts his hands out of the bowl. "Now'd be a good time."

She struggles with the lid, and he's about to tell her to run hot water over it when she twists it off. She drizzles the honey back and forth over the meat, and he watches the side of her face. "That's enough," he says.

She rights the jar and circles a single finger around the glass threads and licks the honey from her finger.

"I need my sleeves pushed back," he says, holding out his hands. She pushes the sleeves up to his elbows, one at a time, and when she sees his right forearm she pulls her hands away and tilts her head for a better look at it.

"It's a dragon." He rotates his arm so she can see that the dragon's tail wraps all around it.

"My mom's boyfriend had one," she says, staring at the tattoo. "But it was like a piece of barbed wire wrapped around his arm. I like yours better."

"I got it when I was in the army." He forms the honey-thickened meat into balls as big as softballs and lays them out on the counter. "I thought it was a good idea the night I did it."

"I think the wings are cool."

"Why don't you crack those vitamins open and poke some into this meat."

She opens the bottle of vitamins. "Did all the soldiers get tattoos?"

"I don't know about the rest of them." He lifts his arm up and looks at it himself. "I guess

I didn't think I'd make it home. It sure as hell didn't dawn on me I'd have to look at this thing the rest of my life."

"Did Mr. Bradley get one?"

He sets the empty bowl in the sink. "Mitch always thought he'd come home."

While he washes the blood and fat from his hands she pushes a vitamin capsule into each ball with her finger, then turns the ball and sticks in another, working at exactly the same pace from ball to ball.

"Mr. Bradley said he dreamed he was flying last night," she says.

"Did he say what he saw?"

"He just said he got so high he could see where the blue turned into black."

He dries his hands and forearms and turns the water back on so she can wash her hands. "Maybe he was too high to get a good look at what was underneath him."

"That's probably what happened," she says. "Did Mr. Bradley have dreams when he was in the army?"

He hands her the towel. "He's just been dreaming lately," he says, hoping it wasn't a lie and wonders if Mitch always had dreams and he'd just forgotten. "I guess when Mitch was younger he was too busy to dream."

NINETEEN

——————

So, it doesn't take a fucking genius to know where she's gone. Roy checks the postmark on the manila envelope. Estherville, Iowa. Iowa Highway Patrol. He reads the letter again.

Dear Mr. Winston,
Please find enclosed your electric and garbage collection bills for this current year dated 9/19 and 9/22 respectively. I hope this paperwork finds you at the address represented on the bills and your late receipt of such presents no problem. Please know that our office processed the above-mentioned within three working days of discovering them in the glove compartment of a green 1984 Chevrolet Impala found abandoned on the shoulder of Highway 9, approximately seventy-three miles west of

Estherville. The automobile, regis-
tered to a Ms. Jean Gilkyson, has been
impounded, and should Ms. Gilkyson
not claim the vehicle and pay for tow-
ing within 90 days, it will be sold at
auction.

Should you have any questions, or
information regarding how I can con-
tact Ms. Gilkyson, please feel free to
call or write me at the address on this
letterhead.

Sincerely,
Sgt. D. Raymond Lopez
Iowa Highway Patrol

"Wyoming," he shouts. "She's heading
straight home, the dumb bitch." And cops, he
thinks. D. Raymond. What's the "D." stand for?
Got to be Dickhead. No doubt about that.

He gets another beer from the refrigerator,
finds a half-empty box of Frosted Flakes and sits
back at the table. Jean told him about her ex-
father-in-law's ranch out there, so hey, follow the
breadcrumbs, D. Raymond. Put one end of a
ruler here at this kitchen table, and the edge of
the ruler along Highway 9, approximately seventy miles west of Estherville, then stop at just
over five inches and where are you? You're in
Ishawooa-fucking-Wyoming, that's where. Five

inches and change ain't more than about twice the length of Sgt. D. Raymond's dick, he thinks, and drops his head back and shakes in a mouthful of Frosted Flakes.

Where else would she go? She's confused. She's lost. She'd need family around her. Sure, she said she hates the old bastard, but hating family's not the same as hating strangers. Hell, he and Jean said they hated each other plenty of times. They've shouted it at the tops of their lungs, but they're still family. Like it or not, that's what you're stuck with. If your car craps out on the highway, you haul ass to family.

The fucking spic. He imagines the short-haired, greasy-haired, thin-limbed asshole. He sees D. Raymond coming home at night to some blond loser white chick with fake tits. He bets D. Raymond loves those white plastic tits. What the fuck's with that? He gets another beer and sits back at the table. "I had such a hard day, baby," D. Raymond Lopez says. "And nobody understands me like these firm, fake boobies do."

Every time Roy opens a skin magazine or has a look at one of the T&A channels on cable, what's he see? Plastic fucking tits. Silicon Valley. Where the hell do those broads think that shit'll be pointing when they're eighty-nine, zoned out in some wheelchair and pissing in their diapers?

To their goddamn ears, that's where. He has to give Jean that much credit. She'll die, God bless her, with the same pair she's sporting now.

He thinks of the hillbilly bitch in **Cool Hand Luke,** the one washing her car. Soaping up her real-deal tits and rubbing those babies all over her windshield for the poor pussy-starved, chain-gang sons of bitches whipping weeds in the barrow ditch. What did George Kennedy call her? He tries to remember if he saw somewhere that George Kennedy had died. Lucille? That was one thing about Jean's kid, the little shit liked movies as much as he does. Not only that **Where the Red Fern Grows** bullshit, either. She didn't always want to watch what he did, but she wanted to watch. And didn't he hold a hand in front of her eyes when there was something she shouldn't see? Like plastic tits, for instance. Sure he did. This here movie's rated Roy, he'd say, and even that made her laugh. Family memories. Do what you've got to do when you're old enough to do it, is what he told her. Navel ring. Sterling post in your tongue. It's up to you, but leave your tits the fuck alone. She just listened, real serious. Somebody's got to tell it like it is.

And shaved pussies, who the hell thought of that? Those Barbie-doll, no-brain fucking bimbos. Give me bush, or give me death. No cunt hair? That's what little girls have. The fucking perverts who get off on that shit should be rounded up and slaughtered. He'd be glad to spread lye on their dead bodies. Shaved armpits, fine. Shaved legs, better. He's not some French faggot. He's just Roy Winston, and he likes bushy pussies, the way they're supposed to be. But don't get me started on that, he thinks.

He wads up the letter and the manila envelope and throws them in the trash. He gets another beer and crashes on the couch. There's nothing on but the news, and he's got all the news he needs.

"Dinner's over, motherfucker," he announces. And then in his best dead-or-alive George Kennedy voice, he says, "My boy Roy here's going to Wyoming."

TWENTY

HERE'S THE DEAL. This is me, and this is where I am. Right where I began, or damn close to it. She sits in the doorsill that leads to the alley behind the café. In the kitchen behind her she can hear the swish of Charlie bricking the grill, and there's a heavy odor of fried food, burnt sugar and fresh bread, the same smells her clothes hold when she walks home from work. She lifts a forearm under her nose and sniffs, then touches her tongue to the back of her hand. Smell and taste both, she's a waitress in the town where she was born. It's like she never got away. She leans against the doorjamb.

The noon and early afternoon rush is over, so what's the hurry? The good people of Ishawooa have been fed. The farmers, the ranchers, a handful of tourists on their way through, the main-street merchants. They'll last until this evening, when she'll feed most of them again. She's served up Nina's meatloaf special and watched it walk out the door. A car idles past at the end of the alley, just a flash of sunlight on chrome and glass. She flicks her cigarette butt away and sips from her can of Coke, then fumbles in her purse for her wallet and slips out her driver's license. She had a premonition this morning that her license has expired, and she feels pretty expired herself.

She lights another cigarette and squints through the smoke. Jean Marie Gilkyson. Donor. No shit. What hasn't she given away? Her pride, her body. She holds the laminated card at arm's length. Dreams, too, it goes without saying. All she's got now are plans, and all she plans next is to get through the rest of the day, and after enough days pass to make a month she'll pack up her kid and take her someplace else. Eyes, hazel. Hair, brown. Five-foot-four, one hundred and thirty pounds. Female. Thirty years old. She looks good in the picture, a real head-turner. Where's that woman now? Hell, she wasn't even that woman when the picture was taken. Just a good day. She puts the license back in her purse. It won't expire for another year and a half, and she wonders where she'll be then, not that it really matters. One week down, three to go. She's saved a hundred and thirty-seven dollars, and half of whatever's in the tip jar by the cash register. It's easy to make money in America. What's not easy is changing your life.

What if she left this afternoon? Stood her sorry ass up, turned left or right at the end of the alley and kept walking? Leaving Griff with Einar and Mitch would give her at least an even chance. The chance for a home. She can feel her one hundred and thirty pounds weighing down her daughter's whole life. She could leave the license on Griff's pillow with a note saying "Mother knows best." The license is the only picture she has of herself, but it's a good one.

She knows damn well that's not what she's going to do. She'll keep Griff with her, and she'll keep this shameful thought locked tight in- side—not to protect Griff but to protect herself. Because without her daughter none of this would be worth it. Without Griff she'd just as soon shrivel up and die. Or at least hasten the process.

She thinks of Starla and her pistol and wishes life were that simple. Come out blazing and just shoot your way through. If it gets too rough, you can always turn the gun on yourself. She kicks her shoes off and stares at her swollen feet. Her toes are swollen too and she arches them back, but that stretches her calves and she winces. She thinks of Crane, wishing he'd run down this alley just like he streaked that football game. She wishes he'd stop, kneel naked in front of her and lift up her feet, one at a time, and massage the pain away. Men as aspirin, as pain-killers. Men who can kill you with pain. That's most of them. If she had to start giving things up, she'd keep right on smoking and never look at another naked man in her life. But what are the chances of that?

Nina steps past her and leans against the Dumpster. She waves the flies away from her face and holds out a snack-size bag of chips. Jean shakes her head.

"What are you thinking about?" Nina asks.

"A naked man."

"I must not be working you hard enough. You shouldn't have that much energy left."

Jean pulls her left foot into her lap and kneads her thumbs into the heel. "My feet feel like I served everybody in town today."

Nina wads up the empty chip bag and tosses it in the Dumpster. "Good thing it's a small town," she says. "How come you don't like living out there with Einar?"

"Because Einar's an asshole."

Nina waves again at the flies and steps away from the trash. "He's never been one to me. He's been a good friend."

"You aren't related to him."

Nina laces her fingers behind her back, drops her chin and bends toward her shins. "Aren't you practically his daughter or something?"

"I used to be married to his son."

With her head upside down, Nina's ponytail hangs in the alley dirt. "It's a good thing we don't have to whore for a living. We'd have more than aching feet then."

JEAN STARES at the truck-ripened vegetables and fruit, and thinks the market hasn't changed much since she left. The same butcher must still be married to the same woman, who every Saturday night still must bleach his white aprons. The ceiling fans whir, the cart wheels stick and wobble. There's a new high-school boy mopping the black-and-white-tile floor. Probably a boy who's good at math, but not scholarship good, whose father drinks, who dreams of studying engineering at the university in Laramie, who needs the job enough to work hard.

Jean stands at a bin of avocados, picking

them out one at a time, squeezing, knowing she can't really afford one. She buys a bunch of over-ripe bananas and a package of pork chops on sale, a carton of skim milk. She wonders what it's like to push a cart down a supermarket aisle without doing the math. Ounces, pounds, bulk weight, allowing for settle, generic, brand name, figuring the price per.

At the checkout she's third in line. She stares at the rack of bubble gum, the batteries, **Good Housekeeping.** The **National Enquirer** has something about alien abduction, easily one of her top five fantasies. How would it be, she thinks, if aliens snatched her, held her for only three Earth days while in their world three years passed? What if they taught her how to sit serenely in alien meditation, to connect directly with an alien god, to realize the simple true happiness of life, and then plopped her back on Earth, enlightened and satisfied, with all of her teeth capped? And what if the aliens abducted some good-natured Earthman along with her, a man who they recognized as her soul's twin? A gentle man. A man without a wife and three kids back home. A man who'd feel lucky for the love of a woman with a good driver's license photo and a little girl.

She moves up in line and can feel the comfort of a man chosen by aliens. She sees them growing closer as the alien years click by. In the evenings they learn to play card games with their wise and patient almond-eyed abductors. Later, they make love. The man wouldn't smell like stale beer. Hell, she thinks, they could be abducted early one Thursday morning and returned on Sunday, just as church is letting out, prepared to spend their lives together. He could have all his teeth capped too.

"Jean."

She turns to the sound of the voice, and there's Crane. Not naked. Dressed in his brown uniform, gun on his hip, but looking at her like he's off duty. He's looking at the pork chops in her cart. He's also looking at her ass.

"Heard anything from your boyfriend?" he asks. He lowers his voice so only she can hear. He lowers his head too. Enough to check out her breasts.

God bless him. This isn't icky, she thinks, but it is a little bit alien. There's appreciation in the way he's looking at her. As Griffin might, if he were still alive. She shakes her head and says, "Ex-boyfriend."

He shrugs and smiles at once, and his teeth don't look like they need capping. "Well, I'm glad there's no problem," he says, suddenly interested in the frozen dinners stacked in his basket. He holds it up. "I'm not much of a cook."

"Me neither."

He nods like he didn't expect her to be and doesn't want anything from her except her company. To stand in line with her in a Wyoming supermarket, looking at her as if she were interesting and alive and more than just something to use.

"You going to carry all that stuff out to Einar's?" he asks.

"There isn't much."

"Still."

"You going out that way?"

"I'm heading home," he says. "I can get there any way I want."

IT'S JUST YOUR basic four-wheel-drive rig, she thinks, looking at the dash for a logo or model name. So she can say she likes the brand of SUV he drives if she wants to. She sees BLAZER. There's the radio console between them, crackling with static, and a shotgun propped up between the seats.

"Nice," she says. She turns to look in the back, and right behind the front seat there's a Plexiglas shield.

"Your tax dollars at work," he says.

She makes a fist and raps on the Plexiglas. When he smiles she can feel the tension between them, and she likes it. All anticipation, no disappointment. The radio might not even be on, she thinks. It could be the air between them that's crackling. She lowers her window and breathes deeply to clear her head. Three weeks to go and she's gone. This could be a mistake.

"Are you married?"

"Was," he says.

His voice flattens and he grips the steering wheel tighter, a man braced against judgment.

"What happened?"

He looks at her, glancing at her knees where the breeze ruffles her skirt. "The usual. She fell in love with someone else."

"Did you know the guy?"

He nods. "He's from Sheridan. An attorney. It was messy."

"Ouch."

"We didn't have kids," he offers. "That helped." He slows at the turnoff to Einar's and uses his blinker even though there's no traffic.

"Small-town messy?" she asks.

He smiles, and she can tell he likes it that she

remembers their last conversation and can get in a little dig.

"That kind of messy," he says. "They were at it for awhile."

She sees Einar on the porch, Griff in the yard in front of him, holding a gray cat.

"How'd it feel?" she asks.

He doesn't expect the question. "You mean her and me not having kids?"

"I mean the attorney. That they were at it for awhile."

"I'm old enough to stand it."

"But how'd it feel?" She reaches over the radio and shotgun to hold her hand flat against his stomach. She can feel him flinch. "Here," she says. "How'd it feel here?"

He stops at the yard gate. The radio still crackles when he turns the ignition off. "It felt lousy," he says.

She hears Griff coming toward them and takes her hand away and opens the door. She stands out ready for her daughter's hug, but she's stopped in the yard, still holding the cat. Crane gets out on the other side.

"Are you arrested?" Griff asks.

"No, baby," she says. "Just tired. The sheriff gave me a ride home from the supermarket."

She takes out her plastic bag of groceries and closes the door.

Einar's leaning against the porch rail. "Evening, Crane," he calls.

Crane stands at her side. "How's it going, Einar?"

"Just another perfect day in paradise. You running a taxi service now?"

"Whenever I get the chance."

Griff sets the cat on the lawn and kneels behind it, stroking it, her face tight.

"This is Sheriff Carlson," Jean says.

Griff doesn't look up from the cat. Even when Crane says, "It's nice to meet you, Griff," she still won't.

Jean turns to this man who doesn't need his teeth capped. "Are you hungry?" she asks.

"We already ate," Griff says, jumping to her feet. She brushes the cat away with her ankle.

"I should swing back through the office to check on some paperwork anyway," Crane says, and then looks at Griff. "Well, it was nice meeting you." When she just shrugs, he says, "You take care of yourself, Einar," and starts back around the front of his Blazer.

"Thanks for the ride home," Jean says, but she's watching Griff. She hears him turn around in the gravel and pull away.

"I don't like him," Griff says.

She goes to her daughter and stands there until the girl breaks and looks up. "I don't remember asking what you thought." She watches Griff's eyes flicker and then spark.

"You never ask me," she says.

Jean bends down right in front of her. She gently lifts her chin up, so their faces are just inches apart. She's always liked it that Griff'll look her square in the eye. "You're entitled to your opinion," she says. She looks over Griff's head to where Einar's standing on the porch. "But let's try to remember who's supposed to be the bitch in this family. Okay?"

Griff nods. And then she kneels and picks up the cat again.

TWENTY-ONE

SHE STANDS AT the end of Einar's porch, beside the table she has all set, and watches as
Mr. Bradley hooks his cane over the wire her
mother put up and shuffles toward her. He has
to stop halfway, and when Einar spots him
there—bent over, huffing—he helps him along,
and she slides under the railing and starts across
the workyard.

She carries a milk bottle and a paring knife
Einar said she could use. She doesn't want to
make them wait too long, but she wants to give
Mr. Bradley a chance to get settled in his chair
and catch his breath. She wants to give him
enough time so he can sit at the table as though
he usually eats there, out in the sun, where he
can hear the birds.

She can't find any real flowers along the
creek, but behind the toolshed there's a bunch of
spiky deep-green plants she thinks look pretty

enough. They're higher than her waist and some of them have clumps of lavender-colored bristles on top. Most of the bristles have already dried out and turned white, but she kneels by one that's still purple and holds the milk bottle up to measure, so she won't cut it too long for the bottle, and saws at the stem with the knife. She has to be careful. The leaves are prickly and make the backs of her hands itch. Like she felt when she woke up this morning—not plant prickly, but shivery, like when people are staring at you. And when she opened her eyes her mother was staring at her, already dressed and standing by her bed.

She said, "He's not my boyfriend." It was like she'd been thinking about it all night.

Griff told her: "If you don't think the sheriff's your boyfriend then he's not." She said it like she meant it.

"You don't know everything in the world," her mother said.

Griff got up and walked to the toilet.

She didn't say anything else, because when her mother doesn't know she's lying to herself it's not a good time to point it out. She knows the sheriff is her mother's new boyfriend. Her mother might not know it yet, and maybe even the sheriff doesn't, but she could tell right away, the minute her mother got out of his car. She looked taller, bigger, like her skin couldn't hold all the rest of her inside. Her mother doesn't look like that for just anybody. Her mother didn't look like that for Marvin. If she had, then Marvin's motorcycle would be parked on Einar's front yard right now and Mary would be all alone in Sioux Falls. She's sure of it. Men don't drive away from a woman who's twice as big as her skin. Roy didn't. Neither did Hank. She wasn't old enough to know about Johnny or Bobby, but she knows men want to see what's inside.

"I'm not getting us into another Roy deal," her mother told her. "If that's what you're thinking, you're wrong."

"I don't think the sheriff's like Roy," she said.

That satisfied her mother, and she didn't have to think of anything else to say.

She trims the spiky leaves away from the bottom of the stem so it'll fit in the bottle. They're going to love this, she thinks. They'll wonder how they ever got along without her. She can't do what her mother does—she's just one size all the time—but she can make a special lunch that she thought of by herself.

She hurries, and when she's almost to the

porch she calls, "Don't start without me," but when she gets to the table there's a bite out of Mitch's sandwich and Einar has a milk mustache, and they're both acting like they've just been sitting there with their hands in their laps, waiting for her.

She moves the butter dish and sets the milk bottle in the middle of the table. She thinks she'll write in her diary that she likes it that old men let her feel like she matters. Even if they're hungry. Even if one of the old men is cranky because he lost his son, and his cows and his wife.

She doesn't sit yet. She has plant juice on her hands and Einar's looking at her. So is Mr. Bradley. But they're looking at her like they don't care what she's got on her hands. She thinks she'll also write that sometimes old men look right at you, like they know you, even after only a week.

She's cut the sandwiches into quarters and stabbed a green olive into each one with a toothpick. She thinks they look fancy. And Einar hasn't said anything about the tablecloth she found in a kitchen drawer. Everybody has a glass of milk and a bowl of pear sections. When she opened the can of pears she drained the syrup off and drizzled chocolate sauce on them instead. She's proud of the pears. They're like her own invention. It wasn't a recipe she had to look up.

"That's not a flower." Einar nods toward the milk bottle. "I don't want to ruin your occasion, but you ought to know it's not a flower."

"What is it?" She sits and wipes her hands on her jeans.

"It's a thistle. A weed," he says. "If you cut that whole patch down I'll give you five dollars." He pinches a toothpick out of a sandwich quarter and eats the olive off and lays the toothpick on the edge of his plate. "You'll have to be careful with the seedheads. I don't want more of a problem than I've got. You can stuff the whole works in the burning barrel."

"You won't have to pay me," she says.

"All right, then." He's got his mouth full of sandwich, but she can tell he's pleased.

"I think it's the prettiest thistle we've raised," Mitch says. The healed, slick part of his face is shiny in the sunlight, like it's wet, and when he smiles it lifts the shiny part higher.

She slips her napkin out from under her fork and opens it on her lap. She wants to do something fun, something she's never done before, but knows she can't come right out and ask.

That's not how you get to have fun. She needs to create a diversion first. She sits back in her chair.

"You guys are gay, right?"

She thinks as far as diversions go that that ought to do it. If she said the same thing to Roy he'd take her to some muscle movie, like with Vin Diesel, and laugh at all the he-man parts and stab her with his elbow and grin when there were naked ladies bouncing all over the screen.

But it doesn't do anything but make Mitch stop chewing. He looks at Einar like he's thinking about being gay, then nods and starts chewing again. Einar doesn't even nod back. She should've thought of something more shocking, but it's too late now. Too many diversions and all you get is an argument.

Finally Einar says, "I think one of us would've noticed by now."

"It's okay. I had a teacher who was a lesbian."

They put what's left of their sandwiches back on their plates. Now we're getting somewhere, she thinks, but Mitch just leans across the table. He moves the milk bottle with the thistle in it so he won't have to look around it and lowers his voice.

He asks her, "Are you bored?"

She can't admit it. That would blow the

whole deal. All she wants is to ride Einar's horse. She shrugs.

Mitch sits back in his chair. "It's probably tough being stuck out here without any other kids around."

"I'm fine," she says. It'd sound too weird to tell him she doesn't really like most kids. Most of the kids she's been around make noise, and she likes it quiet.

Mitch is tapping at the hole in his head and watching her. She thinks it's something he does when he needs to sort things out in his brain. "I do think Einar's got beautiful hands," he says. He looks at Einar. "I just wish he'd take better care of them."

Einar curves his fingers down over his palms to look at his nails.

Mitch leans across the table again. "I like his ears too. I've always liked men with small ears."

Then they both just stare at her. She never noticed it before but on the side of Mitch's face where there aren't any scars, where his skin's just brown and smooth, he's got freckles. The freckles are dark brown.

"You have something planned for after lunch?" Einar asks.

She won't look at him. This isn't fair. She just squints at Mitch's freckles. It's like they've read her mind. It's like they knew where she was going before she even started.

"I thought maybe we could ride your horse," she admits.

Einar picks up his spoon and jabs at the pears with the chocolate sauce on them. "He'll need new shoes before he's ready to go anywhere."

She's not sure what that means. Maybe he's teasing her.

"What about the bear?" Mitch asks. "Have you ever seen a bear?"

She shakes her head. She'd helped Einar mix the honey in with the meat but hadn't really thought about seeing the bear. She was just helping to show him she could and that her living here isn't the worst thing that's ever happened to him.

"Is it safe?" she asks.

"Course it's safe. They've got him locked up." Einar's working the toothpick around in his mouth. "What's that you put on the pears?" he asks.

"Chocolate sauce," she says. "There was a squeeze bottle of it in the refrigerator. I didn't use it all."

"I've never seen that combination before," Mitch says. He's tapping at the side of his head again. "I might save mine for dinner."

Einar still works the toothpick around his mouth. "If you haven't got anything better to do, why don't you ride into town with me? If you think it's safe enough you might like looking at the bear." He smiles at Mitch like they really are gay, like they've got secrets she hasn't even thought about. "Who knows," he says, "it might be a whole lot like fun."

SHE CLEARED the table and stacked the dishes in the sink and stretched Saran Wrap over the bowls of pears while Einar helped Mitch to his cabin. She could hear them talking and laughing but she didn't care.

And she doesn't care now. She's sitting on the edge of the truckseat with her left hand on the gearshift. The grocery sack with the balls of frozen meat is on the floorboard by her feet.

"Now third," Einar says.

He stomps down on the clutch and she pushes the gearshift up and to the right, and it doesn't make the grinding sound this time.

"That's better," he says.

The truck windows are down and the top of the grocery sack shuffles in the wind.

"Do you think Mr. Bradley wanted to come?"

"I'm not sure he could." Einar has his arm hooked out the window. "It'd wear him out too much. Now let's try fourth."

She makes the shift and moves her knee away to make room for the gearstick. Each time she can feel her heart rev up like the engine does. "Did my dad shift the gears?"

"When he was your age he could pretty much drive by himself."

She looks down at the clutch and brake. "I don't think my legs are long enough."

Einar looks at her legs like he hadn't thought she had any.

"Maybe not. Maybe not today." He turns on the windshield wipers and they just swish back and forth over the dried bug guts. She thinks he must not have any water in the squirters. "You confused about how to treat a guest?" he says.

She scrunches up her face.

"Last night. The sheriff."

She looks away from him out the window. "He's just some guy who brought my mom home."

"But he brought her to my house," he says. "I expect you to be pleasant to whoever comes to my door."

She just says, "Yes, sir," but maybe this afternoon's not going to be so much fun after all.

And when she keeps looking out the window he shoves her a little bit. Not hard, just like a kid would so she'll look at him. It makes her feel better, like she's not really in trouble.

"Unless it's somebody trying to sell you their angle on God," he says. "There's no excuse for that bullshit. You can treat those folks any way you want."

And then they're close to town and he tells her to make the shifts back down the gears, one at a time, while he works the clutch. At the zoo he shows her how to put it in reverse and then shuts off the truck.

SHE CARRIES the grocery bag and follows him. They don't stop at the other animals' pens. They walk right up to the chainlink fence and stand and look down at the bear.

He's in the middle of the hole. He doesn't look up at them or anywhere else. He just swings his head back and forth, staring at the ground and making a low sound, like little boys make when they're playing in the dirt with trucks. Only there's nothing happy about this sound. It's more like a low, sad whine.

There's a family, a mom and dad and three kids, standing across the pit from them. The dad picks up the smallest kid and puts him on his shoulders so he can see better.

"How come he's stuck in a basement with no roof?" she asks.

Einar's still looking at the bear. "Because he quit being wild."

"I mean, why doesn't he have a cage like the other animals?"

"This pit is what Angie already had. She didn't have time to build another cage."

The bear doesn't look like Winnie-the-Pooh. He looks old and tired and sort of tattered, like the homeless people she saw when Roy and her mom took her to Des Moines once. He acts nervous and flinchy, and maybe a little bit crazy. She tries to imagine how he'd look if he were standing next to them. How much bigger he'd seem.

"Is Angie the lady with the rattlesnake on her hat?"

"Yeah. She's the one."

There's a gang of boys bent over the circular wall, and one of the boys drops a stone in and they all laugh.

"What are they doing?" she asks.

"They're bothering the snakes."

"Is today a holiday?"

Einar looks at the boys, then back at the bear.

"No, it's not," he says. "Those boys must take their lunch break here. Reach in that sack and throw him one of those balls we made."

Einar doesn't look at her while she unwraps the ball of meat. He's watching the bear. He doesn't even look when she wads up the white butcher paper and puts it back in the sack so it won't blow away. He doesn't check to see if she's doing it right.

She throws the ball into the pit. The meat's still mostly frozen and it bounces and rolls toward the bear. He quits swinging his head and looks up at them, but just with his eyes, like he thinks they're playing a trick on him. Then he walks to the ball real slow and sniffs it, then picks it up in his mouth. He tilts his head back and chews with his eyes closed. He's stopped making the whining sound.

"What would happen if I fell in there?" she asks.

Einar doesn't answer right away, and she thinks maybe he didn't hear her because he's watching the bear so hard.

"I wouldn't have a granddaughter anymore," he says. "Throw him another one."

She unwraps another ball of meat and throws it in.

"Would he eat me?"

"He might not if you curled up real tight and acted like you were already dead."

She looks back at the boys teasing the snakes. "I couldn't make any noise, right? Even if he bit me?"

"That'd be what you'd have to do."

She watches the bear eat the second ball and thinks about him chewing on her. "He likes the honey," she says.

"I believe he does."

She throws in a third ball without having to be asked. "I think he's the saddest thing I've ever seen," she says.

Einar finally looks at her. "Sadder than Mitch?" It's the look he has like he's known her a long time.

"Mr. Bradley's just sad on the outside. I think he's happy on the inside."

When she hears herself say it she knows it's true. Einar nods. Like he knew it too but needed her to say it.

"Throw him one more," he says.

TWENTY-TWO

———

CRANE'S HUNGRY, ready for lunch, and he hasn't felt like eating for months. Not since the divorce. He sits back in his chair and stares at the bleak walls of his office. When she was sitting across the desk from him the other day, the room seemed alive. It seemed that way even after she left. Now it's gone dead again. She's what improved his appetite, no doubt about it.

What he doesn't want is the drama. The midnight phone calls. The headlights shining in his bedroom window at two in the morning. The screaming, the tears. He's had enough of that for this lifetime.

Outside the window there's old Dan Hanson dragging an oxygen bottle down the sidewalk on a wheeled stand, the type of outfit you see for carry-on luggage in airports. A clear plastic tube snakes up the old man's back and splits around the sides of his head. Dan stops and lights a cigarette without even taking the cannula out of his nose. He's a dried-out old fart, dry as kindling, and if one of those cigarettes ever sets the oxygen off, the rest of him would go in a flash.

Crane finds the police report on his desk and reads it again. He's read it a dozen times. Roy Winston. A regular name, an irregular guy. No doubt he's hungry too. Everybody's hungry for something sweet. He hears Starla walking up to his doorway. "You going to Nina's for lunch?" she says, grinning like a striped-ass ape. Like she saw it coming the instant Jean walked in the office.

He pushes back from his desk. He thinks he liked Starla better when she was Susan. "I guess I am," he says.

HE STUDIES the menu so he won't have to look at her. She's standing beside him, waiting to take his order. She smells salty and sweet.

He puts his menu down. "What was the special?"

"Pot roast."

The café window's behind her and it's like she's stepped right out of the glare. Something solid and warm and unexpectedly beautiful. He wonders if she's uncomfortable with her beauty.

Or maybe she doesn't care how she looks. His mother always told him to marry a beautiful woman who doesn't know it. His ex-wife knew.

"You told me that already, didn't you?"

"Twice," she says.

He hands her his menu. "I guess the pot roast'll be fine." He feels like this could be the start of something.

She sits at the table and her hands are shaking and she puts the menu down and clasps them together as if she's about to pray. Her smile's the kind he'd expect from her daughter. "Do you think a man and a woman . . ." She stops, looks toward the kitchen and leans farther over her hands. "Do you think a man and a woman can have a sexual relationship with no emotional involvement?"

He sits back in his chair. She's still leaning toward him over her hands.

"Bing, bang." His voice cracks. "Go on about their day. That sort of thing?"

She nods. "Nobody gets hurt."

"I don't know."

She reaches across the table and takes his hand in hers. Her hands are cool. "What if the woman was me?"

He stares down at their hands.

"I still don't know."

"But you've thought about it, right? I mean, like a fantasy? With someone you've just met and might never see again."

He nods. "Yes, I have."

She takes a pen from her apron and opens his hand and writes on his palm. The pen tickles, but he can't tell what she's written. She closes his hand and holds it closed.

"Was it harder when you were thinking about saying that, or was it harder just now?" he asks.

"It wasn't easy either time." Her eyes flick toward the kitchen again. "I'm only going to be here three more weeks and I'm falling to pieces. I mean, falling to pieces. I need . . ." She pauses and bows her head. He can't tell if she's closed her eyes. "Something to sort of settle me out."

He hasn't lied to her. He has fantasized about a conversation like this, more than once, but the woman's never been this beautiful. He says, "Three weeks isn't much of a relationship."

Her head snaps up like she's been waiting for him to say this very thing. Like she's thought it all through. "The kind of relationship I'm talking about can be over in twenty minutes." She realizes she's spoken too loud and lowers her voice. "I'm not kidding. Really, I don't want to be in love."

"You just want sex?"

She stands and straightens her apron, then picks up the menu and holds it against her chest. "I just want something that's easy to leave."

He watches her walk toward the kitchen, and then opens his hand. Written on his palm is PLEASE.

SHE'S WAITING for him in the alley after work, and he hurries around to her door, but she already has it open before he gets there. "Thanks anyway," she says, and he says, "You bet," but that's all they say.

She doesn't tell him anything about her afternoon, and he doesn't tell her he drove home after lunch and showered and shaved and splashed on aftershave, and then showered again to wash the aftershave off. He doesn't tell her he almost didn't come. Or that he prayed, actually got down on his knees and prayed he wasn't making the biggest mistake of his life.

He parks by the river in a dirt turnaround under the cottonwoods and kills the engine. They sit for a minute and listen to the wind in the leaves and then step out of the Blazer and into the backseat. They hurry.

They're awkward at first, silent and urgent.

Then he bangs his head on the doorframe and they laugh a little. They're better after they relax. It shocks him how much better. It's as though he knows her body and what to expect from her, how she'll move or rise or float away from him, how he can bring her back. It's as though he's heard the sounds she makes, knows that she'll grind her teeth and gasp, that her face will appear frightened for a time and then, finally, wondering. It's not the way he's ever made love. It's not even close. At the end she holds on to him and won't let go. It's surprising to him that he doesn't want to let her go. They lie together on the seat in the tangle of clothes, until the afternoon starts to cool their damp skin.

She's the first to struggle up. She sits on the edge of the seat and folds an arm over her breasts, then looks down at her arm and drops it. There's a wide, yellowed bruise across her ribs that starts just above her right hip.

He touches a fingertip to the edge of it. "I'm sorry," he says.

"It wasn't you."

"I know it wasn't. But I'm still sorry."

She pulls his shirt out from under her and holds it up. The front pocket is ripped. "I don't sew," she says.

"It's all right. I've got another in the back."

She nods and rubs a footprint off the Plexiglas divider. Then she wipes her face with the shirt, and under her breasts, and steps out into the breeze and wipes between her legs.

He pulls on his pants and stands out of the car. He opens the back hatch and takes out the clean shirt, watching through the side window as she gets into her bra and panties and jeans. The sun's low, the air fuzzy with pollen, and he doesn't know what to expect. He looks at his palm as if for a clue, but there isn't even a smear of ink left.

When he closes the hatch she says, "You don't have to worry. My head's not going to start spinning around or anything." And when he doesn't say anything, just buttons the shirt, she adds, "Like in **The Exorcist.**"

"I'm not worried about it," he says. But he is worried. He's worried that what happened only happened to him. That for her it was just exercise.

"I'm not going to start blubbering about us being soulmates, either." She draws her hair into a ponytail and gets into the passenger seat.

He opens the front door and sits back against the edge of the seat and pulls on his boots. His elbow nudges the horn, and when it blares he jumps. She starts to laugh and he does too. He rubs his head where he'd banged it on the door-frame.

"You're dying to ask me how it was," she says. "Come on, admit it."

He gets behind the wheel. "I don't ask questions unless I think I can stand the answers."

"That's a good rule."

He backs them around, facing the sun, and lowers his visor. He lets the outfit idle. "Why me?" he asks. She hasn't turned the visor down on her side, and her face is lost in the glare.

"Ishawooa may have two restaurants, but there aren't that many attractive men," she says.

He pulls ahead until her face falls in shadow. He wants to see whether she's mocking him, but she just looks ready for a nap. "You think I'm attractive?"

"I wouldn't let it go to your head." She shrugs. "My tastes aren't exactly what you'd call a résumé builder."

He pulls onto the blacktop, driving northwest.

"I'm sorry about your shirt," she says.

He likes the whine the tires make on the pavement. He's liked the sound since he was a boy. And the air's just started to have some snap in the evenings. Fall is his favorite time of year. "So, how was it?" he asks.

AN UNFINISHED LIFE

She leans across the console and he can feel her breath on his neck. "Thank you," she whispers. "It settled me right out." Then she straightens up and draws her heels onto the edge of the seat and rides with her arms around her legs and her chin on her knees.

TWENTY-THREE

I T FELT LIKE something new had broken but that's how it always feels, like something was just hanging on, waiting to give out. Last night it gave out after midnight and woke him up. Not so much the pain but the sound the pain makes inside. Like starved animals keening.

Mitch crawled out on his porch. Every time it happens he thinks he'll die and he crawls outside. He doesn't want to die in bed. He doesn't want Einar to find him like that, or Jean or the girl either. He'd found his own father dead in bed and doesn't want to be remembered as just some chewed-to-shit old black man with the covers drawn up under his chin.

But he didn't die. He lay in the dark under the stars and shook and slobbered, and finally slept for a few hours. He woke just at dawn and got back to bed before Einar came in with the morphine. He didn't ask for more than the usual dose. He didn't say a thing. He felt like he was on the other side of it, just a little worse. Each time weakens him. He didn't tell Einar there was blood in his piss.

But now the pain's making another little run, just to show him it can, so he's come back out onto the porch. He shifts on his chair and waits until he thinks he might have to call out, or gasp, then he shifts again and the pain rolls to the other side of his gut, catches low in his hips and starts to build all over again. He can't fool it all day, but it's working so far. He doesn't want another shot. Two a day and then three and he'll just lie in his bed, numbed and ready to die. No, he means to hold at one shot for as long as he can.

Karl picks up his head and whines, and they watch Griff coming toward them from the corrals. Up looking at Jimmy, he'd bet. He knows she can see herself on the horse, sees him as a part of her life she can't quite reach yet. He wishes he was well enough to tap on some new shoes. He's talked to Einar about it, told him to take his granddaughter for a ride, but if he were well enough he could have the pleasure of it himself. If he were a well man the girl wouldn't have to wait.

"Good morning, Mr. Bradley." She sits on the porch in front of him.

"You lose Einar?" he asks.

"He's helping Mr. Hanson."

"Curtis or Dan?"

"Curtis, I think. I think he needed help with the cows." She looks around at him. "Did you have a dream last night?"

"Sure I did." He shifts in his chair and keeps his face calm, and as long as he can trick the pain he'll be able to keep his face that way. She's still watching him.

"I dreamed I was surfing."

She smiles. "Did you have your hat on?"

"Bareheaded," he says. "All I was wearing was a swimsuit."

"What color was it?"

"What color was what?"

"Your swimsuit. Mine's blue."

"I think mine was blue too," he says. "That's how come I was sure I was having a dream. I've never owned a swimsuit."

She stretches out on her belly on the porch-boards and tickles Karl under his chin. The old dog closes his eyes, and Mitch shifts on the chair.

"Was there anybody with you in the dream?"

"Just me and the sharks. The water was lousy with them. It kept me up on my board."

"That's why I'd never go surfing," she says. "My mom wants to move to the ocean, but I'd just like to see it. Just once is all."

"What did you think of my bear the other day?"

She sits up and kneels right in front of him, crossing her arms on his knees. "He didn't look very happy." She picks at a thread in the pant seam on the inside of his knee. "I wondered what would happen if I fell in with him."

"You want to practice?"

She cocks her head like a small dog might.

"If you'll run up to the toolshed and find us a rake, we can practice what you ought to do if a bear's got you."

He wants her away from him for a minute. The pain's caught on.

She says okay and jumps down from the porch. He watches her walk with her arms straight out from her sides, pretending to be on a tightrope, and then she starts running.

He eases out of the chair and lies on his back with his knees drawn up. When his head clears a bit he realizes he's staring into the sky and blinking like he just woke from a dream. He moves his head and can hear his hair scrape against the worn boards. He remembers when these boards were still rough. He remembers an evening at the end of his first week on this ranch. With Einar, in town for a beer. After Korea. The first time they'd gone to town together. He remembers the big man standing at the bar, a man who'd never been to war. Just some big overworked son of a bitch feeling sorry for himself.

He'd turned on his stool and faced the table where they sat and told a joke about Sammy Davis, Jr., out on a golf course, told it loud enough for the whole place to hear: "'Handicap?' Sammy says to his caddy. 'Well, I guess I am. One-eyed, nigger, Jew. That enough of a handicap for you?'"

Einar had finished his beer and got up real slow. He walked his empty glass to the bar and set it down and beat the man unconscious with his fists. Just set the glass down and went to work.

It took Mitch and the bartender and the sheriff, when he got there, it took all of them to pull Einar off, and then he just stood to the side and stared down, breathing hard, watching the blood run from his knuckles and spot the floor.

There were tears in his eyes. He was twenty-two years old. They both were.

"Did I kill him?" Einar asked.

The sheriff knelt by the man, put his ear close to the man's mouth and stood up again. "Not yet," he said. "Did you mean to?"

Einar shook his head, and the sheriff asked the bartender what happened and he told him the joke and said, "I guess Einar didn't think it was funny."

"Did you boys serve together?" the sheriff asked.

Mitch told him they had, for two years, and the sheriff asked if they'd seen action.

"We saw more than we wanted to," Mitch said.

"I don't think it's funny either," the sheriff said. He looked down at the beaten man and touched him with the toe of his boot. "John here's always been a prick, but this won't stand if he dies." He turned to Einar. "If he dies I'm going to have to come out and get you."

"I know you will," Einar said.

The sheriff stepped over the body and the bartender poured him a shot of whiskey. "I imagine he's had all of you he wants," he said to Einar. He drank the shot and wiped his mouth. "If he lives I imagine he'll cross the street to stay away from you. I don't believe he'll want to press charges."

Mitch wishes he had fought that man. He should have been the one. When he turns his head to tell Einar he's sorry, there's Griff with the rake.

"Are you okay?" she asks. She looks worried.

"I'm just resting," he says, but he stays on his back and after a minute he tells her that a grizzly bear's faster than the fastest horse. He can't get up yet, and he doesn't want to say anything about the big man in the bar or why he's on his back, but he knows he's got to tell her something so she'll stop looking worried. He explains that grizzly bears can smell better than they can see, and when she asks if they can climb trees he says there've been plenty of guys who thought they couldn't and got dragged out of one. He props himself up on one elbow, and from there further up until he's sitting. He swings his legs over the edge of the porch and sucks himself full of air.

He raises an arm above his head and curves his fingers into claws and growls, and she drops to the ground, fast, and curls into a ball in the dirt, just like Einar told her she should.

"That's what you've got to do," he says.

He grabs the handle of the rake and works the ground between them, and she curls tighter.

He gets too close, scraping her leg with the tines, and she flinches and squeals. Then the pain comes sweeping up from his heels and he feels the blood leave his head. He falls back on an elbow. "You can get up now," he says. "But don't look me in the eye."

She stands with her head turned to the side, concentrating on the ground.

"I've just wandered off a little ways," he says. "I'm still watching you."

Karl's gotten to his feet by Mitch's head. He licks his face and whines, and Mitch wonders if the pain's at a pitch that's easy for dogs to hear.

"I'll do better next time," she says.

Mitch blinks at the sky. It's no longer blue, just pale. "You did okay this time." And then, "I didn't fight that man because I didn't feel I had the right."

When his eyes clear again she's on the porch beside him. He can hear the dog still whining.

"Mr. Bradley?" Her face is just inches from his. Her breath smells like chewing gum.

"Do you know where Einar keeps my medicine?"

"In the refrigerator," she says right away.

"You better run and get it for me."

"Now?" She's started to cry.

"Just as quick as you can."

He can hear her crying as she runs toward the house, and she's still crying when she kneels by his head and holds out a vial and a syringe. A lot of kids, he thinks, would've had to make two trips.

"What do I do?" she asks.

He can hardly hear her. The pain's howling, and he raises his voice to be heard above it and tells her, step by step, push the air out of the needle, stick it through the rubber stopper, turn the bottle upside down, draw the plunger back to the second blue line, tap the bubbles out, and then he starts crawling away from the pain. He doesn't want to go back inside, but he doesn't want her to hear him beg.

"Where are you going?" she asks. She's up on her feet. Her voice is shrill but light, like the wind.

He's halfway through the door. "I don't know," he says.

"What do I do next?"

"Just mash it in me." He has to shout to hear himself say it.

"Where?" She's quit crying, but she looks like she wants to run. She's up on the balls of her feet.

"Just stab it in my butt. Like a knife. Just stab it in through my pants and push the plunger down."

He hears a scream and when he realizes it wasn't him he knows she's done it. He rests the side of his face on his arm and waits for the warmth to spread. He waits for the howling to stop.

When he opens his eyes again she sits cross-legged on the floor in front of him. She holds the syringe in her lap, her thumb still on the plunger.

"Hey?" he says.

Her face is blotched red and streaked with tears. "Did you curl up in a ball?" she asks. "When the bear had you?" She isn't sobbing, but tears are running down her cheeks.

"No, I didn't," he says. "I ran."

WHEN HE COMES AWAKE again Einar's dragging him toward the bed. He gets a foot down to help.

When he's on the bed he says, "Where is she?"

"I sent her to the house."

He lies quietly long enough to be sure he's okay, that it's only Einar's voice he can hear.

There's the hazy drug hum, but that's all. It sounds like men sound, whispering in church.

"Can we afford one of those little refrigerators?" he asks.

"Sure we can."

"I might need one out here," he says. "I don't want this to happen to her again. If I can keep the stuff out here with me I can make sure it won't." He looks up at Einar. "I can strike a balance."

"I'll pick one up first thing."

He pushes with his heels and wedges himself up against the headboard. Einar's sitting in the chair by the workbench. He's taken the antler out of the vise and holds it on his lap.

"You've got a good scald on this one," he says.

"I have, haven't I?"

Einar lays the antler down on the bench and looks at the pencil sketches tacked up on the wall. "You didn't hear anyone prowling around last night, did you?"

"I was indisposed."

Einar smiles. They both know that in fifty years neither one of them has ever used that word.

"Do you think you did?"

"There were some footprints."

"Maybe it was Curtis."

"Maybe. I should've asked him." Einar gets up from the chair. "I'm going to go in and see how she is. She was pretty shook up. You going to live the rest of the day?"

"I'll just need that little refrigerator. I know this looks bad, but I've been this bad before. I've even been worse."

"All right."

Mitch pushes up higher against the headboard. "You tell her that for me. I don't want her to worry."

"All right, I will."

Mitch brings a hand up in front of his face and slowly turns it. It looks as sharp and clear as if he'd got new glasses. He drops the hand in his lap. "Why did you beat that man like you did? In the bar, when we got back from the war?"

Einar stares at him now just like he did the day Mitch is asking about, like he's stunned and not sure who he is or what he's capable of. He shakes his head hard and shrugs. "That was a lifetime ago."

"I want you to set the bear free."

"Why in the hell would I do that?"

"You'll do it because I asked you to."

Einar sits in the chair again. He rests his elbows on his thighs and stares at the floor between his feet. He sits long enough that Mitch forgets he's waiting for him to respond. Then he nods and stands up. "I guess you're right," he says. "I guess that's why I'll do it."

TWENTY-FOUR

J EAN'S CAREFUL WHERE she steps and
watches for snakes. The road's grown over in
weeds, studded with aspen and cottonwood
saplings, the dirt tracks rutted by years of runoff.
This isn't where anyone goes anymore. High
school kids haven't even come up here to
park and make out or drink beer. Maybe she
shouldn't have come.

She stops between the house and the barn.
The north end of the calving sheds have fallen
in. She remembers holding a lantern in there as
a kid, bundled against the twenty-below night
air, her dad with his sleeves rolled up, his arms
wet with blood and afterbirth, his hat off and
his bald head steaming, grinning like a clown.
And later, when the price of beef dropped, there
were the wire cages filled with the fast, fierce
mink. They frightened her. She hated feeding
them, hated cleaning the cages and picking up

the piles of shit with a scoop shovel, hated the stink and getting bit. After the mink there were llamas. Her father kept two dozen as pack animals, so he could walk tourists into the Bighorns, camp with them and tell them stories of weather and isolation and self-reliance. She liked the llamas and thought of them as smarter, lankier sheep.

Her dad ran out of life before he ran out of ideas. And he never once bitched, that's what she remembers. He grinned and joked as one enterprise failed after the other. She loved him for his optimism. She loved his bald head.

After he died and her mother followed, her mother's parents moved into the house to care for Jean. They were decent people who didn't try to raise anything except her, from one Social Security check to the next, and she never felt on edge, desperate, like she feels now.

When she married Griffin, her grandparents moved back to a trailer they kept in Arizona and died there a few years later, the old man first. They'd already let the bank take this place for back taxes. She kicks at the weeds. That's what a bank raises.

They were good, honest people, every one of them. They're no excuse for how she turned out, and the bank isn't either. It's just that she felt useful as a kid, like she was part of something better than herself, a real family.

She wonders how Griff must feel. She certainly hasn't had much of a family. But God knows she's been useful. She's held her mother's head while she puked up an evening's worth of tequila. Helped her clean herself up after some man's smacked her hard enough to bruise. Of course that doesn't mean she feels useful.

Jean looks toward the southeast. It's just the beginning of evening, and the shadows stretch away over a prairie as calm and indistinct as an ocean. It's the way Griffin would ride up here in the evenings, from the southeast. Bareback, on a sorrel gelding, and he'd bring a horse for her too. When he was old enough to drive, there was a Chevy truck.

"Go," her father'd say, grinning, waving her away. "You're only young once."

And she would. She'd swing up behind Griffin, loop her arms around his slim waist and clamp her legs tight to the ribs of the sorrel horse. They'd lope away through the alfalfa, through the wire gate at the corner of the field and into the pines, slowing. He's all she ever wanted. He's where she always saw herself—behind him, beside him, stretched out in the sunlight on top of Griffin Gilkyson.

His was the first naked male body she ever saw. They weren't even in grade school yet. They'd slipped away from her father and helped each other out of their clothes, shyly, and lay in the lush grass behind the calving sheds. They trusted each other and were curious. His little boy's dick stood up and away from his tight body, and she touched the tip of it with her finger and pulled back, and it sprang away against his stomach. They laughed, and she lay on her back and spread her legs so he could open her, gently, staring at her with wonderment. They held each other. They wrestled. They tickled their young bodies with the long stems of native grass, giggling, writhing, until their curiosity was satisfied. Until they were older and their bodies wanted not only to know, but also to own.

She can't remember Griff ever bringing a boy to any place they've ever lived, or a girlfriend. She's always come home right away, alone, always seeming satisfied to be there, not so much curious about what she hasn't seen, as about when the things she has seen will happen again. And she's seen men's bodies, that's for sure. What Jean's not sure about is whether she's ever seen something as innocent as a boy's body.

She steps up on the porch. The door's lost its lowest hinge and hangs by just the top. She swings it against the wall and steps sideways into the house and the smell of animals, of birdshit and mouseshit, musty as a nest.

There's no furniture. The jagged glass that remains in a broken windowpane catches the light, and when she looks back she can see her tracks in the dust in the hallway, every surface coated with years of dust and pollen.

She walks to the room at the end of the hallway where she woke up most of the mornings of her life, and stands wondering why it seems like a room from someone else's life.

She kneels down in the closet and works the boards loose and sets them aside, then takes out the red box her prom dress came in. It's still tied with a red ribbon. She sits on the floor under the window with the box on her lap. She doesn't even have to open it.

Her 4-H ribbons are inside. She was the only girl along the range to win a ribbon for a prize llama. Baby teeth. Valentine's Day cards she made for her mom and dad. A pair of spurs. A pale-blue garter belt she shoplifted from a store in Sheridan when she was fourteen. She wore it only once, for Griffin. There's a brooch her mother wore. Her father's fountain pen and a lock of his hair. Her grandmother snipped it from just above his ear once he was laid out in the coffin. A picture of Madonna she cut out of **Seventeen** magazine. Scraps of leather and lace. There's a list of names for the children she was going to have. When she was alone she'd call them out, pretending she was calling her family to dinner. Photographs of Griffin starting when he was ten, though not many after their wedding day, when he was twenty. Photographs of her parents' wedding and her grandparents' wedding. All the rings they wore. She dropped in her ring and Griffin's after the funeral.

She puts the box back in the hole and stacks the loose boards on top of it, then walks into the hallway. She believes in memories, not ghosts. And she's come to believe in chance as random as the weather.

She steps onto the porch and looks at her watch. She should have called. Griff'll be worried. She could've called from the café after work and told her she wasn't out with a man, that she just wanted to walk. She starts down through the pasture where Griffin rode the sorrel horse to see her in the evenings. She looks at the sky and thinks she'll get to Einar's before dark.

TWENTY-FIVE

Einar's got Jimmy's front left foot up on his knee. He's set the last shoe and caught the nailends where they've come through the side of the hoof and worked them off, back and forth, with the hammer's claw. He saws a groove under the nailends with the flat rasp and tosses it toward Griff. The rasp skips in the corral dust at her feet and she picks it up and sits back on the handle of the shoeing box. She tests the rasp with a fingertip and then looks closely to see what it did to her skin.

"Why doesn't he jump around?" she asks.

Einar stands away from the horse and picks up the shoeing hammer from where he dropped it. "He doesn't jump around because if he did I'd whack him in the ribs with this hammer. Find me that little chunk of iron."

She stands again and bends over the box.

"It's about the size of a candy bar," he says. "A thick one. You found it before."

She hands him the iron block, and he bends over and lifts Jimmy's front foot up again and keeps it pinched between his knees. The sweat drips off his nose and onto his chaps. He holds the chunk of iron against the broken nailends and strikes the heads of the nails until the ends crimp into the groove he's made with the rasp. Then he drops the horse's foot, takes off his hat and mops at his head with his bandana.

"I'd jump around if you pounded nails into my paws," she says.

Einar taps the side of Jimmy's hoof with his boot. He takes the nails he's got stuck in his mouth and hands them to her. "Hooves. Horses don't have paws. They've got hooves." She wipes the nails on her jeans before she puts them back in their carton. She doesn't seem to care that he's slobbered all over them. "They're hard," he says. "This doesn't hurt him. Hand me that rasp back."

He takes it and sets Jimmy's foot up on his knee again and works the edge of the hoof until it's flush with the shoe. The gray cat's jumped down from a rail to rub itself against Jimmy's other front leg, and the horse looks down and snorts. Einar scuffs at the cat with the side of his boot. "I'm not milking this son of a bitch."

Griff crawls forward, looking up at the horse, and snatches the cat away. "Jack doesn't know that," she says.

Einar drops the hoof and puts his hands on his hips and arches his back. "I ought to hire this done," he says. "Or at least have the good sense to think about it."

He unties the halter rope and leads Jimmy to the gate. He's stood his saddle inside the gate, turned up on its fork, the pads laid over the back skirts. He squares the pads on the horse's back and swings the saddle up. Griff stands by the gate with the shoeing box. She's had to drag it part of the way, but now stands there with her legs spread, gripping the handle with both hands and holding the box just off the ground between her feet. Her face is red from the effort.

"Where do you want this?" she asks.

"Right there's fine."

She's stuck with him all day. They've cleaned the barn and replaced a U-joint in the truck, and she's been as much help as she knows how. Hell, he probably couldn't have driven her away with a stick.

"I could be a cowgirl," she says.

"Yes, I think you could." He snugs the cinch and ties the latigo off. "I agree with you."

He takes the bridle from the gate latch, shucks the halter off Jimmy and bridles him. When he buckles the throatlatch the horse comes up higher on his feet, all business.

"Have you ever ridden a horse before?"

She shakes her head. "We lived in Roy's trailer house. He was my mom's boyfriend. He put in guardrails," she says. "He didn't have any horses." She adds, "I don't even think he knew anybody who did."

Einar catches her under the arms and swings her into the saddle before she can think of anything else to say. He wants to surprise her and see it in her face. Not give her time enough to make her face go flat like there's not a thing in the world she hasn't seen.

She grips the saddlehorn with both hands and blinks like she's been slapped. "Wow," she says softly. It's what he wanted her to say.

He opens the gate and leads Jimmy out of the corral.

"You can see a lot up here."

He closes the gate and turns the near stirrup toward the horse's head and steps in and stands up into the saddle. She scoots closer to the horn, hooking her legs over the saddle's swells to make room for him.

"How long did you live with this guy who didn't have horses?" he asks. He lightly rests the heel of his left hand, where he holds the reins, on top of hers.

"Since I was eight," she says.

She tilts her head to look at him, and he puts Jimmy down through an irrigation ditch and spurs him up across the pasture toward the mountains. The horse wrings his tail and farts and crow-hops and lines out. His ears are pricked and he's looking for cows.

"Did he try to buck us off?" she asks.

He could feel her hands tighten under his. "He's just feeling good. He hasn't been used in awhile."

She nods but doesn't relax her grip on the horn. They can see Curtis at the far end of the pasture. He's got his truck parked below a new post he's stretching wire to.

"My mom had three other boyfriends before Roy," she says, "but not at the same time. They didn't have horses either."

Jimmy breaks into a trot, and her hair slaps against her thin shoulders and blows back into his face. It smells clean in a way he only barely remembers.

"The other boyfriends didn't hit her." She looks back at him. "They just used their words real mean." She lifts her eyebrows. "Like somebody else I know." She keeps looking at him until he nods, then squares herself forward again.

"I can see where living in a trailer house might be a disadvantage for a cowgirl," he says.

He reins Jimmy to a walk, and they watch Curtis hammer in a fencing staple. They sit the horse and watch until Curtis pulls his hat off. His head's streaming with sweat and he brings his shoulder up to rub his face dry. His shirt's soaked through, front and back.

"I thought I'd get this done before it snows," he says.

"This is my granddaughter," Einar tells him. "Her name's Griff."

Curtis steps to Jimmy's shoulder and offers his hand. "I've noticed you. Seen you down by the barn," he says. "My name's Curtis. I guess your grandfather told you he's letting me use his land."

"Yes, sir." She shakes Curtis's hand and grabs for the horn again.

Curtis seats his hat and looks up at Einar. "I'm surprised to see you ahorseback. Thought you'd bounce up through here on that new trike of yours."

"I'm giving my granddaughter a riding lesson, if that's okay with you."

"I guess I can see that."

"My legs aren't long enough to reach the pedals," Griff says. She looks back at Einar. "I tried it the other day."

Curtis steps toward his truck. "What's Mitch been dreaming about these days?"

"He dreamed he was surfing," Griff tells him.

"Like in the ocean?" Curtis has half a dozen two-liter Coke bottles in the bed of his pickup. He refills them with water each night and sets them in his freezer so he'll have something cool to sip the next day.

"Where the hell else do you think he'd surf?" Einar says. Jimmy paces, and he tightens the reins.

Curtis finds a Coke bottle that's mostly thawed. "Well, I don't know. That's why I asked. In a dream he could've been surfing on the river if he wanted."

"It was the ocean," Griff says. "There were owl feathers mixed in with the waves."

Curtis nods and takes a drink, then wipes his mouth with the back of his hand. "Tell him I said hi if you get a chance."

"Yes, sir. I will."

"You take care of yourself, Curtis." When

Einar reins Jimmy away, the horse pivots like he's been asked to cut a cow away from the fence.

"It was nice to meet you," Griff calls over her shoulder.

"Don't you worry about your legs," Curtis calls. "All they've got to do is reach from your butt to the ground."

Einar skirts the west end of the pasture and rides the fenceline toward the rise to the south. Griff relaxes back into him. He can feel her shoulder blades against his chest.

"When I get real good at riding," she says, "maybe we could buy some cows." She thinks for a minute. "The red-and-white ones are pretty."

"Herefords."

"Herefords," she says. "When you were in the war with Mr. Bradley, did he save your life or something?"

He pulls Jimmy up at the grave markers and steps down. "Mitch has saved my life every day for the past fifty years."

"What's that mean?"

She's looking down at the pair of tomb-stones, at her father and grandmother.

"It means he's the best friend I'm ever likely to find."

"Is that why you take care of him?"

"I take care of him because I can."

"Is that my dad?" She points at her father's stone.

"That's him." Einar lifts a hand toward Ella's marker and lets it drop. "And there's your grandmother."

"Did you love her?"

He looks up at her. "Yes, I did. I loved them both."

She shifts in the saddle. "I don't remember my dad."

The wicker chair's been moved to face the house, and Einar steps to it to move it back.

"You would've if you'd known him." There's a bald spot in the grass in front of the chair, and five cigarettes ground out in the dirt. He steps on them and looks up at her again. "Your mom's boyfriend—did he smoke?"

She nods, and Einar rights the chair and leads Jimmy away from the chair.

"You feel all right up there?" he asks.

She's sitting farther back in the saddle but still grips the horn with both hands. She's smiling and not trying to hide it.

"I feel just perfect," she says.

Halfway to the barn he says, "Did that man ever hit you, or was it just your mother?"

"Once he did," she says.

He doesn't turn to see if she wants to tell him anything else. He just walks on and when they get to the corral he ties off the bridle reins and lifts her down and loosens the cinch and carries his saddle into the tackroom. He's heard everything he needs to hear.

She stands in the doorway, stepping up and down and pulling at the inseams of her jeans.

"Are you hurt?" he asks.

She's still smiling, like her father used to.

"I'm just perfect," she says.

WHEN EINAR WALKS past Starla she looks up just long enough to tell him the sheriff's in, but he doesn't stop until he's standing in front of Crane's desk and staring down at him. "Jean capture your interest?" he asks.

Crane leans back in his chair. "I guess she has."

"I would've thought you'd seen enough of her by now you wouldn't need to come out and peep through my windows."

"Why don't you sit down, Einar."

"Just because you're the law doesn't mean you can't do sick shit on your time off."

Crane stands up. "Her ex-boyfriend's in town."

Einar looks toward the door. "Here? You've got him in jail?"

Crane walks to the window and opens the bottom sash. "He's staying down at the Timbers. I can't do a damn thing unless he bothers her, and he knows it."

"Have you talked to him?"

"I sent my deputy down. I wanted everything to be done professionally." He turns to Einar. "I wasn't sure I could trust myself. But if he was out trespassing on your place we've got a whole different deal."

Einar's stepped to the doorway. "Does Jean know he's here?"

Crane shakes his head. "I haven't told her yet."

"Where is he right now?"

"I believe he's over at the motel or the bar next to it. Would you tell me if he'd been out bothering you?"

Einar opens his hands at his sides. They'd been clenched into fists. "That's good of you, Crane, but the man doesn't bother me one little bit."

TWENTY-SIX

―――――

M ITCH HEARS Einar park in the workyard
and slam the pickup door shut, then he
drifts back to sleep. He's been sleeping most of
the afternoon. He wakes again when Einar
comes in with a tray holding his dinner, a box of
morphine vials and one of syringes.

He looks over where Einar's set the tray next
to the vise. "I won't need all that at once," he
says. "It hasn't got that bad."

Einar carries his plate and silverware and
milk to the table at the foot of the bed. "Why
don't you wait just a little and see what I'm
doing."

While he's eating, Mitch can hear Einar outside and metal scraping on the truckbed. He's
mostly finished his meal when Einar wheels in
the dolly with the little refrigerator strapped
to it.

"Where do you want this?" He tilts the dolly

back with one hand, like it's something he does every day.

"Right there's fine." Mitch points to an open span of wall next to Karl's bed, and Einar unstraps the refrigerator and walks it into the space and plugs it in. He sets the box of vials on one of the plastic-coated shelves.

"Was that the only color it came in?"

"They call it caramel down at Sears. They've got one that's white and another that's dark brown. So if you don't like this color you ought to tell me now."

"I like it fine. I was just curious."

The refrigerator hums and Karl noses it and lifts a leg, and Einar shouts him out onto the porch before he can get his stream started.

"I don't know what you're laughing at," he says. "That's not real funny."

"I thought it was." Mitch puts his fork down on his plate.

"I can run you out something to snack on. That cheese you like and some fruit. Stock you up, now that you've got a place to keep it."

Then he wheels the dolly out and comes right back in with a small television set and a boxed VCR in his arms. Mitch lifts his plate away, and Einar sets them on the table.

"Jesus, that must've been one hell of a sale."

"I rented this stuff here." Einar sets the VCR box under the table and stands with a coil of black cable. "I thought you and Griff might watch a movie."

"The last movie I saw was **The French Connection.** I hope you didn't rent that one."

Einar examines the end of the cable and then the ports at the rear of the TV. He shakes his head. "I guess I don't know how to hook this bugger up."

"Are there any instructions in that box?"

"If there are I couldn't find them."

Mitch holds his plate under his chin so he won't spill his last bite of supper. "Maybe Jean knows how to hook it up."

Einar sets the cable on top of the television. "She's out with the sheriff. This is for you and Griff."

"Where are you going?"

Einar pauses, then looks toward the bathroom. "I'm going back to town."

"You never could lie worth a shit."

"I'm not lying."

"Well, you look like you are. You look like you're about to rob a bank."

Einar squints at the back of the television

again, like he's remembered something they might've told him at the video store. "I'm just going back to town. That's all there is to it."

Mitch sets his plate on the corner of the table and wipes his mouth.

"I'm not going in for the bear, if that's what you think," Einar tells him. "Not tonight."

"Then why are you?"

"I just am."

Einar won't look at him, so Mitch slides the cable off the top of the television. He turns it in his hands. "Griff can stay out here with me just as long as she likes," he says. "If you'll get me a stove and another bed she can live here if she wants. You tell her that."

"Okay, I will."

Einar lets Karl back in and watches him until he lies down and curls up staring at the refrigerator.

"What movie did you rent?" Mitch asks.

"It's called **Star Wars.** The girl at the video shop said it was something anybody'd like."

"I've heard of it."

Einar steps to the table and carries the dinner plate and silverware over to the tray. "You're not just saying that?"

"No. I believe I have."

Einar holds the door open with his hip and looks out over the workyard. "You ever wish you'd lived a different life? Instead of working this place with me?"

The aspen leaves shudder outside the cabin window. They're starting to turn, both gold and green in the evening light.

"I've always felt lucky to have work that was right for me," Mitch says. "When I was a kid all I ever wanted was to be a cowboy."

"Not a soldier?"

"No." Mitch looks at him. "That was a mistake. Just something we had to get done. If I could do it over again I think I wouldn't."

"You think it ruined us?" Einar looks down at the tray he's holding. "I mean, do you think it ruined me?"

"I don't think it helped either one of us."

"What about now? You still feel lucky?"

"Yeah, I do."

Einar looks back at the refrigerator. "That color looked better in the showroom."

"It's fine."

Einar nods. "You might want to keep an eye on Karl. Until he gets used to it."

"He lives here too. He can keep an eye on his own damn self."

"I guess he can," Einar says, and closes the door.

MITCH GOT UP and worked on an antler for an hour and then stabbed himself in the thigh with a second round of morphine and hobbled to the bathroom and managed a bath. He was tired when he got back to bed, not wondering anymore if he wanted to watch a movie. He just lay there quietly, looking forward to seeing Griff.

Now she's standing by the side of the bed with a bowl of popcorn.

"I guess it's down to you and me," he says.

"Yes, sir."

He doesn't know whether it's the morphine or the girl, but he's feeling better than he has all day.

"The guy your mom's out with." He watches her face and it doesn't change. "He's not as good as your dad was, but he's not a bad man either." She nods and he raises a hand toward the television. "You know how to hook all that up?"

"It's easy," she says. She sets the bowl beside him on the bed and walks to the television.

"There's a box under the table, but Einar couldn't find any directions in it."

She bends behind the television with the

black cable. "They're all the same," she says. "I've done this before."

She comes around the table and slots the movie tape in the VCR machine and drags a chair beside the bed and takes out the three smaller bowls she's stacked on top of the popcorn. She scoops out a bowl for Karl and carries it to him and sits back in the chair. "I put butter on it," she says.

He tells her that that's how he and Karl like their popcorn, even though it's been at least twenty years since he's had any and the dog never has. She presses a button on a little black box she holds, and the movie starts.

They watch silently for a half hour, and when Karl whines at the door she turns the sound down and puts him out. She comes back and stands by the chair.

"Are you doing okay?" he asks.

"My bottom's a little bit sore," she says. "Einar let me ride the horse."

"Good for him."

They look at the screen with the sound still off.

"I've seen this before," she says.

"It's a good movie," he tells her. "Kind of like a western without horses."

Light sabers are flashing on the screen.

Mitch pats the side of the bed. "You want to get up here with me?"

"If that's okay." She puts the big bowl on the chair seat and he slides against the wall, then she lies down beside him, propped up against the pillows. She lifts his arm from where it's wedged between them and loops it over her shoulders, then wiggles right in against him and looks up to see if it's all right. He can feel the warmth of her slim body, and every breath she takes.

"I met Mr. Hanson today," she says.

"He's a big sort of ape-looking fella, isn't he?"

She smiles. "I didn't think he was until I saw him up close. From far away he looks pretty normal."

"Kind of makes you believe in evolution, Curtis does."

She thinks for a minute, like she's trying to remember what she's been taught about evolution, and then nods very seriously. "Yes, he does."

The sound's still off and Darth Vader's on the screen, and she huffs like he does and squirms in tighter against Mitch's side.

"It's better this way," she says.

"I think so too."

He lets her fall asleep against him, and he's careful not to jostle her. He's taken a strand of her hair between his thumb and forefinger, working it back and forth against the pads of his fingers. He thinks it's been a long time since he's felt anything so fine.

She turns into him and curls her knees against the side of his leg, and he watches the movie until it ends and then closes his eyes. He keeps his arm around her, holding her close, and dreams he's a bear. A large bear out on open land. An animal satisfied with its life, prepared to lie down and sleep forever.

TWENTY-SEVEN

———— ▬ ————

Roy's lining up his next shot when he sees the old prick come into the bar. He chalks his cue and watches him stand inside the door for a minute, blinking, letting his eyes adjust. Roy sinks the fifteen in a side pocket, and the cue ball spins against the cushion and stops right where he needs it to be to put the last striped ball down. Backspin and English, he thinks. It's all about the leave. He grins at the young cowboy he's playing. He's having a very good time.

He watches the old man move toward the bar, then bends over his next shot, thinking about where he wants the cue ball to end up to give him a decent line on the eight. Put this village-idiot son of a bitch out of his misery, three games in a row at twenty bucks a throw. This is better than panning for gold. Hell, if this hayseed'll play him all night he could retire up here with Jean. Buy himself a hat and a pair of fancy boots. Open a bar of his own and let Jean and Griff help him run it. A family business, like Roy Rogers and Dale Evans. He's always had a good singing voice. Put some real country into these backwater assholes. The last striped ball falls.

"Eight in the corner," he says, pointing at the pocket with his cue. The cowboy starts digging in his jeans, and Roy hopes he's got a year's wages in twenties stuffed in his pants. The eight drops with a soft thud, and the cue ball spins back and stops flat.

The old man's sitting at the bar as the cowboy racks the balls for the next game. Roy tilts his beer back and drains it.

"You want another one, Claude?" he asks.

"It's Clyde," the young cowboy tells him. He's arranging the balls in the rack.

"Whatever. You ready or not?"

"Are you buying?"

Roy picks up the cowboy's twenty from where he'd laid it on the bumper, and waves it in his face. "You're the one paying, Earl. Go ahead and break 'em if you think you can."

The cowboy stiffens, and Roy hopes he's pissed him off. Nobody shoots good pool when they're tightened up for a fight. You've got to be loose. And he knows the boy won't fight. The silly hick thinks he might win his money back. Good fucking luck, sucker.

He walks to the end of the bar and leans into it, watching the old man scan the backbar. He knows this rummy old bastard wants a drink more than a fat broad wants pantyhose that fit. He can see it in his face. The old man runs his tongue around the inside of his mouth, gets his handkerchief out and blows his nose.

"Long time no see, Einar," the bartender says.

"Just a club soda this evening, Katie."

That's it: Einar. A good square-head name. He couldn't remember what Jean had called him.

The bartender nods like the old man made the right choice, the used-up fucking cunt. Roy watches her fill a glass with ice. She's looking down so she doesn't press the Seven-Up or the Coke button on the pop nozzle. She wants to make sure she doesn't have to give him a second run at ordering a drink with booze in it.

Then the old man looks right at him, and Roy works up his best smile. That's right, ass-hole, get a good look. After all, I've been looking at you for a couple of days. He almost laughs. He's looked at the old man so often through binoculars he thinks he ought to appear in a circle of light.

When the bartender sets the club soda on the bar, Roy lifts his empty beer bottle toward her. "Two more just like this one," he says, and watches her walk to the cooler. He hears the cowboy break the balls, but he's in no hurry. He feels like he's on vacation, and that clodhopper sure isn't going anywhere. Where else could he blow his paycheck so fast? It's either stay in here where the beer's cool or drag his sorry ass home and fuck his cousin. Which is probably why he's in here in the first place: He's got a butt-ugly cousin.

Roy smiles and leans forward on his elbows. "How's Jean?" he asks. But the old fucker doesn't miss a beat. He doesn't spit out a mouthful of club soda or blow his nose again. He doesn't even wince. He just turns a little on his bar stool.

"She's all right, I guess."

The bartender sets the two bottles of Coors in front of Roy.

"I'll bet she misses me." He lays down the cowboy's twenty for the beers. Of course she misses him, just like he misses her. They belong to each other.

AN UNFINISHED LIFE

"I don't believe I know you," the old man says.

Roy smiles and lights a cigarette. He can feel the bulge of the little velvet box in his pocket and can picture the ring inside. A diamond ring. He can almost hear the wedding bells ringing.

"Sure you do," he says. "I'm the guy that's been watching you and your crippled nigger for the past couple days."

And he sees something he didn't expect, just a flicker of it in the old man's eyes, but there it is. Cold, real cold. A shiver rises into the back of Roy's neck, along the tops of his shoulders. He picks up his beers, not yet ready for the good times to end.

ROY'S ASLEEP when he hears the knocking. He sits up and looks at the clock. It's just after one in the morning. He throws the cheap-ass motel bedspread back. He's still dressed. He remembers playing another dozen games of pool, drinking a dozen more beers. His head throbs. Natural springwater my ass. He presses the heel of his hand to his forehead and there's another knock.

"In a minute," he calls.

He stands and wobbles into the bathroom to piss. He doesn't turn on the light. That'd send the headache into overdrive. There's the knock-ing again, probably the cowboy wanting his money back. Or maybe he wants to trade some inbred-cousin pussy for the money he lost. It's got to be the cowboy.

Or Jean. The old man could've told her that Mr. Roy Winston's in town and she's come to see for herself. Why wouldn't she? She's got to be tired of this game-playing shit by now.

He finds an empty beer bottle on the floor by the bed and holds it at his side when he swings the door open. Just in case it's not Jean. And then he drops it.

"Step back," the old man says.

Roy doesn't step back because he's pointing a rifle at him. It's what's in the old man's eyes. Not the flicker he saw at the bar anymore, it's steady. It's not a look that needs a bark to go with it. It's a look that says "I'm all done barking."

"Pack up your shit," he says.

Roy looks around the room. The television's on, and he can see his suitcase open on the table. He picks up his clothes as he goes to it. The old man watches in the doorway while he gathers his shaving gear and shampoo and drops the toi-let kit in his suitcase.

"Is that it? I don't want any part of you left behind."

Roy checks the room again. He wants a drink of water but thinks it can wait.

"I already settled your bill," the old man says.

THE OLD MAN sits in the passenger seat with the rifle across his lap, the end of the barrel against Roy's lower rib. He's told him where to turn and where to stop and how fast to go, and now they're a mile out of town on some little two-lane. The barrow ditch weeds grow right up to the sides of it.

"I just came out here to tell her I love her," he says. That ought to be something even this old asshole can understand.

"She had your love all over her face when she got here."

Roy turns to look at him. The old man just looks tired now, his face drawn in the dashboard lights. "You mind if I smoke?"

"It's your truck."

Roy gets the pack of cigarettes out of his shirt, shifting against the rifle barrel. "Are you telling me you never had to hit a woman?"

"What do you think," the old man says.

A car approaches and passes, and Roy blinks against the flash of the headlights. He knows damn well there isn't a woman in the world who can keep her mouth shut long enough, not through a man's whole lifetime, where she won't need to get smacked at least once. And he knows you wouldn't have to if you didn't love them. That's just a law of nature.

"She wanted me to find her," he says. "If she didn't she wouldn't have come back here. She told me where she grew up."

The old man's looking straight ahead. "I imagine she came home because she didn't have anyplace else to go."

His voice sounds as tired as his eyes look in the dashlights.

"Pull over," he says.

Roy eases the pickup onto the weedy shoulder and stops, and the old man opens his door.

"It's a long walk back to town." Roy smiles. What the hell. Why not? He'll have to see this old fart at Thanksgiving and Christmas dinners.

The old man stands out of the truck. The door's still open, and the rifle's still between them. The sight of it makes Roy's eyes water.

"Where I walk isn't any of your goddamn business. Your business is to keep driving." He slams the door, then leans in through the window. "If I see you again I'll kill you. I'm sorry, but I will." He's holding the rifle at his side.

"You've seen too many westerns, you know that?"

The old man steps back from the door. "That doesn't exactly work in your favor," he says.

Roy snorts. Then there's a flash of light, and in the rearview mirror he sees the merry-fucking-Christmas jumble of lights from a cop car. How much more fucked up can one evening get? He turns the ignition off and sits back in his seat. At least he won more than three hundred bucks off of Jethro. He can feel the wad of bills in his pocket next to the ring box. Three hundred and twenty for the ring. It's like the cowboy bought it for him.

He hears the cop walking up to the side of the truck. He hopes it's not one of those Highway Patrol assholes. They're the absolute worst, state-in and state-out. Then he hears the cop ask the old man if he needs a ride back to town.

"A ride'd be fine," the old man says, like this happens every Thursday.

And here's what's worse. Country cousins. Welcome to Bumpkinville. Roy looks to the sides of the road. No lights. Just dark. Let the butt-fucking begin.

The cop leans in the window.

"I suppose you want to see my license." Roy tries to sound bored.

"That man threaten you?"

Roy takes a better look at the guy. Maybe he was wrong. He's not Highway Patrol, and he's not the local doofus who already talked to him. "Yes, sir," he says. "He held a gun on me. He said he'd kill me."

The cop nods. He steps back from the truck and scuffs at the pavement with his boot. "Jean Gilkyson's a friend of mine," he says. "I don't believe she wants you here."

The cop's hands are at his sides, away from his pistol, but there it is. No rings on this man's hands. Take one look at his face and it's plain as day.

Roy glances through the back window. The old man's moved away from the truck. "You don't know her like I do," he tells the cop.

The cop nods again. "You're right about that. I don't." He's got his best cop face on, stern but fair. "But I still don't want you here."

Roy lights another cigarette. He's been warned. What the fuck, he's been warned before. This poor bastard thinks he stands a chance. Roy wants to laugh in his face. Jean's his. She always will be. "It's nice up here," he says.

The cop says, "Yes, it is. It's just the way I like it."

Roy starts the pickup and lets it idle. Shame

on you, he thinks. He wants to wag his finger at the cop. He wants to tell this lovesick yokel, "Thou shalt not covet thy neighbor's wife, motherfucker," but he just smiles. Backspin. English. It's all about the leave.

TWENTY-EIGHT

E INAR PARKS the truck next to the corrals and cuts the lights. He levers the cartridge out of the rifle's chamber and lays the rifle back on the seat. It can stay where it is until morning. He's home now. It's over. He steps out and shuts the door and stands listening to the night sounds. There's an owl, the yips of a coyote hunting the deep timber. Most of the world's violence happens after the sun goes down, he thinks. In the dark, blood just runs black, or gray under a moon. Tonight there's only a half-moon. Except for the light in the loft, the house is dark.

He hangs his hat on the peg inside the door and sits in the chair under the hat. He's not ready for bed. He walks into the living room and looks up at the loft, wondering if it's Griff who's up. He'd like to ask her what she thought of the movie. He starts up the stairs and stops short of the top.

He can see Griff asleep in her bed and Jean in front of the freestanding mirror beside the dresser. She wears a dandelion-yellow dress, at least it used to be. It's paler now, more the color of ripe wheat. The dress falls open in the back, unzipped, like she's just put it on. He feels the anger rise up and shorten his breath. He clears his throat, and she turns.

"That doesn't belong to you." It's a struggle to keep his voice low enough that he won't wake the girl.

Jean motions toward the open trunk. "I was looking for more clothes for Griff."

"It still doesn't belong to you."

She looks at where she's tossed her everyday clothes on her bed. He thinks she might strip the dress off right away, and he turns on the stair to start down.

"Was it hers?" she asks.

He hears her take a step toward him.

"Yes, it was. It was her favorite." He's feeling light-headed and grips the banister.

She shucks her arms out of the yellow sleeves and holds the dress up in front, over her breasts, with a single bare arm. "I'm sorry."

"I want it put back like you found it. I had tissue paper around it."

"I haven't hurt it, Einar." She checks to make sure Griff's still asleep. "It's not like you come up here in the middle of the night and dance around with it in the dark, do you?"

He stands on a single stair, one foot drawn up next to the other. He's staring at his boots. "Not so much now." He's still managing to whisper. "Not for a long time."

"Shit," she says quietly.

"I need to talk to you downstairs."

HE SITS at the kitchen table with a glass of milk. He doesn't hear her in the kitchen, but when he looks up she's standing across the table from him in her jeans and a sweatshirt. She's barefoot.

"Mitch said they liked the movie. It was sweet of you to think of it." She pulls a chair from the table but doesn't sit. "I carried her up to bed," she says. "She fell asleep out there with him."

He takes a drink of milk. He wipes his lip and stares into the glass. Swirls it. Watches the cream turn under and rise.

"I put the dress back," she says. "I won't take it out again. I wrapped it up like I found it." When he just nods, she says, "It's the middle of the night, Einar. If you can't remember what you wanted to say then why don't we both go to bed."

He sets the glass in the middle of the table, at arm's length, like he's afraid he might knock it over. "I had a little chat with your ex-boyfriend." He looks right at her. "I thought you'd want to know he was in town."

She sits in the chair, studying him like she thinks he's lying. "You mean Roy? He's here?"

"Not anymore."

She turns toward the wallphone. "We should call Crane."

"Crane knows all about it."

Her elbows are on the table. She drops her forehead into her hands and runs her fingers back through her hair. Her hands are trembling. "I'm sorry, Einar. I didn't come up here so you could solve my problems."

"I think you did." He's still charged up.

When she looks up her cheeks are wet. She wipes at them with the backs of her hands. "I'm truly sorry."

He doesn't care. If she fell over dead, he thinks he'd cover the body with the afghan from the back of the sofa and carry it out in the morning, lay it in the truck and bring the rifle in. He finishes the milk and walks the glass to the sink, flicking the little light on over the sink. "You screwing Crane Carlson for sport or protection?"

He hears her scrape the chair back from the table, turning to face him.

"That's none of your business." She pauses. "But I'm with Crane because it feels good."

Her voice almost cracks with the effort, and he thinks she's still trying to act tough, like she did when she was a kid. He leans against the counter, watching her.

"Maybe you haven't noticed," she says, "but there isn't a hell of a lot up here that does. Not for me, anyway."

"Why don't we wake up your daughter and ask her what she thinks about your problems?"

"This isn't really about Roy or Crane, is it? Or Griff either."

"It's about what it's always been about. It's about you and me."

"And Griffin."

He hates that she can even speak his son's name. "Yeah. It's about Griffin."

She gets up slowly and pushes the chair in under the table and stands holding on to its back. "He was the one who flipped the coin. Did I ever tell you that?"

"I don't know what you're talking about."

"I'm talking about chance, Einar. I lost a coin flip. That's why I was driving and he wasn't."

"Is that what you tell yourself? Is that what keeps you from putting a gun in your mouth when you remember how you killed your husband?"

She takes a step toward him. She's mad now. Good.

"Was it a quarter?" he asks.

"You want to know what coin we flipped?"

"I want to know what you're saying killed my boy. Was it a dime?"

"I killed him, Einar." She's raised her voice and glances toward the loft. "Is that what you want to hear?" She steps back to the chair and holds onto it with one hand. Her hands are shaking again, and the chair is too. "It wasn't the change we had in our pockets, or Highway 2 south of Calgary, or the weak-ass coffee, or the rain. It was me. I fell asleep and rolled the car six times. I'm the one that killed Griffin Gilkyson. No argument. It's not something I'd forget."

He turns the light off. He feels tired now, finally. He feels leaden. "That's what I wanted to hear you say." He starts out of the kitchen. He thinks he'll be able to sleep.

"I'm not done." She takes her hand away from the chair. "I'm trying," she says, "and you aren't. I didn't kill you when I killed Griffin."

"Yes you did."

"Then why don't you lie down and we'll bury you." She takes a step toward him again. "What's the matter? You afraid no one'll come to the funeral? No tears and wailing?" Her hands are at her sides, but they're clenched into fists. "I guarantee you I'll cry, Einar. And so will your granddaughter."

The window's open over the sink, and the wind comes up and lifts the curtains. It sounds like the wings of a small bird. It's that quiet. When the wind slackens, it's only their breathing he hears.

"We'll talk about you leaving in the morning."

She looks at the light still on in the loft. "We're done talking," she says.

HE'S SITTING on the porch when she comes out. He's sitting there because he wanted away to be from her, because he felt sick and didn't want them to hear.

The girl leans into her mother's hip, still mostly asleep, still in her print nightgown. She's wearing tennis shoes but the laces aren't tied. Jean's got an arm around her shoulders, holding her tight. In her free hand she carries the shopping bag and the girl's orange backpack.

Griff opens her mouth like she's got something to say, but Einar looks away and they stumble down the porch steps and across the lawn. He doesn't want to hear it. He stands when the gate hinges squeal, but only to watch them move up the road. He doesn't call for them to stop. He can't tell if the girl's looking back. He hears the owl again, but the coyote's quit.

He hurries to Mitch's cabin and doesn't bother to knock. He turns the light on over the workbench and searches the shelves. A can of lacquer falls from the bottom shelf. He doesn't pick it up. He isn't trying to be quiet.

"It's behind Karl," Mitch says.

The old dog hears his name and lifts his head from his paws.

"She walked out of here and took her kid with her."

Mitch gets up on an elbow. "Was that your idea or hers?"

"It doesn't matter. They're gone."

Einar kneels by the workbench, and the dog struggles up and stands at the door.

"Leave him alone. He's just a dog."

"I didn't touch him." He pulls the carpet scrap back from the wall and takes the bottle from where it's wedged under the base log.

"You ever wonder why I'm all the family you've got left?"

Einar stands, holding the bottle at his side. "I've got my boy. I've got Ella too."

"They're dead."

"Their memory's not."

Mitch works himself up higher on his elbow. "I guess you don't remember how bad Griffin wanted off this place. How much he wanted a life of his own." He sweeps an arm toward what's beyond the window. "He wanted a life with the woman he married. You think Jean or Griff would be here if he'd lived?"

Einar can feel the blood in his face and pulsing in his temples. "If you weren't a fucking cripple I'd jerk you out of there and kick your ass. You better know I would."

Mitch looks down at the side of him that's

caved in and scarred. "If I weren't a fucking cripple," he says, "I wouldn't be lying here listening to your whining bullshit."

HE TRIPS in the yard and falls to his hands and knees, then holds the bottle up in the moonlight. It's not broken.

He gets up slowly and crosses the workyard and huffs up through the sage and sits in the wicker chair and knows that that's where he'll sleep. He's not getting up again tonight. The gravestones stand before him, dull but distinct under the weak and setting moon. When the light goes off in Mitch's cabin he uncaps the bottle.

"Sweet dreams," he says. It sounds just as silly as he thought it would. He tips the bottle back and drinks. And then again. It tastes like he remembers, as sour as his memories.

He doesn't try to form another thought, a sentence or an explanation. He's got nothing else to say. He's not going to tell Ella, or his boy either, that forgiveness isn't as easy for the living. He guesses they've figured that out.

TWENTY-NINE

S HE WAKES with her back against a cool plas-
terboard wall, and her mother turns in the
narrow bed next to her. She crawls off the end of
the bed and stands there holding her breath, and
when her mother turns again in her sleep she exhales quietly. She doesn't know what time it is,
but it's still dark.

She expected the floor to be cool, but it's not.
She digs her toes into the carpet. She remembers
Nina leading them to this room, but she doesn't
remember what was on the floor or the walls or
where the furniture is.

She reaches out with her hands so she won't
bump into anything and finds their shopping
bag and her backpack by the bedroom door.
There's a night-light in the bathroom at the
end of the hallway, and she carries everything
in there and puts on a pair of jeans and a

shirt that belonged to her father and now are hers.

She brushes her hair away from her face, then rolls the brush up in the brown towel with her toothbrush and toothpaste. Her mother didn't know where her diary was or it'd be here too. It's still under her mattress in the loft. If she had it now she'd write that she hates her mother. That's all she'd write. She wouldn't say what she hated her for. She'd need a bigger diary for that. She doesn't feel like crying. She's just mad. Like a tornado came and ruined everything and nothing's left.

She leaves the shopping bag and backpack in the bedroom and finds her tennis shoes and sits in the living room to put them on. It's still dark. She thinks she'll wait to leave when she can see where she's going. She wants to make sure she doesn't miss the turnoff to her grandfather's, and the walk home won't seem so scary once the sun's up. Plus she wants her mother to see her leave.

In the living room there's a little bit of light from the streetlight on the corner, but it's not like Mary's house in Sioux Falls. It's just dim, and there's nothing to look at except the rounded shapes of the dark furniture.

She draws her knees under her and leans

back in the soft chair with the rolled brown towel beside her.

When she wakes again her mother and Nina are in the kitchen, and it's like the sun's just a little bit up. Her legs feel all pinpricked and stiff, and they're hard to get out from under her. She sits on the edge of the chair to wait until her legs wake up too. And then she clamps the towel under her arm and walks right past her mother where she sits with Nina at the Formica table. She can smell the coffee they're drinking, but she walks past like she doesn't even know they're there.

"Where do you think you're going?" her mother asks.

She's made it all the way to Nina's front door. She opens it and turns toward her mother. "I'm going back."

"You're going back where?"

Her mother doesn't even smile good morning. She doesn't say anything about being sorry for ruining their lives. And her hair isn't brushed and her face looks puffy.

Griff reaches up and flips the little hook on the inside of the screen door. She's not sure she can outrun her mother, but she's sure going to try. "I'm staying with my grandfather and Mr. Bradley."

Her mother sets her coffee cup down on the table. She doesn't raise her voice. She just says, "The hell you are," but it comes out like she's screamed it really loud.

Griff knows she must've flinched. She can tell by the way her mother's looking at her.

"You make decisions like they don't matter for anybody but you." It doesn't sound like her voice but it is, and now her mother flinches. She thinks they're doing what Roy always does. They're hitting with their words.

Her mother looks at Nina, then down at her coffee cup. "I always think about you, Griff. You know I do." She's trying not to hit back this time.

"Then it should start to show."

She doesn't wait to see if her mother flinches. She turns and walks right through the screen door and keeps on going across Nina's little brown front yard. The grass is crunchy under her feet. She can hear her mother's chair bounce on the kitchen floor and the screen door open and slam. She can hear her mother coming after her, and she starts to run.

She hears Nina call, "Let her go, Jean. For Christ's sake, let her have her grandfather for another week or two."

And she hears her mother stop behind her in the rustly grass.

A MAN in a pickup stops at the edge of town by the zoo where they keep the bear and asks if she wants a ride, but she says no and keeps walking. A boy slows his bike and pokes at the towel under her arm with a rolled-up newspaper and asks if she thinks she's going to the beach. She doesn't say anything at all, but in her mind she says **asshole** over and over, and he pedals away from her laughing, looking back over the canvas bag slung over his shoulder that says ISHAWOOA ENTERPRISE.

She decides that if a man on a horse offers, she'll take a ride. Or maybe a woman might ride past on a horse, a spotted one. She likes them best even though Jimmy's all one color. But no one comes on a horse, and when she looks for Curtis in the pastures above Einar's house he isn't there.

SHE'S AT the stove frying eggs when Einar comes in from the barn. She's making enough for both of them.

She's been home long enough to wash her face and hands and drink from her cupped hands under the tap and take her diary out and write that she hates her mother for everything there is. Not just her life, but everything. She thinks that ought to do it.

Einar sets the pail of milk in the sink. He hasn't remembered to take his hat off and hang it by the door, then he does and walks back.

"Where's your mother?" he asks.

She turns to look at him and the eggs spit grease on her hand, and she drops the spatula and steps back from the stove. She waves her hand in the air to cool it. "She's staying at Nina's."

Einar wets a cloth at the sink and gives it to her. He moves the big black skillet off the burner and turns the heat down. "Your mother and I had an argument last night."

She holds the wet cloth to her hand and lifts it away to look. The skin isn't bubbled but it's red. "It wasn't your fault." She wants to tell him it isn't the first time she's left a house with her mother in the middle of the night, but she just says again, "It wasn't your fault."

"Yeah it was. Mostly." He picks the spatula up and turns the eggs. "But I didn't expect her to leave like she did."

She watches him put two slices of white bread in the toaster. "My mom's good at leaving."

"It looks like she taught you how to fry eggs. She must be good at other things too."

She puts the washcloth back in the sink. "She didn't teach me," she says. "I taught myself."

He reaches for the butter dish, and she can smell him and wonders why she didn't before. It's kind of like the eggs smell. Sulfury and sour. Like Einar is Roy now—fighting with her mom and drinking and smelling sour in the morning. Like her mother's turned him into Roy. The thought scares her and she starts to cry. She spreads her hands over her face.

"Does your hand hurt that bad?"

"My hand's okay," she says.

IN THE AFTERNOON he pulls the truck to the toolshed, and she watches him bring out a drill and drill holes right through the clutch and brake and gas pedals. He cuts blocks of wood and drills holes in them too, and she stands behind him while he bolts the blocks of wood to the pedals. She hands him a wrench when he asks her to. He's laid the wrenches in the dirt by the pickup.

"Why are you doing that?" she asks.

"I'm going to teach you how to drive this rig."

"Really?"

"Yes, really." He's kneeling on the ground, tightening the last bolt. He taps the block of wood with the wrench. "These are so your legs'll reach."

She looks at the side of his face. He looks more like a stranger now, like he's somebody she knew a long time ago and now they're both here but hadn't planned on it. He looks like somebody she's going to have to get to know all over again.

"How come today?"

He stands up and puts the wrenches in his back pocket and picks up the drill and starts toward the toolshed, looping the extension cord like she's seen him loop his lariat.

"We've already been horseback riding," he says, "and I can't think of what else to do with you. You've got to learn sometime. Everybody does."

"Do you have a hangover?"

He stops in the doorway to the toolshed and looks down at the black cord in his hand. "I guess this isn't the first time you've ever seen a man hungover."

"No, sir." She doesn't want to tell him how many times.

"It won't happen again."

She looks back at the truck, and the door's still open. "Did my dad learn this way?"

"Yes, he did." He puts all his tools away and starts back toward her. "Did you figure I thought all this up just now?" He pushes his hat away from his face. "Well, I didn't. This was something I thought of twenty years ago."

When he smiles he looks more like her grandfather again. Like somebody she's already used to.

SHE SITS in the truck, and he has her practice shifting and looking in the side mirror and telling him what she sees. He gets out of the truck and adjusts the mirror so she can see along the side. When he gets back in he adjusts the rearview mirror until she can see through the back window. What she sees is the steel mesh that covers the window. There's a steel frame that stands up over the whole back of the cab, and the mesh is welded to the frame. So whatever's on the truckbed can't break through the window.

Einar's sitting sideways on the seat watching

her, when he tells her to push in the clutch and hold it and start the truck. But when she can't get the gearshift into reverse he does it for her, and then tells her to back away. He tells her she's as ready as she'll ever be, and she lifts her foot and the truck jumps backward and throws him against the glove compartment and he has to pick his hat up off the floor. He rubs the side of his head, still watching her, and tells her to push in the clutch and try again.

For most of the afternoon they bounce across the big pasture. She drives next to the fenceline, around and around, and she's surprised at how good she's getting at the shifting. She doesn't make the grinding sound anymore. She gets so good she's almost bored when he says, "Now out through that gate."

He points to a wire gate that's already open.

She pushes in the clutch and then the brake. "Are you sure?"

"I'm sure tired of driving in a circle."

She wets her lips with her tongue and swallows and lifts herself higher on the seat. Then he takes off his jacket and folds it and shoves it under her butt like a pillow.

"Is there a bigger gate?" she asks.

"They're all the same size." He puts on his seatbelt and she does too.

She looks at her hands. She has the steering wheel gripped at ten o'clock and two o'clock like he's told her she should. "Did my dad do this part on his first day?"

"No, he didn't. He wasn't as good at it as you are. He was good at other things right away, but he wasn't a born driver. I think you might be."

She feels a little bigger on the seat. She doesn't even mind that he still smells sour. "I'm glad you're not mad anymore."

"I never was," he says. He looks toward the gate again. "I was a little bit. Maybe I was just cranky."

"Because I left?"

"I guess that was it."

"I came back."

"Yes, you did. Now get us through that gate, and when you're out by the barn just keep going past the house and up the drive." He pulls his hat down tight on his head. "When we get up close to the oiled road I'll tell you what to do next."

She eases the clutch out and does just what he told her to, and when she gets to the road by the mailbox he tells her to turn left. He says it's clear, and when she looks at him he says it again.

"Just keep it in second," he tells her.

When she's almost to town she looks in the

side mirror, and there's a whole line of cars and trucks behind her. Nobody honked, so she didn't even know they were there.

"Should I pull over?" she asks.

"Just keep your eyes on what's in front of you. We're almost there. When you get to the stoplight turn right."

After the light he tells her to nose it in at the curb, and then he tells her to shut it down. He unfastens his seatbelt. "There's a lot to be said for diagonal parking," he says.

He opens his door and steps out, and they both take a deep breath. That's when she sees where they are.

"I'm not going in there," she says.

"Yes you are." He reaches across the seat and takes the keys out of the ignition like he thinks she might drive away. "We're both going in."

HE STANDS on the sidewalk and holds the café door open until she walks through. Her mother stands by a table next to a man who's looking at his open menu. He closes the menu, but Griff can tell her mother isn't listening to his order. Jean's watching her walk to the counter and sit down next to her grandfather.

Einar takes his hat off and sets it on its crown

on the floor between their stools. "Have you got any pie today?" he asks Nina. It sounds phony. Like the man on the five o'clock news sounds when he's talking about a whole lot of people who got killed and wagging his head and smiling at the same time. Like he can't tell the difference between happy and sad.

Nina steps out of the kitchen, wiping her hands on her apron. "We've got two kinds of berry left, Einar. And a slice of chocolate pecan." Nina smiles at her like she didn't just see her this morning in her own kitchen. She says, "All my pies'll make your teeth ache."

Einar looks down at her for her choice, and she says, "I'd like the piece of chocolate pecan, please, with vanilla ice cream on it."

"This girl's got young teeth," Einar says. "Just coffee for me."

He still sounds like the man on the news. He looks over his shoulder at her mother, and she looks too. Her mother's writing down the man's order.

Nina takes the plastic dome off the silver pedestal where the last piece of chocolate pie is and slips it onto a plate. "How's Mitch doing?" she asks.

"Not good," Einar says. "He's worse than he was just a week ago."

Nina bends over the little freezer where she keeps the ice cream. "I'll send something home with you. You tell him I said hi."

"I'll do that."

"You tell him I'll want to hear about his dreams. Maybe I'll drive out next week."

"I'll tell him."

Her mother comes behind the counter and takes the pie plate from Nina and sets it in front of her.

She looks right at her mother. "We're just visiting," she says.

"I'm glad you are," her mother says, but she hasn't looked at Einar yet. It's like it's her first time onstage and she has to play the piano or sing or do something she's not very good at and she can only look at one person in the audience at a time.

Griff takes a bite of ice cream and pie. "We came into town for a snack. I drove." She tries to sound casual. "My grandfather's teaching me."

Her mother's eyes dart toward Einar. "You drove what?"

"The flatbed truck," she says.

Her mother looks at Einar now, and doesn't look away, and he says, "It's a ranch, Jean. Kids learn to drive when they're big enough."

Her mother thinks about it for a minute. "I guess it's okay," she says. "You're here. Was it fun?"

The pecans are too sweet, like Nina really used pecan-shaped cubes of sugar instead of nuts, so Griff finds them with the tip of her fork and pushes them into a little pile at the side of her plate. "It was okay." She looks up at her mother. "I even drove on the highway and in town."

Einar steps off his stool. He doesn't get his hat. He just walks to the cash register and digs in his pocket. When Nina sees him she starts to come out of the kitchen, but he shakes his head. "Can I talk to you for a minute?" he says to her mother.

Jean looks at where Nina's acting like she's busy in the kitchen and goes to the cash register. She stands there looking at Einar like she's glad the counter's between them.

"She's fine with me," her grandfather says.

Griff mashes the pie and ice cream against the roof of her mouth so she won't have to listen over the sound her chewing makes.

"I never thought she wouldn't be." Her mother sounds impatient, like she wishes Einar would just pay for their pie and coffee and leave.

She hates it when adults talk like she isn't there. Or like they don't care if she's there, like she's not smart enough to understand what they're really saying. She'll write in her diary that she hates it when her mother does it, and hates it when old men do it too.

"I thought you might worry." Einar hands her mother some dollar bills. "I just wanted you to know she's safe."

"Is that it?" her mother asks.

"Do you care if I take her camping?"

Griff stops mashing the pie and holds her head real still.

Her mother hands Einar his change. "When were you thinking about going?"

"Tonight. In the Bighorns. Just car camping. We could sleep in the back of the truck."

Her mother looks at her, and she keeps her head down.

"Is she going to drive?"

"I am," Einar says.

The man at the table calls that he'd like iced tea instead of coffee, and her mother says sure thing, and tells Einar it'll be all right.

She has to listen real close because Einar lowers his voice. "She's a good girl," he says.

"I know she is."

"That doesn't happen by accident. I guess you know that too."

"No, it doesn't," her mother says. She's pushed the cash drawer shut and is leaning into the register.

"All right, then," her grandfather says.

THIRTY

———

J EAN POKES a finger at the row of buttons on the blender. It takes her three times, but she switches it off and the kitchen's quiet again. Just the neighbor's dog and the slap of the neighbor's sprinkler against the side of the house.

She holds her cigarette under the tap and throws the wet butt in the trash can under the sink and wonders just exactly what the hell **frappé** really means. They shouldn't sell blenders in Wyoming with a word like that on them. Stir, mix, liquefy. Got it. **Frappé** would be okay for a second middle name, like your maiden name. It's one of those words people think they know, but they haven't got a clue. Like she didn't about Crane.

She fills the two water glasses from the blender and walks back to the yard. Her arms and legs tingle and her face is completely numb. She likes the feeling from head to toe. It suits her. When she hands Nina her glass Nina doesn't even open her eyes. Her head hangs over the back of her lawn chair and she's whistling a Dwight Yoakam tune, sitting in her panties with her shirt still on. Her feet are in the wading pool in front of their chairs. She just holds out her hand and Jean puts the glass in it.

"How many is this?" she asks.

Jean steps into the pool. The water comes halfway up her calves. She hasn't taken her jeans off, just rolled them up under her knees. She stares down at the seahorses and octopuses and fish that decorate the bottom of the plastic pool. They're all smiling at her. "This is number three," she says, staring at the treasure chests dripping with jewels and gold coins.

"Is that it for the tequila?"

"There's enough for another round." Jean rocks back on her heels and almost falls. "Maybe two." Her heels are as numb as her face.

Nina rights her head and raises her glass in a toast. "Happy Margaritaville, Jean Marie."

Jean sips from her glass, and the cold, sour liquid makes the hinges of her jaw itch. She chatters her jaw without clicking her teeth together, like she's seen cats do sitting at a window staring at a bird feeder. "Jean Marie Frappé," she says, "a bad judge of men and mother of none."

"Don't tell me you're feeling sorry for your-self."

Jean sits in the second lawn chair, her feet still in the pool. "They ought to put a warning label on bottles of booze. 'Makes the worst parts of you more noticeable.'" Dried grass floats on the surface of the pool. "How come you don't water your yard?"

"So I won't have to cut it."

A car goes past in the street and honks, and they lift their glasses.

"Do you think I'm a shitty mother?"

Nina studies her, blinking against the late-afternoon light. She wrinkles her nose. "I think you're doing the best you can."

Jean sips her drink. Slower than the last one. She drank the last one too fast and it gave her a sharp, quick headache between her eyes. "I don't think I'm very good at being a mother. I could be a whole lot better."

Nina leans down over her knees and scoops water over her face and the back of her neck. A late-season grasshopper jumps in the pool and strokes in a small circle on the surface, and she splashes it out onto the brown grass. Then she takes a picture from her shirt pocket and holds it out to Jean. "That was her school picture.

Second grade. She was my daughter. Her name was Becky."

"Was?"

"Yeah."

Jean sets her drink beside the chair and holds the picture with both hands. Her jaw has started to chatter again. "Jesus Christ," she says. "Oh, Jesus Christ, Nina."

Nina takes the picture back and slips it in her shirt pocket. She pats the pocket and keeps her hand held to her breast. "She drowned in the river five years ago this summer. On the Fourth of July." She tilts her glass and slowly pours her drink into the wading pool, spelling the letter B in margarita. They both watch the green liquid spread in the clear water and drift to the pool's blue plastic bottom.

"I looked away for about two minutes, and she was in the water." Nina stands out of the chair. "As far as shitty mothers go, I probably top the list." She picks up her jeans where she's dropped them by her chair and starts toward the house. "I'm as drunk as I want to get."

"Nina?"

Nina turns back to her. "It's harder to lose a kid," she says. "You've got to give Einar that much." She looks at the house. The paint's peeled and chipped, the clapboards weathered to the same color as the yard. "A parent expects to have their kids around forever."

His shadow wakes her, or she thinks that that's what it must have been, because he doesn't look like he's waiting for her to answer a question. He's standing on the other side of the pool with the sun at his back.

She sits up straighter in the lawn chair. "Fuck you," she says.

His county Blazer's parked at the curb.

"Where's Griff?"

"She's with Einar. They went camping, and don't change the subject. Why the hell didn't you tell me Roy was in town?"

"He's not anymore."

"I already heard that from Einar. But I should've heard it from you, first goddamn thing. Right when he got here."

Crane looks back at the Blazer like he wishes he'd never gotten out. He shrugs like some little kid. If he'd told her about Roy before Einar had to take care of him, the gesture might've even seemed cute. Now, it just seems chickenshit.

She drains what's left of her margarita. It's warm and burns the back of her throat. "You think you have the balls to ask me what you really want to know?"

He folds his arms across his chest and sticks his hands in his armpits. She thinks she ought to buy the simple son of a bitch a book on body language.

"Will you have dinner with me?"

"You're so full of shit."

She stands out of the chair and slips against the bottom of the pool. She has to skate sideways to catch her balance. She picks up her glass where she's dropped it in the water, then turns and tosses it onto the seat of the chair. "What you really want to know is why I didn't leave Roy right away." She shuffles toward him across the wading pool. "After the first time I got hit. How could I let it happen? Haven't I got an ounce of fucking pride? How could I put my daughter through that?"

She stands close enough to feel his breath on her face. His forearms almost touch her breasts. She lights a cigarette and blows the smoke in his face.

"I thought you might like to have dinner." He drops his arms to his sides. "That's all."

She smiles. She juts her chin out and turns her cheek to him, and when she holds it there he kisses her. Up high, near her temple, like any spineless asshole would. Like she's his fucking Auntie Jean Marie Frappé.

She smiles again. So he'll be double, triple sure that it doesn't mean shit. "And now you can kiss my ass," she says.

She watches him walk to his car. She watches him climb in and shut the door and drive away without looking back. At least he got that part right, she thinks.

THIRTY-ONE

H E HAS THE GIRL help him load the acetylene tank and the tank of oxygen. They
tilt them both against the back of the flatbed and
push them up, one at a time, onto the wooden
decking. Then Einar climbs up and rights both
tanks, and walks each one to the steel frame built
against the cab, and cuts lengths of yellow baling
twine and ties them upright against the frame.
When he's done he closes the blade of his pocketknife against his leg and slips it into his pocket.

Griff stands at the back bumper. "We aren't
really going camping, are we?"

He can hear the disappointment in her voice.
"Why don't you run into the house and make us
some sandwiches. Make enough for Mitch too.
And get a warm jacket. Find one in the mudroom that'll fit."

She kicks at the trailer hitch. There's just her
head showing above the edge of the flatbed.

"You can tell me," she says. "I won't say anything to my mom. I won't tell her where we're going."

He walks to the back of the flatbed and drops what's left of the baling twine to her. She looks smaller standing below him. "You and I are going to set that bear loose."

She smiles at him like his hair's turned purple.

"I'm not kidding."

"The bear in the zoo?" When she says it out loud he can see the real possibility of it register in her face. "The bear that hurt Mr. Bradley?"

She looks toward Mitch's cabin. She doesn't look happy.

He sits on the back of the flatbed and slides to the ground from there.

"Is Mr. Bradley coming with us?"

"Later on he is. Not at first. At first it's just you and me."

He starts back toward the shop, and she walks at his side, looking up at him.

"Have you already talked to him about it?"

"Yes, I have. He's why we're doing it. He asked me to."

He coils the red and blue hoses for the welding tanks and finds his cutting torch and striker.

"You don't have to do everything he tells you."

She looks like she wants to hide, and her voice is higher than it was a minute ago.

"I think I do. And he didn't tell me to do anything. He asked. That isn't something he's done a lot." He loops the hoses over his shoulder and starts back for the truck. She stays right with him. "Anyway, you were the one who said you thought it was like Mitch and I were married."

"I was just trying to be funny," she says. "I couldn't think of anything else to say."

He tosses the coiled hoses and the cutting torch onto the bed behind the cab, then carries out a coil of cotton rope and the big green canvas tarp and hefts them up onto the flatbed too.

"I should stay here," she says.

He squats down. He grips her shoulders and holds her in front of him. "Look at me."

She bites her lip and stares at the ground. "I'm not brave enough," she says.

"Yes you are. You're good help."

She doesn't look up. "What does that mean?"

"It means I wouldn't ask you if I didn't think you could do it. I'm not going to let anything happen to you."

He stands and brushes off his jeans and she turns toward the pasture.

"I can't," she says.

"You don't have to, not if you don't want to."

He watches her relax, but just a little.

"Are you just going to get him out of the pit at the zoo?"

"I'm going to trailer him back to Yellowstone."

"In what?" Her voice has gone up again and she spins back around.

"I'm going to borrow one of those cages from the Fish and Game. One of the ones they've got on wheels." He starts toward the house. He can hear her behind him.

"How do you know the bear used to live in Yellowstone Park?"

"I don't. But I don't know where else he used to live, and the park'll be a good place for him. It's far enough away. I don't think he'll come back."

"Do you think he'll die if he stays in the zoo?"

"Yes, I do."

She comes closer to him. "He didn't look very happy when we saw him. Did you think he looked happy?"

"No, I didn't. It didn't seem like he had much of a life." He looks back at her. "You think about it," he tells her. "I'm not going anywhere till the sun's gone down."

THE LIGHTS are out in the cabin when Einar goes in, and he turns on the hinged lamp at the workbench. Mitch sits in a chair at the table by the foot of his bed. He's dressed and his canvas chorecoat lies across his lap. His good brown Stetson's turned upright on the table.

"Are you ready?" Einar asks.

"Yes, I am. I'm as ready as I'll ever be."

Einar opens the little refrigerator. He sets three vials of morphine on a shelf on the refrigerator door and takes out what's left in the box.

"I just got done with that awhile ago," Mitch says.

Einar puts the box on the workbench and sits in the chair, swinging the light away so he's out of the glare. "It's for the bear. If I get him in the cage I won't want him jumping around in there. Not all night long. I've got a horse syringe from the barn."

"That's a good idea. I wish I'd thought of it."

Mitch takes a pack of cigarettes from his shirt pocket and lights one. He blows out the match and drops it in a water glass on the table.

"I thought you quit those."

"I did, but I've always missed them. I've missed them for thirty-two years." He pats his shirt pocket. "I had Jean get me these from town."

"Were you saving them for tonight?"

"I had her get me a whole carton. I'm trying to start again."

He exhales, and the pleasure registers on his face.

"I guess they won't kill you. Not now."

"That's what I thought."

Einar checks his watch and stands. "I'll be back for you. You just sit there and enjoy your cigarettes. If I'm not back in an hour or two then I probably got caught and you ought to go to bed."

"I'm not so old and fucked up I wouldn't have figured that out for myself."

"I know you're not. I'm just talking. I'm not ready to go yet."

Mitch lifts a .45 from under his coat and sets it on the edge of the table. The blued barrel glows dully in the light. "You want to put this in your belt?"

"No, I don't. I never was any good with a handgun. I almost shot myself in the foot when we were overseas. If I had that in my belt I'd probably shoot my dick off."

"That wouldn't mean as much now as it used to."

Einar sits on the bed. He turns the .45 on the table so it's not pointed at him.

"I brought it back with me," Mitch says.

"All the way from Korea?"

Mitch waves at the footlocker under the workbench with his cigarette. "I kept it in there."

Einar bends to look at the locker. "You have anything else in there? I might take a hand grenade with me if you brought one of those back."

"There's just this old pistol."

"You're full of surprises tonight, aren't you?"

"I guess I am."

"I might try a cigarette, since you have so many."

Mitch hands him the pack and the book of matches, and he lights one and sets the pack and matches on the table.

"You could sit in here with me and smoke all night if you wanted. You don't have to do this, you know."

"I've made up my mind." Einar taps his ashes in the glass.

"Are you taking Griff with you?"

"She's in the truck. She didn't want to go at first, but after supper she said she felt like she'd come."

"Is she all right?"

"It just took her a little while to get used to the idea. I guess it took me awhile too." He drops the cigarette in the glass and stands beside the bed.

Mitch picks up the pack from where it sits on the table. "Do you want to take these with you?"

"I'll just bum one if I want."

Einar walks to the workbench and turns off the lamp, and the room falls into shadow and the yellow runs of light from the yardlight.

Mitch taps another cigarette out of the pack. "You've been a good friend to me."

"I know I have. It wasn't hard."

"I wanted to say it anyway."

"You didn't have to."

"I know. But I wanted to hear myself say it." He lights the cigarette.

"All right then. There anything else you need before I go?"

"I'm fine where I am."

EINAR TURNS OFF the two-lane with only his parking lights on and coasts to the gate in the chainlink fence. There's a sign wired to the fence: WYOMING GAME AND FISH. He sets the emergency brake and steps out and pulls the seatback forward. Griff turns and kneels on the seat and holds the seatback against her chest while he finds the bolt cutters and brings them out. The dome light shines in her hair.

He closes the door and leans in through the window. "If you see anyone coming you call out."

She looks through the back window and then over her shoulder, north along the highway. "Should I honk the horn?"

"I don't think you'd want to make that much noise. Just call out."

She nods and he walks to the gate and cuts a link out of the chain that holds it shut and pulls the chain free. He throws it in the weeds grown up against the fencing and swings both sides of the gate open and returns to the truck.

"Have you got your light ready?" he asks.

She holds the flashlight under her chin and turns it on and moans like she thinks a monster would.

"You're a very spooky kid," he says. "You know that?"

She's smiling. She's proud that he thinks she's spooky. She's proud she decided to come.

He drives through the gate and behind the squat brown building and turns in an arc through the graveled lot. When he stops she jumps out.

She points to the wheeled cage parked against the fence. "Is that it?"

"That's it. You remember everything I told you?"

"There wasn't that much," she says. She's still smiling.

He watches her in the side mirror as she runs to the cage and straddles the tongue at its front. He backs up slowly and stops when she waves the light.

When he gets to the back of the truck she's shining her light on the ballhitch but she's turned to study the cage. "It's just one of those tubes they put under the highway so the water can run through."

"A culvert pipe," he says. He cranks the tongue down until it seats over the ballhitch.

"Yeah," she says, still looking back, "a big culvert pipe. That's all it is." She shines the light over her shoulder. "They just put metal screens over the ends."

"You want to pay attention here?"

She brings the light back to the hitch, and he

snaps the footed stand up against the trailer's tongue and secures it.

"I thought about it," she says, "and this part doesn't scare me. Even if we get caught they won't send me to prison. I'm too little."

He straightens and stretches his back. "If we get caught you can tell them I made you come with me."

"They won't send you to prison either," she says. "If they sent you to prison then there wouldn't be anyone to take care of me or Mr. Bradley. They won't do that. And the sheriff's going out with my mom."

He loops the safety chain over the hitch. "It'll probably take these government boys a day or two before they even notice that somebody stole their cage."

She snaps off the flashlight. "Before, you said we were just borrowing it."

He walks to the trailer and kicks the cinder blocks away from where they're wedged in front of the tires.

"It's the same thing. I'm never going to get back in Social Security what I've paid in taxes."

She makes a sound he doesn't recognize, and he takes the light from her and shines it on her face. She's brought a hand over her mouth, and she's giggling hard enough that her shoulders are shaking.

"Did I say something funny?"

She drops her hand but she's still giggling. "I'm glad I came with," she says.

"SHOULD I STAND outside and wave which way you should drive?" she asks. She's kneeling on the seat, watching him back the cage to the fence at the edge of the pit.

"I'm fine," he says. He eases the cage back against the fence, snug, until he can see the fencing flex against the pressure. He shuts the engine off and they both look toward the zoo entrance. The truck windows are down and they can hear the other animals, the bobcats and coyotes up in their pens, the coyotes yipping.

"You still glad to be here?"

She nods and they get out of the truck. She helps him ease the welding tanks off the flatbed and walk them along the trailer, clear back to the fence.

"Don't you need one of those black helmets?" she asks. "So you won't burn your eyes out?"

"How do you know about welding helmets?"

"Roy had one."

"I'll just be cutting." He's hooking up the hoses to the tank valves. "You don't need the helmet when you're just cutting."

The bear stands in the middle of the pit, rocking back and forth, his eyes half closed, just as he has every day Einar's seen him. They watch him turn and pace in front of the undercut at the far end and then return to the middle, still rocking.

"He looks worse than before." She has her hands hooked in the fencing, looking down at the bear.

"Yes, he does."

"Do you really think he'll get in the cage?"

"Yes, I do," he says. "Come on." He stands at the side of the cage, bent over, with his hands laced in front of him like a stirrup. "Let me boost you up there."

"I forgot what was next," she says. She steps in his hands and grips his shoulders and he lifts her up, and she swings a leg over the top and sits straddling the cage, her legs splayed out. "Jimmy's not this fat," she says.

Einar's watching the bear start up the ramp toward them, stop and sit, then walk back down and stand. He looks at the top of the cage again, at Griff's dark outline against the sky. But he can't see her face and it panics him.

He steps up on the runner and grips her leg. "Come down off there," he says.

"I haven't put the rope through yet."

"I don't care." He holds her by the cuff of her jeans. "I don't want you up there."

The bear huffs, and they turn and watch it start up the ramp again and stop.

"I can do it," she says.

Her face is still in shadow. Behind her there's the vague swell of the lights from Ishawooa.

"I want to do it." She doesn't sound scared, just determined. "I'm half Viking," she says.

She turns her head just enough that he can see the flash of light in her eyes and on her teeth.

"All right," he says. He keeps a hand on her leg as she scoots up to the angle-iron housing above the very back of the cage. She grabs hold of it and looks down at the bear.

Einar can see her face clearly now, and she nods at him like her father might've done—with confidence—and he steps back and watches her thread the rope through the pulley at the top of the housing. He looks back down and the bear's watching her too.

"This is cool," she says. She drops the soft cotton rope over the side of the cage.

"That's it," Einar says. "That's as much as I can stand."

She raises her arms over her head, turns at the waist and lets herself slide toward him. Like they've done it a thousand times before and he's always been there to catch her.

He takes her under the arms and sets her down, and she stands at his side while he pulls back on the rope, hand over hand, and the mesh door at the rear of the cage raises into the metal housing.

"Now?" she asks, standing by the open pickup door.

He ties the rope off. "Yeah, now," he says, and she scrambles up over the seat and slides back down with the grocery bag of honeyed meat.

She holds the bag open as he unwraps the balls and drops them one at a time through an eight-inch hole cut into the side of the cage. They hear the meat drop onto the floor and so does the bear. He growls deeply in his chest, still rocking, but his eyes are fixed on where they stand.

"That's enough," he tells her.

"There's still one left."

"Get in the truck." He takes the bag from her. "Right now," he says.

He watches her climb up on the seat and shut both doors, and once he can see her kneeling on the seat, looking through the glass and steel mesh at the back of the cab, he moves to the rear of the cage. And the bear's right there, nearly at the top of the ramp, pacing, his head back, tasting the air with his open mouth. When Einar lights the cutting torch, he steps away from the hissing blue flame and growls, but he stands his ground.

Einar starts on the fence from the top down. On this side of the cage first, then the other. The metal pops and sizzles and he can see the flame's reflection sparking in the bear's eyes.

THIRTY-TWO

ROY DROVE AWHILE and stopped when he started to tremble, then lay down across the truckseat and fell asleep. When he woke he drove a little farther but had to stop again.

He can still hear the smirking son of a bitch. "Jean Gilkyson's a friend of mine." Friend, my ass. You didn't have to be there to hear what he was really saying: "Hello, you used-to-be-motherfucker, I'm the one boning her now."

The waitress asks, "Are you okay?"

Roy stares into his coffee, afraid he might cry again. He'd cried in the car and that's why he stopped now. He nods with his head looking down. "I'm just fine," he says.

But he's not. He's a long fucking way from fine. Why the hell did he let those hillbilly bastards think they could run him off? It was the shock of it all. It had to be. Hell, he might still be in shock.

"Well, I think she's a fool," the waitress says.

Roy looks up. He doesn't have to look very far because she's bent down over the counter. She smiles real sweet and lets her eyes fall more open, like she's listening with her eyes.

"How'd you know?" he asks.

"Big, good-looking guy like you," she says. "There's not a lot that's going to bring a man like you down to his knees." She tucks her chin in a little. Glances down at her fine set of knockers like she's making sure she didn't leave them at home.

"I'm okay," he says. "Really. I just think I'm one of those people who fall in love too easy."

She pushes back from the counter. "I hear you there." She pinches her skirt where it's ridden up a little at her hips and works it back down.

"I came up here to ask her to marry me," he says.

"To Casper?"

He shakes his head no. "Ishawooa."

"That's three hours north."

"Every bit of three hours," he says. "I drove straight through from Iowa to get there." He shakes his head since this seems to help. "And then I started back and stopped here."

What kind of woman can do what she did?

THIRTY-THREE

SHE FEELS BEAT UP. Dizzy. Her muscles ache and so do her joints. There's a damp spot on the throw pillow where she's drooled in her sleep, so she turns it over and leans it against the arm of the couch and wipes her mouth with the back of her hand. Her jeans are still rolled up to her knees and she unrolls them before she stands.

She drinks a glass of water at the kitchen sink, shakes two aspirin out of the bottle above the sink and takes them with a second glass of water. She lights a cigarette and walks outside. Nina's sitting on the front step in her shirt and panties, and Jean sits down beside her.

"I thought you'd be in bed," she says.

"I can't sleep when I drink. I mean I sleep okay when I first go down, but then I wake up and can't get back to sleep."

"Is it late?"

Nina holds her wrist up to catch the light from the kitchen. "It's five to midnight. How do you feel?"

"Like warmed-over shit."

"That's warmed-over dogshit."

"Are you sure?"

"That's the way I've always heard it." Nina reaches across and takes the cigarette from Jean's hand and takes a drag and hands it back.

"I'm sorry about Becky."

"I'm sorry about her too, but that's how things turned out. Nothing's going to change because we're sorry."

"Do you want an aspirin?"

"I already had some."

A mosquito buzzes at Jean's ear and she slaps her neck.

"It's nice it warmed up again," Nina says, "but we aren't going to get many more nights like this."

"No, we aren't." She flicks her cigarette into the yard, and they watch the red glow at its tip fade and burn out. "When Griff was little she told me she didn't want to get old and die. She said she didn't want somebody to come along and take all her stuff."

"What'd you tell her?"

"I told her it was a good thing she didn't have

very much." Jean stretches her legs and rests her bare heels on the walk. She can still feel the warmth in the concrete. "Which is about like I feel now. Like it's good I haven't got much."

Nina stands and opens the screen door but doesn't step inside. "You're welcome in this house for as long as you like, but you're making my head hurt more than it should."

Jean turns at the waist. Nina stands above her, outlined by the kitchen light. A moth bounces against the screen to the side of her shadowed face.

"Is that something you've wanted to say for awhile?"

"It's something you say to someone you care about. If you don't care it's easier to keep your mouth shut."

Jean lights another cigarette and drops her chin to stretch the back of her neck.

"I'm sorry your husband's dead and I'm sorry you were driving the car when he died, but I'll bet he's not tickled about it either. I think that's another way to look at it."

"I have looked at it like that."

"Well, you should try again."

Jean exhales and watches the smoke lift in the warm air. "It isn't your fault Becky drowned."

"Yeah it is, and yeah it's not. But I've quit

screwing up my own life because I can't figure it out."

"You think I am?"

"Well, of course I do. Don't you?"

Nina's chest rises and falls, the outline of it, standing sideways at the screen, her hand still on the door.

"Do you think I'm screwing up my daughter's life too?"

"I don't think it stops with your daughter."

A car turns at the corner, and Jean watches the headlights sweep the front of the house. A man sits alone in a pickup parked at the curb. He raises a hand to shield his face, and Jean draws her feet under her.

"That's just Curtis."

"Curtis Hanson?"

"Yeah."

"Is he drunk?"

"We're the ones who were drunk. I might still be a little bit." Nina swats the moth away from the screen. "He's parked there because none of us think your old boyfriend's gone for good."

Now that she knows it's Curtis in the truck she wonders why she didn't notice him before. "Did you ask him to park there?"

"No, I didn't. I didn't ask Starla or Jimmy J.

from the Conoco either, but when Curtis goes home in a couple hours one of them will be sitting out there."

Then they watch as Crane pulls up behind Curtis. He's driving his own pickup, not the county Blazer.

"This is a good place, Jean. There's good people here, and you don't have to, but if you'd pull your head out of your ass you might notice."

"I'll leave right now if you want me to."

"Nobody wants you to leave but you. I don't even think Einar does."

"Oh, he sure does."

"Well, that's between you and him. At the café today he didn't look like he wanted to put Griff on a bus. Do you think he did?"

"No, I don't."

Crane's walked up to Curtis's truck. Jean can hear them talking but can't make out the actual words.

"I'm going to start a pot of coffee. If Curtis didn't bring a thermos he might like a cup."

Jean hears the door shut and turns to it. Nina stands just inside the screen.

"Are we still friends?"

"I'm probably one of the best friends you're ever going to have."

"I could make the coffee."

"I know you could, but I'm known for my coffee."

Jean watches Crane coming across the lawn. Her neck's still tight, so she rotates her head first toward one shoulder and then the other.

"Are you okay?" he asks.

"I took a nap and had a couple of aspirin a little while ago." She draws on her cigarette and flicks the butt into the yard.

"Those things'll kill you. I guess you've heard that."

"Maybe that's why I smoke as much as I do. Have you come back to arrest me?"

"This isn't California. You can pretty much smoke in Wyoming anywhere you want."

"I mean for when you were here before. For me being drunk and disorderly."

He looks past her to where Nina's running water in the kitchen. "You were right when I was here before. I was thinking everything you said I was."

"About why I didn't leave Roy before I did?"

"Yeah. About that." He puts his hands in his pockets. He widens his stance and stares down at her legs. "And I should've told you right away when he got here. First thing. I was wrong not to." He pulls his hands from his pockets and stands straighter. "I was afraid you'd leave with him. I was afraid I wouldn't see you again."

Jean lets him see her smile, a real smile. "You want to stay for a cup of coffee?"

"I'll stay a little while," he says, "but I can't drink coffee this late."

THIRTY-FOUR

———— — ————

K ARL STANDS and whines, and Mitch gets out of his chair. He braces up against his canes and shuffles to the window and sees the headlights in the drive and the dark shape of the trailer. "Well I'll be damned," he says. Karl whines again.

Mitch leans against the table and pulls on his canvas chorecoat. He buttons it halfway and checks the safety on the .45 and slips it into the side pocket. He wants this single night more than anything he's wanted for years and means to get through it like a man. From front to back, from now until tomorrow morning. That's what he's asked for. He asked God, and he's never asked for much, not from God or Einar or anybody else. He feels like his prayers have been answered. He feels better than he has. He feels good to go.

"Get back to bed now," he says, and Karl circles on his carpet scrap and lies down, and when Mitch steps onto the porch Einar's already come up in the yard.

"By God, you got him." He thumps a cane on the porchboards.

"Did you think we wouldn't?"

"I wasn't certain you'd get him in that cage."

Einar steps up on the porch. "He walked right in. I dropped the fencing down and he backed away from it and pranced around some, but that was it. In he went. Like he was ready."

"Maybe he was."

"I guess so."

They look toward the cage.

Einar asks, "You're sure you want to do this?"

"I wouldn't miss it for anything in the world."

"Just so you're sure."

"I had another shot an hour ago. I'll be all right till morning." He wants to add "God willing," but doesn't. He throws an arm across Einar's shoulders and that's how they get to the cage, where Einar steps away and he leans on his canes to catch his breath. "You know I want to see him."

"I thought you might."

Griff stands at the far side of the truck, looking up the lane like she thinks they've been followed. "We should go," she says.

"We can go in a minute. Mitch needs to look at this bear first."

Einar unties the ropes at the nose of the trailer and folds back the tarp and steps away, and Mitch leans in close.

"Go step on the brake lights," he says, and Griff runs to the cab and the brake lights flash and hold steady.

He works a cane in through the mesh and lifts the bear's lip with the tip of the cane. The animal's canine shines pink in the red light. He opens an eye and lets it fall shut, and Mitch draws the cane back. "You ought to look at this big son of a bitch," he says.

"I already have." Einar's watching the lane. "I've had a good look at him."

Mitch pivots around on his better leg. "How much medicine did you give him?"

Einar steps past him to retie the tarp. "I figured he weighed about five times what you do, so I gave him about that much. A little more to be on the safe side."

Mitch finds where the moon is on its arc across the sky. He forgot to check his clock when he left the cabin. "Well, hell," he says, "I guess we better get gone."

GRIFF SITS between them with a leg on either side of the gearshift. She stays awake watching the road until they top out over the Bighorns, and then she leans against Mitch and squirms and settles and goes to sleep.

He loops an arm around her so she won't sway in the curves. "How'd she do?"

Einar looks down at the sleeping girl. "She did everything just right. I even think she liked it. She got excited."

They come off the last switchback at the base of the mountains and Mitch watches the shadows the moon casts over the Bighorn Basin, gray and tan and slate, and the Absarokas farther west, the mountains black and jagged against the sky. He lowers his window an inch and sniffs at the night air. He tries to remember the last time they came this way and decides it must have been ten years ago. They'd sold a bull to a man in the Wapiti Valley and trailered him over. That animal's no doubt dead by now. He thinks the man might be too.

"We should've done this more when we were

younger," he says softly, so as not to wake the girl. "Gotten out now and then."

"There was too much to do when we were younger."

"You telling me you can remember everything we did?"

"Sure I can. I can remember most of it."

"Well I can't, by God. But I would've remembered a trip like this."

They drive down the main drag of Lovell, under the row of streetlights, and Mitch holds a hand above Griff's closed eyes. He looks back at the trailer.

"You think we ought to check him?"

Einar glances in the rearview mirror. "I was thinking we would when we got on the other side of Cody."

They drive through Byron and Powell and in and out of Cody without speaking. It's how they've mostly traveled in the past, and worked and taken their meals, for over fifty years, in an easy silence.

Einar pulls into a National Forest campground forty miles west of Cody and they sit for a minute and listen to the engine tick. Griff repositions herself against Mitch's side but doesn't wake.

"We good on gas?" Mitch asks.

"We've got plenty. You hungry? She packed some sandwiches if you are."

"I'm fine."

Einar steps out and eases the door shut, and Mitch watches through the back window as he lifts the tarp away from the trailer and steps back and then ties it down again.

When he's back in the truck Mitch asks, "He's awake, isn't he?"

Einar starts the truck. "Not all the way. He'll be just right by the time we get there. I was thinking we'd turn him out when we get over the pass. By the lake."

"I've always liked it there. It's a pretty spot."

Einar checks the side mirror when he pulls out. "I don't think I've seen five cars all night."

"There was eight."

Einar works up through the gears, gaining speed. "You counted?"

"Yes, I did."

He can see Einar smile in the dashlights. "That's something old men do."

"I am an old man."

"Well, you're just a month older than me."

Mitch shifts against the sleeping girl. She's

warm and limber as a cat, and it makes him glad to think of her like that. If the pain was bad she'd just be weight. "You remember that fella we sold a bull to back down this valley?"

"Sure I do, but I imagine he's gone. That was some time ago."

"Ten years."

"Well, he wasn't a young man when he bought that bull."

There's a mile of palisade to the right of the truck, knobby and dull in the moonlight.

"I hope there's not a park ranger at the gate," Einar says. "If there's a ranger I haven't thought how we ought to explain the trailer."

"They won't have a ranger there this time of night." Mitch watches the Shoshone River below them off to the left, its rapids flashing in the weak light. "Not this time of year either."

Griff sits up straight and stares through the windshield and closes her eyes and lies down against Mitch again.

"I can remember being able to do that when I was a kid," he says.

"Sleep in a truck?"

"Yeah, that too. But I meant wake up and go right to sleep again." He smooths her hair away from her face. "I'm not sure I'm prepared for her to leave," he says. "I don't think I could stand it."

"She's not going to stay with us without her mother."

"I know it." Mitch holds his hand cupped against her cheek. He can feel her breath on his fingers. "That's what I'm saying. I'm saying I don't think I could stand it."

Einar lowers his window enough to spit and rolls it back up again. "I'm not sure I could either."

THE LIGHTS are out in the ticket booth at the east entrance to Yellowstone and they don't even have to come to a stop. There's no traffic over Sylvan Pass and it's only four in the morning when they park by the lake. There's a wind from the west and the water slaps at the pebbled shore. A pair of white swans float a hundred yards out, rising and falling on the waves. When Einar opens the door, the cab fills with the wet early-morning air.

"You aren't planning on dragging that trailer back, are you?"

"No, I'm not. I plan on cranking it up and driving away from the son of a bitch."

"I'll wake her."

"Why don't you." Einar watches the swans. "If I was her I wouldn't want to miss this part of it."

Mitch jostles her and then again, and she sits up and looks around.

"Are we there?"

"We're by Yellowstone Lake."

"Where's Einar?"

"He's out getting the tarp off the trailer."

She slips across the seat, under the steering wheel, and out of the cab. She doesn't even seem drowsy. "I should help," she says.

"You come back in here with me before he opens that cage."

She stands at the open door, holding on to the armrest but looking at Einar. "I will."

Mitch watches them lay the tarp out flat next to the cage and fold it and lift it onto the truckbed. Einar helps Griff up onto the bed, and she pushes the tarp snug against the cab next to where the acetylene tank's tied upright. She presses a hand against the steel mesh, and Mitch raises one against the inside of the window, and her face lights up in a wild smile. He sees the bear stand up behind her and lets his hand drop away.

It swings its head and paws at the front of the cage, and Mitch can hear the rasp of its claws on the metal. The sound makes his thighs and the small of his back tingle.

Griff jumps off the truckbed and climbs in the cab. Her hair's tossed and she smells damp and piney.

"He's awake," she says, kneeling on the seat beside Mitch with her arms folded on the seatback.

Through the back window they watch Einar coil the ropes and toss them on top of the tarp. He blocks the trailer tires with stones from the lakeshore and cranks the tongue off the ball-hitch.

"Shouldn't he do that last?" Griff asks.

"I don't think he wants to be out there once the bear's loose."

She nods.

The release rope's coiled and tied at the side of the cage, still fed through the pulley mounted at the top of the angle-iron framework at the rear of the cage. They watch Einar untie it and walk back toward the flatbed uncoiling the loops as he comes. The rope's long enough for him to stand between the trailer and the truck, where he looks back at them. Most of his chest and his shoulders rise above the flatbed, and he's grinning like Mitch hasn't seen him in a long while.

"He looks happy," Griff says, as if she's known him all his life.

"Yes, he does."

"What do you think, boys and girls?" Einar calls.

Mitch holds a thumb up in the back window and Griff holds up both thumbs as Einar grips the rope tighter. He's still smiling like he's twenty, looking back at them and pulling hard on the rope, quick as he can, hand over hand, and as the cage door raises into the angle-iron framework with a sharp, solid slap the bear charges against the mesh at the front of the cage, right in Einar's face. He rocks back, and Griff yelps and pushes away from the seatback, and totters for just an instant before losing her balance. She throws her arms up to catch herself and falls against the dash and then the gearshift, knocking the truck out of gear. That's what Mitch sees happen, all at once with no way to stop it. And then the night slows.

He watches the nose of the cage drop and the rear of it rise up in the night, the bear backing out of it like he's shot from a cannon. Then the truck drifts back over the trailer's tongue and Einar's pinched between the edge of the chest-high flatbed and the nose of the trailer like he's no more substantial than a shaft of dried grass. Mitch watches him disappear, just drop, when the truck rocks forward from the impact. That's what he'll remember for the rest of his life about how they set the bear free.

What he won't remember is sweeping an arm against the gearshift to fix the truck in place, or getting out of the truck, or telling Griff to stay put.

The next thing he remembers is standing between the bear and Einar. He'll remember looking down and seeing the pistol in his hand, seeing the metal foot that held the trailer tongue snapped in half, watching Einar writhe in the sandy soil by the truck's back axle. He'll remember hearing, as if it wasn't his own voice at all but that of a stranger speaking clearly and calmly, "I'm not curling up in a ball this time either, you ugly son of a bitch."

And he'll remember the bear tilting his big dish-shaped face like he understands, then turning slowly and loping away along the edge of the lake, just in the water, the beads of spray all about him.

"AM I ABOUT to get mauled?" Einar asks.

Mitch looks to where Einar lies holding his

side. He can hear the swans trumpeting out on the water. "He's gone," he says.

Einar drags himself out with just one arm and gets to his knees and then raises that hand to grip the side of the flatbed and pull himself to his feet. His other arm's pressed against his ribs, and he's breathing in short, shallow bursts. His face shines slick with sweat.

"How bad is it?" Mitch asks.

He's seen Einar hurt. He knows that when he's just skinned up or stunned or needs a few stitches he'll curse and raise all kinds of hell. And that when he's hurt bad he'll go quiet, like this.

Griff jumps out of the truck and stands lifting herself onto her toes, up and down, one foot and then the other, like she's getting ready for a race.

"I just got the wind knocked out of me. That's all," Einar says. His mouth hangs open, and he's watching Griff. "I just got mashed a little. Get back in the truck."

"I hit the gearshift," she says. She puts a hand over his where he holds on to the steel edge of the flatbed. "I didn't mean to. It was an accident."

"I know you didn't." Einar looks away from her. He's still having trouble breathing.

"Your grandfather's fine," Mitch says, with all the confidence he can muster.

EINAR DRIVES them back over the pass and through Cody, and they're on the east side of the Bighorns when the sun comes up. He drives with just his left hand and holds his right arm pressed against his side, his forearm in his lap. Mitch watches him, and the girl, and sometimes the road. He doesn't feel tired or hurt or anxious. He doesn't feel like he needs another shot yet. He feels fine.

He watches Griff make every shift. She sits on the edge of the seat and stares at Einar's legs to see when he depresses the clutch. She cried for half an hour when they first started back, but Einar told her it wasn't helping and she quit. Mitch kept his hand on her shoulder so she'd know she wasn't alone and still she wouldn't look at him, wouldn't even glance away from Einar's legs, and for some time he wondered if he was there at all. He imagined that the bear had killed him and he was allowed this sweet reprieve as simply a passenger, feeling fine.

At the top of the Bighorns Einar said, "Why don't you light me one of those cigarettes?" and

Mitch lit them both one, and they cracked the windows and the blue smoke swirled around in the cab. When he inhaled he knew he was alive for sure and felt more than just fine. He felt lucky.

IT'S TEN in the morning when they get to Ishawooa and Einar pulls the truck into the emergency room lot at the hospital and shuts it down. He leans against the door panel and closes his eyes, his face nearly as white as the ambulance parked in the lot.

"I'm going to say I fell out of my barnloft." He opens his eyes and looks at Griff.

She just nods. When Einar looks at him Mitch nods too.

Einar looks back at the girl. "If they ask any questions I want you to say you saw it happen. You shouldn't say a word about the bear or the little trip we just had."

She nods again. She's still sitting on the edge of the seat, holding the round knob on the end of the gearshift with both hands, and Mitch leans forward and lifts her hands off the knob and lays them in her lap.

Einar opens the door and slides out and stands there bent over, his right arm still tight against his side. He looks at Mitch and laughs up high in his throat. "Shit," he says. "That wasn't as bad as I thought it would be."

"You need some help?" Mitch asks. He feels like it wouldn't be any trouble at all to pick Einar up in his arms.

Einar shakes his head and grimaces and chuckles in his throat again. "Just so you know," he says, "I wouldn't have missed last night for anything in the world. Not one bit of it."

"It was a fine night." Mitch looks down at the girl so Einar will look at her too. She sits staring at where her hands are crossed on her knees.

"You think you can drive home?" Einar asks.

"Yes, sir," she says. She snaps her head up. "I know I can."

Einar raises his left hand toward the clutch and brake pedals. "Your blocks of wood are behind the seat. If you have trouble with them Mitch can lay over and help you get them bolted on."

She says, "Einar, I didn't mean to," and starts to cry again.

"I know you didn't. Quit that."

She holds her hands over her face, and Einar steps toward her.

"Look at me," he says. "What you did was

make last night a better story than it should've been. That's all."

She lets her hands drop from her face.

"We couldn't have done it without you," Mitch says. He pats her shoulder. "We couldn't even have come close."

She looks from one man to the other.

"If you hadn't bumped that gearshift with your bony little butt we'd've never known Mitch could get around without his canes like he did. Did you see him sprint out there to keep that bear off me?"

She says she did. She looks at Mitch and dries her eyes on her shirttail and hiccups.

"All right," Einar tells her. "I guess I'll go in there now." He winks at Mitch and grins again like they're young and don't really believe in dying, like these mountains are a sweet, high place they've never had to leave, not a single day in their lives.

THIRTY-FIVE

———————

W HEN HE OPENS his eyes it's Jean he sees, and he's shocked that he expected to see her. She paces at the foot of his hospital bed.

"Griff call you?" he asks.

She stops pacing and sits on a chair by the side of his bed. "She told me you were in here."

When he sits up straighter and breathes in they can hear his ribs crackle, and she starts out of the chair.

"I'm fine," he says, and she sits again but doesn't lean back in the chair or cross her legs to get comfortable.

"I thought maybe you had a heart attack," she says. "That was the first thing I thought of when Griff called."

"I'm just bunged up. I'll try for a heart attack next time."

"That isn't what I meant. I meant I was worried." She steps to the nightstand and pours a cup of water for herself and one for him from a beige pitcher. "You don't look very good."

He plucks at his hospital gown. "It's hard to look your best in one of these little blue nightshirts."

She sits in the chair again, holding her cup with both hands. "How pissed off do I get to be at you for taking my daughter out in the middle of the night to set a grizzly bear free?"

"Is that what she told you?"

"She said you fell out of your loft."

He sips his water and sets the plastic cup on the wheeled table by the far side of the bed. "I'd say you should get as pissed off as you want."

She drinks the whole cup of water and walks to the foot of the bed and stands with her back to him. "Every day I wish it had been me that died in that car and not Griffin." She says it all at once, and it's not what he thought she was going to say. He realizes he's always wished she would've died too, and that he doesn't anymore. He looks down at the IV tube taped to the back of his hand. He makes a fist and looks up at her. What he sees is a nervous woman standing in a small, bleak hospital room. His dead son's wife. A young widow with dark circles under her eyes.

"It would've been better if you'd both lived."

She starts toward him but stops and stands

behind the chair. She opens her mouth to say something but doesn't. After awhile she says, "Crane says he needs to talk to you."

"I'll bet he does."

"He says mostly he wants to know where to find the Fish and Game cage. To tell them where it is."

"You can tell him it's parked up by Yellowstone Lake. You can tell him you heard it from a reliable source."

She sits in the chair again. She has her upper lip sucked back between her teeth.

"I was falling-down drunk when Mitch got mauled. You ought to know that." He raises his chin and breathes in deeply enough for his ribs to crackle again. He clenches his teeth. "If I'd been sober it never would've happened like it did."

She sits back in the chair. "Mitch never said anything about it."

"He never would."

A nurse named Sally comes in and takes his temperature and his blood pressure and checks the flow in his IV. "Have you gone to the bathroom?" she asks.

"Yes, ma'am, I did. Before I got here." He smiles at her. "I'll probably need to go again when I get home."

Sally's taking his pulse, watching the second hand on her watch. "You might need to go before then, Mr. Gilkyson. Dr. Christensen's not going to let you go home just yet." She looks at Jean as if she, at least, might understand what she has to put up with. "The doctor said he wants to make sure there was no internal damage."

"I'll help him to the bathroom if he needs it," Jean says.

The nurse turns to Einar. "Liquid in, liquid out, Mr. Gilkyson. We keep track."

"Yes, ma'am," he says. "I'm sorry, but I still guess I'll wait to get home."

The nurse swings the door shut behind her without looking back.

"I'll take you home right now if you want to go," Jean says. "I've got Crane's truck."

Einar presses a thumb into the elastic wrap around his chest and winces. "I better stay awhile longer. I think I could get to sleep again if I tried. Maybe you could check on Mitch if you have the time."

Jean stands. "I'll drive out there right now." She takes her jacket from the back of the chair and folds it over her arm. "Can I bring you anything?"

"You could let Griff go to school here."

She drops her head toward him. As though

she needs glasses and can't quite focus on him. "Here in Ishawooa?"

"It's a good school. There's nothing wrong with it."

She sits back on the edge of the chair and bites her lip again, then crosses her arms over her chest. "I'll think about it," she says. "Thank you, Einar."

"Course I couldn't be counted on to help her with her homework. That's something you'd have to do all by yourself."

THIRTY-SIX

———

SHE GOT the afternoon milking done and turned the cow into the pasture and stood by the gate watching Jimmy run along the far fenceline with his neck arched and his tail twirling behind him like a pinwheel. She thought it must be the best thing in the world to be a horse on a clear day. Einar's told her that it's less than best in winter, or in the rain, or when the flies are bad, but that's not today.

She watches her mother leave Mr. Bradley's cabin and climb the little hill where her father's and grandmother's tombstones are. She watches her mother sit in the chair that her grandfather keeps on the hill.

When her mother came home she wasn't even mad. She said maybe someday real soon they could take a ride on Jimmy, and when Griff told her they'd better ask first she just smiled and said Jimmy used to be her father's horse. She said it would make his soul happy to see them riding his horse together.

She looks at Jimmy turning at the end of the pasture and tries to see if there's any sign of her father's soul on his back. She can't tell, and then she wonders what else her mother knows that she hasn't said anything about.

Her mother had unpacked her shopping bag into the dresser in the loft and knelt down in front of her and kissed her and hugged her for a long time and told her they wouldn't sleep in different houses again. Not until she got old enough to have a family of her own.

Her mother told her that Einar wasn't too sick, that he'd only cracked a couple of ribs, and he was lucky that that's all the damage he did falling out of the barn. "A man his age trying to learn to fly from a barnloft," she said, and winked. Then her mother went out to talk to Mr. Bradley.

Griff got her diary out and looked at the list of things she hates about her mother but couldn't think of anything else, so she wrote that she liked it when her mother winked at her and talked about Einar learning to fly. Like it was a joke just between the two of them. Like she wasn't just a kid and her mom wasn't just a grown-up with bad taste in men.

And then she turned the page to her other list and wrote that she likes it that old men are real tough. A lot tougher than they look. She carefully printed out that they can get hurt and act like it doesn't mean a thing. Like the bunny in the commercial for batteries.

She walks back into the barn and lifts the piece of plywood off the top of the milk pail. She'd laid it over the pail so the cats wouldn't climb in and drink all the milk, or even drown.

She picks up the pail with both hands and walks straddling it, like she has to when it's full, over to the cats' saucers and fills each one to the brim. She takes a deep breath before she picks the pail up again. She still doesn't trust the raccoons, and when she gets to the granary she's surprised they aren't there. She's relieved, too. She sets the pail next to the rocker and looks out the window. She watches Curtis walking along the bank of an irrigation ditch and wonders what the pasture will look like with snow on it. She can hardly wait. She wishes it would snow today, but it's still too warm. Her mother said she might go to school here, and if she does she thinks she might make a friend. And then when it snows her life will be perfect.

She feels her calf tickle and jumps away because she thinks the raccoons have come back.

But it's just Jack. She picks him up and when she turns around Roy's standing in the doorway. He looks fidgety and mean, just like he always does, and he's holding Einar's rifle in front of him with both hands.

He smiles his Roy smile, which never means he's happy, and says, "Hello, little girl. Did you miss me?" He steps closer. "What's the matter? Cat got your tongue?" He laughs his Roy laugh, which never means he's happy either.

She puts Jack down at her feet. She's surprised she isn't even scared, and she smiles to show Roy she isn't.

Roy grins. "See there," he says. "I think you missed old Roy."

"That's my grandfather's gun."

Roy holds the rifle up like he forgot he had it and he's glad she reminded him. "What, this?" And then he doesn't even bother with his fake smile or his fake laugh. He just says, "I heard your dear old granddaddy got himself laid up." Real mean, like he's the reason Einar's in the hospital.

She turns to the window. She can still see Curtis in the pasture, loading something into the back of his pickup truck. She can't see the hill where her father's buried, so she doesn't know whether her mother's still there.

"Don't do it," Roy says.

"I was just looking outside."

She makes sure that absolutely nothing shows on her face. She has the same tight feeling she used to have when she lived in Roy's trailer, and she doesn't want to let it show. She won't let him see her feeling tight or scared. She's done with Roy Winston, and he ought to know it. She wants to prove she's as tough as Einar and Mr. Bradley, that she lives here now, and doesn't care if he's got a gun in his hands.

He takes another step toward her and she smiles to give him something to look at and bends her legs a little bit. She doesn't want him to guess she's going to run. She turns to the window again like she's going to yell for Curtis to come save her. She doesn't think Curtis could hear her, but she wants to give Roy something else to think about. She doesn't want him to know she's going to get past him and through the door and run so fast that even if he was on Jimmy he couldn't catch her.

When she turns back around his arm is already in the air. He's already brought it up and it's starting down, and he's closed his dirty-guardrail fingers into a fist. She raises her face up just a little. If she had more time she'd step right into his ugly fist. She wants him to know he doesn't scare her at all, that she's tough enough to take anything he could ever give her.

WHEN SHE WAKES UP it's almost dark, and she has to try twice to sit. Her head throbs and she holds the palm of a hand against her temple, against where her ear rings, and she can feel the sticky blood. And the pieces of hay stuck in the blood, she can feel them too. She doesn't need a mirror to know her face is a mess.

She has to get on her hands and knees and then kneel for awhile, and then she uses the rocker to pull herself up. There's enough light that she can see the pail got knocked over and all the milk's run out.

She goes through the barn next to the stalls, where she has boards to hold on to. She stands in the big opening at the end of the barn, balancing against one of the big doors. Karl's in the workyard, sitting next to something dark and lumpy, like a little bear that's sleeping out there in the open, and he's howling. She starts toward the dog. She tries to run but it's like her head's lifting up and she has to run sideways to catch it. She keeps her legs going.

She can hear Roy and her mother in Einar's house. She can see the lights are on. Her mother screams, "Get out! Get the fuck out of here!"

And she hears Roy use his patient voice. It's the one he uses to show the world that nobody understands him and that he doesn't care, that he can see into any person's heart and find the goodness. It's the voice he uses before he starts hitting.

Roy says, "I wish you could see yourself through my eyes, baby. I wish you could see how beautiful you are. Don't be like this, sweetness. Just be nice. You know you want to be. Don't you know how special we are together, baby?"

Griff falls twice before she gets to Mr. Bradley, and then she kneels down beside him. He's slumped over on his stomach with his back humped up in the air. Karl's still howling. She tells him to quit but he won't.

She reaches across Mr. Bradley's back and grabs her hands full of his canvas coat and pulls as hard as she can. She has to pull again, even harder the second time, leaning back with all her weight to roll him over. His left eyebrow is split and his eye's full of blood. It's the same eye that the bear already hurt, the one that's lower on his face. And farther up in his hair there's another place where he's bleeding.

She strips off her sweatshirt and dabs at the bloody spots with it.

Mr. Bradley moans a little bit, and smiles like her mother does in her sleep, and then the eye that isn't bloody flutters open and blinks, then stares at her. His smile disappears and he sits up fast and keeps getting up. He doesn't even stop to find his canes, he just gets up all at once like he got out of the truck when he thought the bear was going to bite Einar. Like he carries another person around inside him who he only gets to use for emergencies. He looks toward the house and then away he goes, dragging his bad leg behind him. He still doesn't know he's forgotten his canes, so she picks them up and starts after him.

She tries to tell him to stop but when she opens her mouth, nothing comes out, so she runs to tell him she's okay. She knows it's the blood on her face that got him up that fast and she wishes she could have washed it all away.

Mr. Bradley goes right up the steps to Einar's porch and when he gets to the top he holds on to the railing and pulls something out of his coat pocket. Her legs aren't as wobbly and she's running right at him but it's too dark to see what he has. She can hear her mother screaming like she does when Roy's hurting her, and she watches

Mr. Bradley point his hand at the screen door. And then his hand jumps up and the sound stops her, almost slaps the wind out of her, and she takes a step backward. She's at the bottom of the steps, right below him, and it's like the air got clearer all of a sudden. Like you didn't even know it was dirty until all the dirt got knocked out of it. She can see so much of everything that she has to squint her eyes as she goes up the steps so she won't see too much. She doesn't want Mr. Bradley to shoot the gun again, because that's for sure what he's done.

She can hear Roy now, and it's the only time she's ever heard him when he wasn't trying to be somebody else. Now it's like he's just a little boy talking to his mother about something really scary he's seen, saying: "Oh no, oh God, oh no, no, no."

And Karl's not barking anymore. He's just whining somewhere behind her.

When she gets up on the porch she can see the bullet hole in the screen door. The light's still on inside and she can see clearly enough to count the little torn ends in the wire where the bullet's gone through. And behind the screen there's blood on the floor and on the wall, and Roy's all curled up and quiet now in the middle of the blood. She looks up at Mr. Bradley but he's still looking down his arm, still holding the gun in his hand, pointing it at Roy.

When she looks back at the screen door, her mom's standing there holding it open, right between Roy and Mr. Bradley, and her face says she's not trying to save Roy. Her face says she's saving herself, and Griff's never seen her mother like this before, this big and bright. Bigger and brighter than she's ever shown Roy, or the sheriff, or any other man. It's like her mother's on fire and everybody else in the world's cold and in the dark, and her mother's there to make sure they get warm.

Her mother walks to Mr. Bradley and takes the gun from his hand. Just that easy. Like from now on there isn't anything she can't do.

THIRTY-SEVEN

—— ——

HE DOESN'T SLEEP and he doesn't dream, and at some point it occurs to him God has taken his dreams away as a punishment and that he'll never dream again. He's glad for it. It seems only fair.

When the pain falls upon him in the night he doesn't beat it back with the drugs. He welcomes it. That also seems fair. He allows the pain to gather and gain confidence and rage unchecked, as lightning tears through a dark sky. He grinds his teeth with the pleasure of it, as men bent on redemption do, and lies with his fists clenched and finally he just endures. Also as men do. Before he loses consciousness he swears he can smell himself burning.

He doesn't hear Einar come in or draw the syringe of morphine or turn him on his side, and even now he's not sure it's Einar in the chair by his bed. It could be a dream. It could be

God's pity, His grace. He doesn't expect it to last. He knows he doesn't deserve it.

"Tell me the truth," the dream-Einar asks. "Did you even try to get to your medicine last night?"

He lies blinking, but when his eyes feel better shut, he keeps them shut.

"Are you going to talk to me?"

He opens his eyes once more, slowly, and it is Einar in the chair. It's not a dream, no kind of pardon at all. Einar walks to the window and opens it and comes back. A draft of clean air follows him, and there's the smell of coffee.

"Do you think the dead worry about our lives?" he asks. He honestly wants to know. He wants to know if his crime was witnessed. He was going to ask Jean what she thought when she put him to bed last night and cleaned the blood from his face, but he felt too shy to ask.

Einar just stares at him. "Is that something a man thinks about before he curls up on his bed and gets ready to die?"

"That's not what I did."

"It sure looked to me like you did."

"Are you going to answer me or not?"

"Yes, I do. I think they worry," Einar says. "But I think they forgive us too. I even think it might be easy for them."

"You aren't just saying that to make me feel better?"

"No, I'm not. It's something I've thought about. I'm saying it for myself."

His head clears, and with it the last bit of hope that any part of this is a dream. He's glad for that, too. He shot a man. There should be no hope.

"You don't have to come out here in the mornings," he says. "I don't want you to feel like you do." His voice rasps.

"All right."

"I can get myself shaved. And dressed, too."

"I know you can." Einar reaches forward, then winces and tucks his arm against his side and with his other hand takes one of the mugs from the nightstand.

He watches Einar sip the coffee. "I tried to kill that man," he says.

"Well, you didn't. He isn't ever going to use his right leg like he did yesterday morning, but you didn't come close to killing him."

"But I'm telling you, I tried. I meant to kill him. I didn't know I wasn't a good shot anymore."

Einar blows across the top of the mug and holds it to his lips, then sets it on the floor. He gets out of the chair and grips Mitch around his chest and hefts him up against the pillows. He groans with the effort and then stands away and presses his palm into his ribs.

"How bad are you hurt?"

"I'm fine," Einar says. "They brought me home from the hospital last night."

"Maybe you should've stayed another day or two."

Einar drags the chair to the window where he can see the house and the rise beyond it. "Tell me when you're done feeling sorry for yourself," he says.

"That's not what I'm doing."

"You're feeling like you shouldn't have shot that boy in the leg."

"I suppose you wish you'd done it? To have the responsibility of it?"

Einar looks at him, and there's not a speck of doubt in his face. "Yes, I do. I'm the one who should've been here." He turns back to the window and sips his coffee.

Mitch takes the other mug from the nightstand. "How bad was Griff hurt?"

"Bad enough."

"What's that mean, 'bad enough'?"

"It means they gave her ten stitches in her head."

"I want to see her."

"You can see her later. Crane came and got her and her mother too. First thing this morning. He took them down to Sheridan to shop for a used car so they won't be stuck out here without a vehicle." Einar sets his mug on the windowsill and turns on the chair. "Don't you let me come out here again and find you like I did a little bit ago. I don't want that to ever happen again."

"I'm not going to live forever."

"There's a lot of evidence for that, by Christ, but you're going to let me take care of you until you do die. And you're going to make it as easy for me as you can. Do I look like I'm having a good time right now?"

"I'm sorry."

"What did you say?"

"I said I was sorry."

"All right then." He leaves his mug on the sill and finds where Mitch's shirt is hung and takes the pack of cigarettes from the pocket. He lights them both one and stands by the bed, and they watch each other smoke.

"I'd like to be buried up next to Griffin and Ella."

Einar snorts. "Where the hell do you think I'd bury you? Did you think I'd just haul you to the landfill?"

"I hadn't thought about it before."

Einar walks to the door and flicks his cigarette butt out. He fills Karl's bowl with kibble and stands by the workbench. "You hungry?"

"I'm okay. This coffee'll do."

"I don't think she'll scar," Einar says. "Most of the stitches were up in her hairline. They had to shave a little patch of hair away."

"Did she cry?"

"Not even a little bit." He swings the magnifying glass over the antler clamped in the vise and bends to look at the figures carved there, and then he leans back against the workbench and stares down at his boots. "After the doctor was done with her, when we were all coming home, she told me she thought her life could be like this. That this is how she always thought it could be."

"You think she meant living up here?"

"Yes, I do." Einar looks up at him and nods. "I think that's exactly what she meant."

ACKNOWLEDGMENTS

My wife, Virginia, is my polestar. This book was held always against her candid and insightful comments. And, in that she and I coauthored the screenplay of the same title, much of the story reflects her graceful contemplation, her dogged insistence that we strive harder for the truths held in each character.

Richard Spragg, Kent Haruf, Nancy Stauffer, Kate Murphy, Betsy Burton, Donna Gershten and Annette Wenda were all kind enough, at different stages, to give the manuscript thoughtful reads. They brought me back, carefully, to its weaknesses.

And there is not a single page that did not benefit from Gary Fisketjon's precise edit. The surety with which he entered, and walked from front to back, resulted in a leaner and better book. I am indebted to him.

My thanks to Liz Van Hoose. And also, to Chuck Christenson for his medical advice concerning several of the characters in this book.

My thanks to the Mrs. Giles Whiting

ACKNOWLEDGMENTS

Foundation for its much-needed and unexpected Freund Grant-in-Aid.

For the film **An Unfinished Life,** Virginia and I are deeply grateful to have worked with the fine minds and hearts of Lasse Hallström and Leslie Holleran.